A Shot in the Dark

Gregory Payette

8 Flags Publishing, Inc.

Sign up for the newsletter on my website:

GregoryPayette.com

Once or twice a month I'll send you updates and news. Plus, you'll be the first to hear about new releases with special prices. If you'd like to receive the Henry Walsh prequel (for free) use the sign-up form here: **GregoryPayette.com/crossroad**

Chapter 1

It had only been seven months since Alex took the detective job in North Carolina, with the town of Selma's small police department. At the time it felt like she'd been gone for years. After she moved, I took time off from Walsh Investigations, gave up the office above my friend Billy's restaurant, and headed down to Naples, Florida to stay with my parents.

I needed a change of scenery.

By the time I'd gotten back to Jacksonville, I knew I was going to need a restart. And not just in the business. Without Alex around, things were different. We spent a lot of time together over the years, and when our relationship changed from friendly and professional to, well, to something else, neither one of us knew what we were supposed to do. When she was offered the job, I encouraged her to jump at the chance.

Some days, I'd wished I hadn't.

But being a private investigator isn't for everyone. In fact, it's not for most people. I know it wasn't what Alex had wanted. I don't think she ever planned to stick around working with me for as long as she had, so going back to law enforcement was always in the back of her mind.

But she was happy with her decision. At least that's what she said when we'd talk. And I'd do my best to make it sound like all was good on my end too.

Whether either of us were being honest, I'm not sure.

When I first got back from Naples, I took a ride out to Fernandina Beach. I drove to the old house where I grew up, but it was a different house. The family who'd bought it from my parents did some major renovations, to a point where it was twice the size. It had been a while since I went by it, and I didn't notice the bikes and toys in the yard like I did the last time. They were all gone. I thought maybe the kids were gone too... maybe off to college.

Part of me wished I'd bought the house when my parents first decided to sell. But I wasn't exactly rolling in dough at the time. Not that I ever was. My dad always called it a money pit. I'd never be confused for a financial genius, but I always wondered, if you did the math after all those years of owning a house, all the money you dump into it, if you really came out on top the way real estate people like to say you would.

I don't know. Maybe I was just bitter about the whole thing.

I drove away without looking back and headed over to the beach. I drove the Jeep right onto the sand and parked so I could sit and stare at the ocean. I needed to let my mind wander.

Between the sound of the crashing waves and the screaming gulls, mixed with the smell of the warm, salty air, it was hard to find a better place to think things through. As long as there weren't too many other people around.

I'd stepped down from the Jeep with one foot on the sand when my phone buzzed. The call came from a 212 area code, and I almost ignored it but wanted to know who was calling me from a New York number.

I answered, "Hello?"

A female on the other end said, "Oh, I'm sorry, I was looking for, uh... This isn't Walsh Investigations?"

"It might be," I said.

There was silence on the other end.

I waited a moment, then said, "Hello?"

"Yes, I'm... I'm sorry. I was calling Henry Walsh."

"You're speaking to him," I said.

"The private investigator?"

"Well, for now I am. Yes." I don't know why I didn't give her a straight answer, although it was the truth. I hadn't yet decided if I was going to renew my PI license, which meant my days as a private investigator would officially come to an end in another week.

The woman on the other line didn't waste any time. "My father was murdered, and I'd like to hire you, or someone, to help find who did it."

"Your father?" I said. "Here in Jacksonville?"

"Are you asking if the crime occurred in Jacksonville?" she said, and didn't wait for my response. "Yes, it occurred in Jacksonville."

I hadn't followed the news lately. I hadn't even read the paper or looked at anything news related online for at least a few weeks. "I assume the police are involved?"

"Well," she said, and followed with a pause. "Not anymore, that I know of. He was killed eleven years ago."

It was hard to hear her with the crashing waves and wind blowing in my ear. "Eleven? Did you say it happened eleven years ago?"

"Yes. But, let me explain something. I didn't know he was my father, or that he even existed, until a little more than a month ago."

"Oh," is all I said. I waited for more, and started to wish I hadn't answered.

"My mom recently passed away," she said. "She told me about him just before she went."

"I'm sorry." I looked through the windshield at the waves in the distance, rolling onto the shore, where a young boy ran and splashed through the water ahead of a man I assumed was his father, chasing him. They both were laughing. "So all in the same day, you found out about a father you didn't know about *and* that he was killed? Over a decade ago?"

"I know how it sounds," she said. "If you want to know more, I can—"

"Please, go ahead," I said. I wasn't in a hurry.

"I was adopted by my dad," she said. "My dad, I mean, the man who raised me. He's been there my whole life, since I was a baby. And for whatever reason, my parents never told me he wasn't my biological father."

"Is he still around?" I said.

"My dad? Yes. He's a physician in New Rochelle."

A pickup truck, with an American flag blowing in the wind off the back of it, drove by, its wheels bigger than my Jeep. The engine roared as the wheels kicked sand into the air, flying past me, and continuing down the beach.

I said, "But your father—the one you never met—he lived here, in Jacksonville?"

"As far as I know, he did. I don't have a lot of information about him."

"Have you talked to the police already? If it's still open but not actively being investigated, then they should still be able to answer your questions. It's considered a cold case at this point."

"Yes, I know. I have called them, but..."

"The fact it's a cold case, it presents a lot of challenges for whoever you end up hiring to help you," I said. "And, to be honest, it's not really my expertise."

"What's not your expertise, cold cases?"

I said, "There are investigators who specialize in that kind of thing. It's a long process. Longer than normal, I should say." The truth was, cold case or not, I didn't want to string the woman along. If I was going to jump into a new case, I wasn't sure one that had gone unsolved for eleven years would be ideal. Especially if I was going to get back into investigative work so soon. Of course, I could use the money, but I still hadn't made up my mind.

"So how'd you get my name?" I said.

"I looked online," she said. "Then I found some articles... some cases you were involved in."

"You can't always believe everything you read,'" I said.

She went quiet again. "Can you just tell me if you're interested in the case? I need to know. I have some other investigators I was going to call."

I looked at my watch, hesitating. "I'd have to ask you more questions before I can answer that."

"Okay," she said. "Then, can we meet? I can come to your office, or—"

"Do you know where Trout River Marina is?"

"No. But I can find it," she said. "What's it called?"

"Trout River Marina."

"Is that where your office is?"

I smiled, gazing at the water. "Sort of. I live there. On a boat."

The woman paused. Slowly, she recited what I'd said, like she was writing it down: "Trout... River... Marina."

"Are you from New York?" I said.

"Yes. I live in Manhattan."

"Oh, okay. Then just put Trout River Marina in your GPS, hopefully you're not too far away. Give me at least a half hour, and just call this number again when you're in the parking lot."

"Okay."

I was about to hang up. I said, "Wait, you didn't tell me your name."

"Oh, sorry. It's Trish. Trish Williams."

Chapter 2

A DAMP, MUSTY SMELL had taken over the inside of my boat after me being away for so long. And although I tried to clean it, it was still there when I went below, into the cabin. I figured it had been there all along, for years, but maybe I hadn't noticed it until I went away and came back with a fresh nose.

I mean, there was water everywhere. It wasn't that odd of a smell. But I'd locked the boat up tight while I was gone, trapping the odors inside. I was going to have to spend the afternoon doing a thorough cleaning.

I glanced over at the unopened bottle of Jack Daniels on a shelf in the galley. I had gone eight months without a single drink. And for whatever reason, I kept the last bottle I'd purchased, still untouched, sitting there on the shelf waiting for me. Of course, I could've given it to someone else, who'd put it to good use, but decided to hold on to it. It wasn't that I'd imagined falling off the wagon and spending a night drunk on the dock like I used to. But maybe I wanted to test myself, make sure I was strong enough to resist a temptation, not tap into it.

If it sounded foolish to test myself that way, then maybe so. But my personal list of doing foolish things wasn't short.

I heard a faint buzz and realized it was my phone, buried under the clothes piled on my bed. And by the time I got to it, I'd missed three calls from area code 212. I'd tapped the screen to dial back when a woman's voice called for me from somewhere outside.

I climbed the ladder and poked my head out the hole, glancing at an attractive woman, who looked nothing like what I'd imagined. I stepped off the boat and onto the dock. "Trisha?"

"Trish," she said, correcting me as she reached out and shook my hand.

I held up my phone. "Sorry, I missed your calls."

She grinned, looking at the only restaurant in the marina, at the far end of the dock from where we stood. "That's all right," she said. "I asked the bartender which boat was yours." She pulled her sunglasses back down over her eyes. "This is great," she said, looking around the marina. "What's it like living on a boat?"

"It does the job," I said. "No grass to mow."

I told her the same thing I told everyone who asked. There wasn't much else to say about it.

Trish had a nice smile. She was dressed in cut-off jean shorts and a plain white T-shirt that didn't cover her stomach. "How long have you lived here?"

"A few years," I said.

"Do you like it? Living on the water?"

I shrugged, nodding. "As long as I'm near water, I'm good."

She looked around, her hands in the back pockets of her shorts. "So this is the St. Johns River?"

I pointed west. "Technically we're standing right where the Trout River feeds into the St. Johns." I turned to my right, pointing. "It's over a half mile across the water over there, where the two come together."

"Is it fresh water?" she said, seemingly interested.

"It's mostly brackish, here in Jacksonville."

She looked east where the late-morning sun glistened on the water. "Is there anywhere we can talk?"

"If you don't mind my casual office setting, we can sit on the deck of the boat, if—"

"Whatever works," she said.

I stepped up onto the boat from the dock, turned and reached for Trish's hand to help her up. I'd already unfolded the lawn chairs and had them out, with a new canvas sunshade I'd installed over the deck to keep us somewhat cool from the hot summer sun.

"We had these when I was a kid," she said, looking over my lawn chairs.

I told her, as I explained to everyone who asked where I got them, that they were from my parents' house.

She sat down in the yellow one. "Are your parents still around?"

"They're in Naples. Florida," I said. "Not Italy. I actually just got back from there." I pointed toward the cabin. "Can I get you a drink? I made some coffee a little while ago. It's not gourmet or anything, but it's got caffeine."

She shrugged, nodding. "Sure."

I went below, thinking about her. She seemed nice. There was something about Trish that I liked, and it wasn't just her looks. A lot of times a prospective client would show up, and I'd know right away it'd be nothing but business, because there wasn't a speck of personal interest of any kind or real connection.

But she seemed different. For one thing, she wasn't sad like a lot of people who'd show up at my door. It was understandable, of course, considering oftentimes clients had something bad happen to a loved one or someone they cared about, or had a spouse who was unfaithful.

She may not have known her biological father, but the connection between them was there. If it hadn't been, I couldn't imagine why she'd be in Florida, looking to find out what happened to him.

I thought about how the situation had to have been strange for her.

I poured two coffees and brought them up to the deck, handing one to Trish. She looked at the side of the mug. "Sharks? Is this a mug from the baseball team?"

I nodded. "I used to work for them."

"No kidding? Doing what?"

"I was in security."

"They're not here in Florida anymore, are they?"

"No. Moved to Tennessee, even changed the name."

I grabbed a small, square folding table I had tucked in the corner and unfolded it between the two chairs. "See, it's just like a real office," I said. I placed my coffee on the table and sat in the chair across from her. "So, did you grow up in New York?"

"Mostly," she said. "We moved around a little, when my dad first got out of medical school. We lived in Texas for a couple of years, but I was a little girl back then."

"And you never thought of leaving?" I said, although I wasn't exactly sure why I'd asked.

"New York?" She shrugged. "I thought about it, when I first got out of school. But I got a job in the city, right out of college. Next thing you know, I'd become a writer."

"Yeah?" I said. "What kind of writer?"

"Don't laugh, but I was a writer on *One Life to Live*."

"The soap opera?" I said. "Why would I laugh at that? Sounds like a pretty good gig, no?"

"It was, until it ended. It's one of the last soap operas filmed in New York. So when that show ended, I was out of work for a while."

I knew we hadn't gotten into the real reason she was there, and that her career likely had little-to-nothing to do with what might've happened to her father, but I couldn't help wanting to hear more about her. I'd been spending a lot of time alone over the past few months, other than hanging around with my parents.

"Do you still write?" I said.

"I've worked for a few TV shows over the past few years, but the work comes in waves."

"I know how that goes," I said. "Any shows I would've heard of?"

She shrugged. "You must watch police shows, right?"

"Not really," I said. "I mean, I've seen some here and there, but..."

"Oh, well, I just thought you... It's just that I wrote for *Law and Order*. And a show called *Blue Bloods*."

"I've heard of them," I said.

"I wasn't one of the main writers, mainly because I was only hired to write the romantic scenes, whenever they'd come up. I guess they saw that as my niche after working on the soap operas. You get pigeonholed, you know?"

I sipped the coffee. "Are you still working for them?"

She shook her head. "I've written a couple of books."

"Let me guess," I said. "Romance novels?"

She laughed, nodding.

Trish finally took a sip of coffee, but I could tell by the look on her face it wasn't the best she'd ever had. I guessed she was used to ten-dollar coffees in Manhattan. I should've known better than to give her coffee from a can.

"Sorry," I said. "It's not good to the last drop?"

She laughed, wiping her mouth with the back of her hand. "Was it that obvious?"

I said, "The look on your face was like you took a sip of gasoline." I took another sip myself, but didn't mind it.

Trish put the mug down on the table and wiped her forehead. "I think it's too hot for coffee, now, anyway," she said.

Even with the shade cover I had hung over the deck, she was right. It was late spring and still morning, but the summer heat was already creeping in.

"There's a place we can go, not far from here, if you want to go get a decent cup of coffee?" I felt a little off base for asking, as soon as the words left my mouth.

She stood from the chair, nodding. "I don't know how anyone can sit out here in this heat. I'm up for it, if you are."

I dumped both of our coffees into the river and left the mugs on the table, then helped her down to the dock.

I pointed toward my Jeep. "You want to drive with me?"

She appeared hesitant, then shook her head. "I think I'll just take my car, if you don't mind?"

Chapter 3

TRISH FOLLOWED ME OFF North Main Street in her rented gray Ford Taurus, and into the parking lot at the Norwood Plaza. My phone rang just as I was pulling into a parking space, and I answered right away.

It was my friend Billy.

"Good morning," I said. "It's been a while."

"It has," he said. "I'm sorry I haven't checked in. Are you still in Naples?"

"No, I'm in Jax," I said.

"You're kidding? And you didn't come by the restaurant?"

"I thought you were traveling the world?"

"I am. I mean, I was. But the restaurant... It's not as easy as I'd hoped, leaving it in someone else's hands. My name's on the sign, so..."

I watched Trish step out of the Taurus and said to Billy, "Listen, can I come by and see you a little later? I gotta run."

"Of course. It'll be good to see you. Are you at the boat?"

"No, I'm at Java Jazz. I'm having coffee with a potential client."

"Client?" he said. "So you're already working?"

"Maybe. We'll catch up later this afternoon. I'll tell you all about it." I hung up and stepped out of the Jeep and toward the entrance to Java Jazz Café. Trish was already at the door.

Inside, my gaze went right to the table in the far corner from the entrance. It was the table where Alex and I always sat together, mostly because we liked how it was tucked away from the crowd where we could talk.

Jazz played inside, along the lines of what you'd find in an old-school nightclub after hours.

"What would you like?" I said, standing next to her in line.

"I think I'll get a tea," she said, looking at the menu written in chalk, on the wall behind the counter.

"No coffee?" I said.

She shook her head, with a sly smile. "I'm just afraid nothing can top that delicious cup I had at your boat."

We both laughed, and moved up in the line, closer to the counter.

Trish ordered a green-ginger tea. I ordered a black coffee.

We sat at the table, and I thought we should get right into it, just so she didn't think I, for some reason, chose to ignore the real reason we were there. I kept my voice low, so nobody could hear. "I hope it's all right, discussing things here? This table gives us a bit of privacy, so..." I looked around. "Maybe I should've kept my office."

"So you actually *had* an office?" she said.

"I did. But after my partner left for a job in North Carolina..."

"I didn't know you had a partner," she said. "What kind of job did he leave you for?"

"She," I said. "Alex. She's a detective."

She nodded, like she was impressed.

"So, why don't we start with you telling me what your father's name was," I said.

"Stuart Graves." She looked into her cup. "I'm sure you're wondering why I need to know what happened to him?"

I nodded with a slight shrug, because I wasn't sure how much it mattered.

She said, "Whoever killed him took away any chance I had of at least getting to know him. And that really bothers me. And, I..." She paused, looking away from me. "I'm his daughter. I feel like I deserve an answer."

"But, do you understand what that'll entail?" I said. "It's not like the crime shows." As soon as the words left my mouth, I knew it came out as condescending.

"Are you trying to imply that because I wrote for TV, I think that's how it really works?"

"I'm sorry," I said. "I didn't mean... It's just that, on TV, they always solve the crime. They always get their guy. But in real life, a majority of cases are never solved. That's just a fact. And, you know that guy they arrested? The one they believe committed a crime? It often turns out he didn't actually do it."

She stared across the table at me with a look in her eyes, like she didn't appreciate anything I'd said. I guess I couldn't blame her. "If you don't want this case, I'd rather you just come out and say it." She let out a sigh. "It's just... I hoped maybe you would've been a little more optimistic."

"Optimistic?" I leaned closer. "My preference is to be *realistic*."

Trish was quiet, her eyes on mine.

"I'm sorry," I said. "I could easily take your money, tell you it'd be a piece of cake, but…"

"I get it," she said, her pleasant, calm voice replaced with a snappishness only a woman from New York could have. "I'm not going back to New York without some answers. So, if you can't help me, I'll find someone who can." She glanced around the café, then stood from the table. "I'm sorry if I've wasted your time," she said.

"Wait," I said, standing up from my chair. "I didn't say I wouldn't do it." I gestured toward her chair. "Please, sit down. I'm sorry."

We both sat down again.

I said, "My fee is two fifty a day."

She stared back at me, nodding. "That sounds fair. But, just so you know where I'm coming from, if I wanted someone to talk me out of doing this, I'd call my dad."

"Does he know you're down here?"

"He knows," she said. "But he doesn't understand why I need to do this." Trish peered toward the door when it opened. A young couple walked in, pushing a baby in a carriage. She turned to me. "My mom got pregnant when she was a student at SCAD."

"SCAD?" I said.

"Savannah College of Art and Design."

"Oh, right. I've heard of it. Is that where you get your creative genes from? Your mom?"

Trish shrugged, then nodded. "My father, Stuart Graves… he was an artist and a writer. Mom was an amazing artist herself, but gave it all up when she had me. She started painting again a couple of years ago before she got sick."

"What's her name?" I said.

"Joyce. Joyce Williams. Cannon was her maiden name. So, it was her junior year at school, she got pregnant. Then she left and moved back to New York with my grandparents. She ended up marrying my dad. They were high school sweethearts."

"And your father, Stuart Graves, he stayed at school?"

"I'm not sure. But he didn't even know about me until a few months before he was killed," she said. "My mom told me she'd planned to tell me, back then, when I was younger. But he was killed soon after she'd finally reached out to him. She didn't have the heart to tell me, and waited all those years until right before she died."

I was starting to understand what motivated Trish to want to find the answer.

She said, "She told me it was right after I'd graduated high school, when she first tried to find him. But she had trouble tracking him down. She eventually found his sister, a woman who lives in Georgia."

"She's your aunt," I said, as if she hadn't thought of it.

She nodded, with a crooked smile. "I feel funny calling her that."

"So your mom found him through the sister?"

Trish shook her head. "Not right away. It took her a long time. She left her contact information with his sister, but then never heard from him. Then, one day out of the blue, he calls her. He had just moved back from the West Coast, and was living here in Jacksonville with his girlfriend."

"A girlfriend?" I said. "Have you talked to her?"

"No." She brushed her hair back from her face. "But, he called my mom, and the reaction wasn't what she'd expected.

She said he was so happy to hear about me, and that he wanted to meet me right away. He was going to drive up to meet me, but then my mom... I guess she got cold feet. She told him to wait, and she'd contact him again to arrange it." Tears started to fill her eyes. "She told him I was a writer, working on TV shows in the big city, and he started to cry." Trish got up and walked to the counter to grab a napkin, wiping her eyes as she came back and sat down. "I'm sorry," she said.

I watched her, waiting. I didn't know what to say. Normally, it was Alex who would take over when someone needed some emotional support. Not that I couldn't handle it, but I wasn't the type to wrap my arm around someone I didn't know.

Trish took a deep breath and exhaled. "Dad—my dad who raised me—was the one who stopped it."

"Didn't he know your mother was trying to reach him? Stuart Graves?" I said.

"He just didn't think it would be fair to me, to have this stranger show up in what had always been a fairly normal life. But, as it turns out, a few weeks later, his sister called my mom and said my father had been killed." She closed her eyes for a moment. "It had to do with some kind of real estate deal. I'm not exactly clear on it, but I guess he was somehow involved in real estate. He was supposedly helping a friend of his sell a house. The friend found my father in his house, and he was dead."

Chapter 4

I PARKED THE JEEP next to my friend Billy's Lexus by the back door of his restaurant. I glanced up the exterior stairway, toward the second floor, where I used to have my office. At first, I was hesitant to go up and see what it looked like now that someone else had taken over the old space. But I decided to go up, and walked along the covered exterior.

Looking in through the office window, I was surprised to see it was empty.

When Billy rebuilt Billy's Place, he included offices up on the second story. One of the offices became the home of Walsh Investigations, and worked well until Alex left.

But seeing it vacant made me feel a little guilty because I knew it meant Billy's cash flow would be cut. Of course, he did all right with the restaurant. It was one of the most popular restaurants in Jacksonville.

I went back down the stairs and through the front entrance into Billy's Place. I stopped just inside the door and looked at the bar, most of the stools filled with businesslike people, who were eating or drinking alone. The last time I'd sat at the bar was around the last time I had a drink. The dining room was separated from the bar, with tall tropical plants that Billy treated like children. The only plant I ever owned—a gift a client had given me—was proof enough, within a few weeks, that neither thumb I was born with turned out to be green.

I gave a nod to Chloe behind the bar. She was Billy's full-time bartender for as long as I'd been going there, and was now managing the place while Billy tried to pull back from the day-to-day operations.

She smiled and gave me back a nod, lifting a bottle of Jack Daniels so I could see it.

I waved her off. "Not today," I said, stepping toward the bar. She came around the bar and gave me a hug. "Billy said you were back in town. It's good to see you."

Before I could ask for him, the swinging door from the kitchen opened, and Billy walked out, carrying a large tray of plates toward the dining area.

I said to Chloe, "Is this what he considers pulling back from the business?"

She laughed. "He can't let go. And can't sit still."

I decided to take the only available seat at the bar and sat next to a woman who looked up from the phone she left flat on the bar. She glanced at me like she didn't want the company, quickly shifting her gaze back to her phone.

I felt a hand on my back. "How are you, my friend?"

I turned to Billy standing behind me, and rose to shake his hand. I said, "I think I'm all right."

"You *think*?" he said, laughing.

I shrugged, nodding. "Yeah."

"Did you order something to eat?"

I shook my head. "I was thinking about it."

He waved for me to follow him. "I'll have Jake make you something special. Come with me so I can show you my new office."

Billy's office used to be upstairs—an office I shared with him on the second level—until a bomb blew up and leveled the whole restaurant. That's when he decided to rebuild the whole thing and add the new offices.

I followed Billy, but he walked behind the bar. "Wait here," he said, stepping into the kitchen. He came back a moment later. "Jake's taking care of you."

Jake, his head chef, also happened to be Chloe's fiancé. I thought they would've been married already, after their long engagement, but it was none of my business.

Billy brought me down a short hall and into a space, that, last I knew, he'd used for storage. But now there was a thick wood door with PRIVATE engraved on a brass plate affixed to it. We walked into the large space. He had a huge cherrywood desk, two leather couches, and a matching chair with a coffee table between them. There were tall plants in every corner, with dim lighting. A big-screen TV hung on the wall over a pool table.

Two windows overlooked the dining patio on the edge of the St. Johns.

"I could live in here," I said, looking around. My gaze caught a framed photo on top of a set of bookshelves. It was me, Billy, and Alex. I remembered the day it was taken, out on the baseball diamond, back when Alex and I were still working security for the Sharks.

He nodded. "Nice, isn't it? I know I said I was going to be traveling, but then I decided I liked being here, in my restaurant. So I thought I should at least have a comfortable place to get away from it all, without having to leave."

I laughed, walking over to the pool table. I rolled a ball into the corner pocket.

"Initially, I was going to fix it up to be a private party room for guests. But then I realized I needed my own personal space. And with Chloe needing an office of her own, she took over the one I was using on the other side of the kitchen." He walked to the desk and ran his hand over the top of it. "This is custom built," he said. "Gentleman who comes in here, built this for me. He's a snowbird from Maine."

I nodded, impressed.

"So what's this you were telling me on the phone?" Billy said. "You have a new client?"

"It looks like it," I said. "But it's a cold case."

"A cold case? Didn't you turn something like that down last year?"

"Good memory," I said.

He leaned back against his desk, arms crossed. "So, why this one?"

I wasn't sure I had a good enough answer. "I don't know." I stepped to the window and looked outside. "Do you remember a case, back about eleven years ago, where that real estate agent was shot while showing a house?"

Billy was quiet for a moment. "I might. Is that the one? The cold one?"

"She's from New York. My client. The man who was killed was her father." I went ahead and told him whatever I knew.

"You like her?" he said, a sly smile on his face.

"Do I *like* her?" I stared back at him, but he knew I knew what he meant.

"Don't play dumb," he said. "The way you just talked about her, I'm just wondering if—"

"She seems like she'd be a decent client. Sure."

Billy rolled his eyes.

"She's nice," I said. "I haven't even fully committed to the case yet. Not until I have a chance to dig into it a little deeper, make sure there's something there for me to work with." I pointed toward the ceiling. "So what happened to the tenant upstairs?"

"Guy was a flake," Billy said. "Paid me first month, last month, security... and that was it. Never paid another day's rent. I got back from a trip a few months back, and the place was cleaned out. Even took the coffee machine that didn't belong to him."

"He took my Mr. Coffee?" I said.

"Oh, was that yours?" He turned from me and started to walk out the door. "Let me go check with Jake, see how long it'll be for your food."

"Billy," I said. "Do you mind if I get it to-go?"

He shook his head. "Why would I care?" He took another step and turned again. "I guess you're in a hurry?"

I wasn't sure if I was or not, and shrugged.

Billy left the office and disappeared around the corner.

I checked my phone to see if Trish had called, but she hadn't. We were going to meet up in the evening, and, admittedly, I was looking forward to it.

Billy came back into the office, holding a white paper bag stapled on the side. "It's a sandwich," he said. "And it looks pretty good. I'm assuming you didn't go vegan while you were away, did you?"

I laughed, shaking my head as I pulled out my wallet.

"Come on," he said, waving me off. "Put that away. I haven't seen you in how many months? You think I'm going to make you pay for a sandwich?"

Chapter 5

I STOOD ON THE dock by my boat, calling Detective Mike Stone, when Trish pulled into the parking lot at the marina. I looked at my watch; she was fifteen minutes early.

Mike answered and was back to his old ways. "I haven't heard from you," he said. "It was nice while it lasted."

I tried to resist playing his games, but it wasn't easy. "Last I saw you," I said, "you were talking retirement. I guess the good people of Jacksonville couldn't be so lucky."

He huffed a laugh through the phone. "You know how it goes. Not sure what I'd actually do with myself. Maybe next year." The line went quiet.

I thought I'd start with the small talk, regarding something—or someone—we both cared about. I said, "Have you heard from Alex?"

"Yeah, I talk to her," he said. "Why?"

"I was just curious. I haven't talked to her much at all. I hope everything's good with her."

"She's away from you, so it can't be all that bad," he said.

Mike just couldn't help himself. He wasn't a bad guy, for the most part, but could also be like that kid in high school who couldn't have a normal conversation without bullying someone else to hide his insecurities.

"She calls me all the time," he said. "Sometimes, she needs advice from a real detective."

I should've just hung up right then.

Trish stepped up onto the dock dressed a little different than she was earlier, wearing a longer skirt with sandals and a buttoned white shirt, cut short above her waist. Her hair looked different, too, but I wasn't sure why. Maybe it was because she didn't have her sunglasses holding it back.

Either way, she looked good.

I said to Mike, "Are you going to be in the office tomorrow?"

"Why?"

"I wanted to ask you about someone. An old case."

Mike was quiet at first. "Which one?"

Trish walked up onto the boat and sat in one of the two folding lawn chairs under the sunshade.

I kept my voice low and said to Mike, "The name Stuart Graves ring a bell?"

"Graves?" He paused. "The real estate agent?"

"You know much about it?"

"The case? I guess so. It's open. I know that much. But what's it got to do with you?"

I didn't answer, looking up onto the boat at Trish looking out toward the river. "Would it be all right if we discussed it later? I was hoping you could meet me, face-to-face."

Mike said. "I thought you were backing out of the business, now that you don't have Alex around to carry you on her back."

Dealing with Mike involved having a lot of patience sometimes. "Can you meet me tomorrow? I can come out, first thing in the morning."

"I don't know if showing your face at headquarters is a good idea," Mike said. "You seem to forget nobody in the sheriff's office likes you."

I was about to speak, but looked at the screen and realized Mike had hung up on me. Just like that, without another word.

I went up onto the boat. "You're early," I said, and held up my phone. "That was a detective with the JSO."

"JSO?"

"The Jacksonville Sheriff's Office. Mike Stone. He likes to pretend he doesn't like me, even though we've been involved in a handful of cases together over the years."

She said, "Do you work with them?"

"The sheriff's office?" I shook my head. "No. Not directly. But Mike's one of the top detectives in the area. Maybe in the whole state. He's a bit temperamental, and likes to be credited as the man who solves the crime."

Trish stood and leaned against the boat's rail. "Did you ask him about my father?"

"I did. But... well, see... with Mike, it takes some time. It's like dealing with a little kid."

Trish smiled but didn't laugh. "Did he hang up on you?"

"You heard that?" I cleared my throat. "He does it all the time. He does things just to impress himself. Sometimes you just gotta deal with what you've got."

"Is he the only detective you know over there?"

I looked west, toward the orange glow of the clouds, the sun making its way toward the horizon. "He was, or *is* a good friend of my former partner, Alex. If she were here, he'd help out in a heartbeat, without question."

"Is it like the movies, where the cops don't like the private investigators?"

I laughed. "Unless it's one of their retired buddies, it's hard to get the respect. Plus, I don't do it for the glory, where someone like Mike needs a pat on his back... a little blue ribbon to wear on his chest."

She gave me a look like I was making a joke. "But I saw online that you were a police officer in Rhode Island?"

I didn't like to get into my background, unless I had to. So I changed the subject and stepped onto the ladder. "Let's go eat," I said, helping her down. We started along the dock. "Just a fair warning, Jed's isn't fine dining."

Trish laughed, nodding. "I was in there this morning, when I was looking for you. But I wouldn't expect a place called Jed's would be fancy." She kept her eyes on me as we walked, and said, "Do I look like I only go to fancy places?"

"I don't know. Considering you're from New York... a writer. And your dad's a doctor?"

"So you think I'm some kind of snob from the Northeast? Or that I've never been to a dive bar?" She gave me a look, like she was holding back a grin.

We walked past an older couple sitting on the dock by their boat, having drinks, and I waved to them both, raising their glasses to us.

I said to Trish, "You may want to lower your expectations a little. A dive bar would be a step up from Jed's."

She laughed as we got to the entrance.

"It's actually not that bad at all," I said. "The food's good. And you won't beat the service."

The lights were dim when we walked in, the small bar with ten stools that were all full was to the left of the entrance. Everyone at the bar, mostly men, looked at us when we walked in, then went right back to what they were doing.

Johnny Cash played on the old jukebox that'd been there since the original owners, twenty years earlier. It was hard to beat a place that had one.

The smell of mostly grilled meat and fried fish hung in the air, coming from the kitchen. I could see Ronnie, one of the owners, through the pass-through window behind the bar, plates of food under the heat lamp over the stainless-steel-topped shelf.

Trish and I walked into the small, dark dining area with eight round tables—all but one occupied—covered in white tablecloths to hide what the tables looked like underneath. There was a battery-powered candle flickering on each.

The few windows at the front of the restaurant were tinted, blocking most of the natural light coming from outside. The walls were covered in chestnut-colored paneling; the stained, wood-planked floor had been there since the place was built in the fifties. It was an old place, but there was something to like about the way it made you feel comfortable.

We managed to grab a table toward the back of the dining area, and Margaret, Ronnie's wife, came out through a swinging door and hurried toward us.

"Evening, Henry," she said. "Long time, no see." She glanced at Trish and nodded, smiling. "Hi, there, I'm Margaret."

"She owns the joint," I said. "Margaret, this is Trish."

Margaret was getting up there, maybe somewhere in her mid-seventies, although I never asked. It wasn't that she didn't have plenty of energy, maybe as much as someone half her age. But her husband, Ronnie, wasn't any younger either, and I wondered how much longer they'd want to lead lives of restaurateurs, running a somewhat run-down place in a marina.

She said to me, "Are you gonna have a Jack, hon?"

"Not tonight." I said. "I'll just get a ginger ale."

Margaret must've been thinking, *Who comes to a place like Jed's and doesn't have a drink?* She raised an eyebrow, along with a small shrug. "Okay, ginger ale." She turned to Trish, who was glaring at me like she wasn't sure what she should do.

"That's all right," I said. "Order a drink. I'm just taking a little breather from booze for a bit." Whether it was a few nights or not, I didn't need to tell her otherwise. Not at that point, at least.

Margaret waited, looking around at the other tables, maybe seeming a bit impatient with Trish, knowing she had other customers to take care of. But she always seemed to manage.

"Are you all alone tonight?" I said, trying to buy some time while Trish looked over the beer-and-wine menu.

Margaret nodded. "Can't find good help anymore. It's not like it was when I was younger. Nobody wants to work."

I didn't mean to, but it sounded like I'd hit a sore spot.

Trish ran her finger over the single-sheet, laminated menu. "I'll have a glass of this wine here." She looked up from the menu, holding her finger in place. "The Vincent? Chardonnay?"

Margaret smiled, wrote it down on her pad and stepped over to one of the other tables.

The door swung open from the kitchen, and the bartender—Margaret's cousin, or maybe he was her cousin's son—walked out, carrying a couple of dishes he brought over to an older couple sitting together at the bar.

I kept my voice low and leaned closer to Trish. "Like I said, it's nothing fancy. But the food's good."

She smiled, looking around. "I like it."

We both sat quiet for a some moments. I still wasn't sure if the dinner was supposed to be all business or something else.

Margaret came over with our drinks. "You want a few minutes?"

We hadn't even looked at the menus. "At least a few," I said. "We're not in a hurry." But as soon as I said it, I realized I'd spoken for both of us. Margaret walked away, and I said to Trish, "Unless you are?"

"In a hurry?" She smiled, shaking her head as she raised her glass. "Do you think your detective friend will really call you tomorrow?"

I assumed, right then, it was going to be business. "He'll call," I said. "I'll follow up with him. If he can't help, he'll at least be able to point me in the right direction."

I looked at my glass of ginger ale and the red cocktail straw sticking out of it. I wasn't even sure I liked ginger ale that much. "Listen," I said. "Can I ask you a question?"

Trish nodded and sipped her wine.

I said, "Is there something more to why you're doing this?"

"Something more than the fact he was my father? And the fact that after all these years, nobody seems to know who killed him?" She seemed somewhat agitated and didn't appear to appreciate the question.

"I'm just asking," I said. "I can't help but think the man is as much a stranger to you as he is to me, so—"

"Didn't I just tell you he's my father? How does that make it the same for you as it is for me?" She had a twisted look to her face, a slight snarl to her lip.

Our dinner together had gotten off to a bad start.

I said, "I didn't mean it the way it came out."

"Then why don't you say what you mean?" She cleared her throat. "This is the difference between us," she said. "In New York, we say what we mean. People might say we're not nice, but we don't waste people's time beating around the bush."

I nodded, like I understood. And I did. I experienced it firsthand, for the five years I lived in Rhode Island.

"If I can't ask questions, then how do you expect me to get anywhere with this?"

She shrugged. "Then maybe you need to ask better questions."

I looked over at the bar and thought maybe it was time for a real drink. But I resisted.

"Let's forget I asked," I said, sipping the sugary ginger ale. I had to come up with a better drink to keep me from hitting the booze. "Can I ask a favor?"

She nodded, and reached across the table for my hand. "I'm sorry I snapped like that," she said. "It's been a lot for me to handle. All of it. I feel like I need this. I need closure." She let go and leaned back in her chair, throwing back whatever wine was left in her glass. "Do you mind if I get another?"

"Not at all," I said.

Chapter 6

I ROLLED OVER IN my bed when my phone rang, waking me from a deep sleep. I rubbed my eyes and reached for the phone on my nightstand, needing a moment for my eyes to clear so I could see who was calling.

I answered when I saw it was Mike. "Yeah?"

"You're asleep?" he said.

"I wouldn't be talking if I was," I said, checking the time on my phone. "It's barely past five." I sat up on the edge of the bed and pulled on my shorts from the floor with one hand.

Mike sighed into the phone. "I don't have all day. You said you've got something that has to do with the Stuart Graves case. You'd better not be yanking my—"

"I'm not yanking anything. I thought if we could talk, maybe put our heads together..."

"Give me a break," Mike said. "Who's the client?"

I was hesitant to tell him, but I knew I didn't have much of a choice. It would only be a matter of time before he'd find out.

"The victim's daughter," I said.

"His daughter? What *daughter*?"

I said, "He'd found out about her a few months before he was killed. They never even met."

"And she shows up eleven years later? There's got to be more to it."

I didn't tell him I was thinking the same thing. "She never knew about him. Not until a couple of months ago. Her mother was on her deathbed, told her about the boyfriend from college who got her pregnant. Turns out Stuart Graves was the guy. Her biological father."

"Why'd the mother hold out? I'd be upset, someone held something like that from me my whole life. How old is she?"

"Early thirties," I said. "She lives in New York."

"And why would she want to hire *you*?"

"Are you asking why she'd hire me, personally? Or why she'd want to know who killed the father she never met?"

"Well," Mike said. "Both, but... okay, listen. I dug in a little. It's not the most organized case. I had nothing to do with it at the time, so keep that in mind. I don't have a lot of the details. At least not that I'm finding. And I don't want to open up a can of worms by asking about it either."

I said, "I understand the lead detective's retired?"

"Yeah. Name's Detective Holt. Allen Holt. He was old, even back then, when it happened. He retired a few years back now."

"Is he still living in the area?"

"I have no idea where he is."

••••••••••

I sipped my coffee from the cardboard to-go cup, catching a glimpse of Mike on the other side of Friendship Fountain, watching me through the jets of water shooting into the air.

I walked around and there he was, standing, his green John Deere hat on his head pulled low, and wearing dark sunglasses.

I approached him, and said, "How come you always look like you're undercover when we meet?"

Mike waited to answer, watching a man run past us, jogging.

It was early morning, and there weren't many people around. To me, it was the best part of the day, when everyone else was just rolling out of bed. Even the weather was better at that time.

"You think I want someone seeing me talking to you?" Mike said, sipping his own coffee. He looked back and forth. "Sharing public information is one thing. And you know how to find it yourself." He held up a large white envelope. "This is a different story." He handed it to me.

"What is it?"

"Mostly notes," he said. "Printouts, copies of documents, witness interviews... You may find something useful in there, but nobody else ever did."

"Thanks Mike," I said. I opened the clasp on the envelope.

"Hey hey hey. What are you doing? Don't open that here," he said. "Just take it, and keep quiet about it. All right?"

Mike always had an act, like he watched too many cop movies. "I appreciate you *not* helping me."

He nodded, chewing the inside of his cheek. "You sure this woman is who she says she is?"

I thought for a moment. "Why would someone show up in Jax pretending to be a dead man's daughter?"

Mike looked out at the St. Johns River. "I'm just saying, you never know. Why wouldn't she come to the sheriff's office?"

I said, "For what? It's been eleven years without any answers."

"She didn't even know the man. And now she's going to take money from her own pocket to hire someone to solve a crime that may be unsolvable?"

"Maybe you shouldn't always be so distrusting," I said. "And have a little faith. People have their reasons for doing things."

Mike sipped his coffee.

I held up the envelope. "How much of this did you look over?"

"I looked it over," he said, "but didn't get into the details of the investigation. I hate to say it, but it's just another name in a pile of unsolved cases. Hundreds. Thousands. I recognized the name of the main suspect at the time."

"Rick Lilly?" I said. "I read he was a good friend of the victim."

"He owned the house where Graves was killed," Mike said. "But he came up clean. Had nothing on him, other than owning the house. Apparently, he hired his buddy to help sell his house. Supposedly, he had his real estate license, but other than this particular instance, it doesn't appear it was his thing."

"They didn't have anything else on him?" I said.

Mike shrugged, shaking his head. "Like I said, I just skimmed through the notes, and wasn't involved enough at the time to answer your questions." Mike nodded toward the envelope in my hand. "It's all in there. What you won't find is the person Graves showed the house to."

"Because it's not in here? Or they don't know who it was?"

Mike said, "The likely assumption is whoever it was he met there is the killer. Rick Lilly's alibi was strong enough, it wasn't him. It's happened before, but in most cases, it's a female agent."

"What's happened before?"

"Real estate agents, meeting some stranger to show a house, ends up dead."

"Oh."

"They're all so desperate to make a sale, there'd be no thought of the danger they'd put themselves in going into an empty house with a stranger."

I said, "Is the real estate agency he worked for still around?"

Mike huffed. "How many times do I have to tell you I wasn't involved in the case? But you keep asking questions, like I..." He shook his head and took a crushed pack of cigarettes from his front pants pocket.

"I thought you quit smoking," I said.

He acted as if he hadn't heard me and pulled a cigarette from the pack. He stuck it in his mouth but didn't light it.

We both stood, quiet.

"So trying to hunt down this alleged person he showed the house to must've been a big part of the investigation, right? But that's also assuming Lilly was telling the truth?"

"I believe he had a message on his answering machine at the time, Graves telling him he had an hour to get out of the house so he could show it to this potential client. Again, it's all in the folder."

"The recording?"

"A tape?" Mike shook his head and looked at his watch. "I didn't see it. But I gotta get to work. Good luck." He abruptly walked away from me without another word.

· · · • · • · · ·

I drove into the parking lot at Billy's Place and stopped behind a full-size box truck with SISKEY SEAFOOD and a photo of a lobster printed on the side. A large man, with a thick beard, pushed a hand truck down the ramp and in through the back door of the restaurant.

The rest of the lot was empty, Billy's Place still a couple of hours from opening, so I parked in a spot far enough out of the truck's way.

Chloe stood outside the door, clipboard in her hand. She looked up and smiled when she saw me walking across the lot toward her. "Morning, Henry."

"Morning," I said. "How's your day, so far?"

She shrugged. "Just getting started, I guess."

I looked into the truck and could smell the fish, or whatever rotted residue had permeated the inside of it. "Billy around?"

She shook her head. "Not today. He doesn't come in early anymore."

I looked up the wooden steps going up the back to the second floor, with the two offices. "Do you happen to have a key to the upstairs office? My old office?"

She nodded. "I can get it. Are you taking it back?"

"I'm not sure yet. It depends."

39

"Billy would love that. He loved having you up there."

The bearded man walked past us with the empty hand truck, and up the ramp. He came back down, carrying a large box, the sides dripping wet.

Chloe put her finger up to me to wait, looking down at the clipboard she was holding, making a note. "Thanks," she said to the man, smiling as he walked back into the restaurant. "After the last man who leased the space up there, I don't think Billy wants to rent the space anymore. I know for a fact that doesn't mean you." She started toward the open door. "Let me grab the key."

Chapter 7

I SAT IN THE middle of the office on a wooden chair I grabbed from Billy's. Other than a few random wires running across the tile floor, it was so quiet and empty, it seemed even my thoughts echoed off the walls. It felt cold, beyond the air blasting through the vents.

The last time I'd been in there, I remembered looking at Alex's desk, her box packed and ready to go on top of it. And I wondered why I didn't try to stop her from leaving. In fact, I did the opposite. I told her she had to go, that it was the opportunity she always wanted, and she'd be foolish not to take it.

Turns out, I might've been the one who was foolish.

I leaned forward in the chair, elbows on my knees, studying the documents Mike had given me, spread out on the floor. Most of what I looked at included copies of interview notes from suspects and no more than a handful of witnesses the sheriff's office had questioned eleven years earlier, after Stuart Graves was killed.

I read over the notes about Sherry Carter, who turned out to be Stuart Graves' girlfriend, at least at some point before he was killed. She was forty-three at the time of the murder, and cleared of any suspicion.

The office door opened, and Billy walked in with a take-out coffee in each hand. He closed the door behind him with his foot. "Chloe told me you were here early, thought I'd grab you one of these since your coffee maker's gone." He cracked a smile, handing me one of the coffees.

"Thanks," I said, standing up from the chair with the files from Sherry Carter's interview in my hand. I had to stretch my back, sore from the way I'd been leaning over. "I hope it's okay I came up here? I just needed a place to spread out. I thought working off the boat made sense, but not when it gets as hot out as it is now."

"You don't have to explain," Billy said, looking at the mess I had on the floor. "What's all this?"

"Files from Mike Stone. He pulled what he could from the sheriff's office, pertaining to this case I'm working on."

"I thought you weren't sure you were taking the case?"

"I guess I am."

"Didn't you say your license expires soon?"

"I renewed this morning."

"Good call," he said, walking around the large, empty office. "You can use this space as long as you want."

I paused, taking a moment before I nodded. "I appreciate that, Billy. But—"

"There is no 'but.' Nobody else is using it, and I don't know if I want to be in the commercial leasing business at this point in my life. So, no sense in letting the space go to waste." He sipped his coffee. "Whatever you need to do to get back on your feet, get the agency rolling again... just let me know."

There weren't many people in the world like Billy.

"I do appreciate it."

"I know. You said that already. Don't make a big deal about it, all right?" He smiled.

I'll pay you, whatever you need, for however long I'm here. Depending on how this case turns out, I can sign a lease for a few months, six months, or—"

"That's not much of a commitment," he said.

"Oh, okay. Yeah, I'll sign it longer. A year. Whatever you want."

"I'm not talking about the lease," he said. "I don't even want your money. What I'm talking about is your commitment to your business. What are you going to do? Take one case and walk away again?" He shook his head. "Either you get back on the horse and ride it, or..." He looked me in the eye. "You can't keep doing this."

"Doing *what*?"

"Living your life, always thinking there'll be something better out there for you. That something else'll be easier."

I swallowed hard. Billy sometimes treated me like his kid brother, for as long as I'd known him. I didn't always love it when he'd try to give me advice. I wasn't keen on taking advice from anyone at all, in fact, but most of the time, his advice was right on.

I let out a sigh, nodding. "It's just that, doing this without Alex..."

"Everyone misses her," he said. "But she's doing what she needed to do. And you're acting like you can't do anything without her. That's just not the case. As much as you liked to tell people she was the brains behind the operation."

"The brains *and* the looks," I said, smiling.

"But it's just not true," he said. "I mean, the looks, yeah. I won't argue with you there, but…"

We both laughed.

Billy looked around. "I think you should set this place up; make it yours again. Maybe this time put a sign out front."

"I don't need a sign," I said. "Attracts the crazies."

"Okay, well, that's up to you. But electricity is taken care of. I can get the broadband turned on up here, and I have some furniture if you need it. We'll worry about everything else some other day."

I said, "I don't feel right not paying you. Why should you—"

"I said we'll worry about it some other day." He sipped his coffee and looked out the window, at the river. "Still one of the best views of the St. Johns." He turned and walked over to where I had the papers spread out in front of the chair.

"So are you having any luck?"

I held up the file in my hand. "You don't know a woman named Sherry Carter, do you?"

Billy pulled at his chin. "From Jax? Name rings a bell," he said. "Is she married?"

"She was Stuart Graves' girlfriend," I said. "Divorced. Was married to a…" I looked at the papers in my hand. "Ex-husband's name is Jack Carter. Owns some kind of photography business. At least, he did at the time they were married."

Billy said, "Was she a suspect?"

I looked at the papers on the floor, shaking my head. "Not according to the sheriff's office. They were divorced long before the murder."

Billy was quiet, thinking. "Honestly, both their names sound familiar."

I handed him the paper with a photocopy of Sherry Carter's picture. "I don't have a photo of the ex-husband, but this is her."

Billy took the paper, looked at it for a few seconds and handed it back. "I don't know. She looks familiar. If I think of anything, I'll let you know. What else about the ex? They never found any reason he'd kill the boyfriend?"

"I don't know. I'm going to talk to him—to both of them. Nothing in here that leads me to believe the sheriff's office considered some kind of love triangle. And they'd been divorced a few years already at the time of Graves' death."

Billy put his coffee on the floor and sat on the edge of the windowsill, his back against the glass. "So what else have you got?"

I shrugged. "I'm not sure yet." I looked at the papers and sat back down in the uncomfortable wood chair. "Mike grabbed what he could for me, but the investigation went on for at least a year. I mean, it's still technically active, but there are over nineteen thousand unsolved homicide cases in Florida. Stuart Graves' case is just another needle in a haystack."

Billy sipped his coffee. "So, Stone's actually helping you out?"

"He claims he's not helping. I'm not supposed to mention it, so keep it between us," I said. "But it was never his case either."

"Who was the detective?"

I picked up the folder and looked inside. "His name's Allen Holt. He's retired. " I picked up another sheet of paper from the floor. "Apparently Stuart Graves had an on-again, off-again girlfriend he moved in with when he came back from a business trip to the West Coast."

"What was he doing out there?"

"I'm not exactly sure."

Billy said, "And she still lives around here? What'd you say her name was?"

"Sherry Carter." I nodded. "She runs a pottery studio called Jacksonville Pottery, in Murray Hill."

"I like Murray Hill," Billy said. "Not as hip as Riverside, but one of the nicer historical neighborhoods in Jax. I think I actually know this pottery place, right there near the Murray Hill Theatre on Edgewood, right before you get into Avondale."

"Oh, okay," I said. "I'll take a ride over later." I held up the sheet of paper. "She had an alibi, apparently teaching a pottery class at the time of his murder. She also claims she knew nothing about his meeting with a prospective buyer or helping his friend sell his place."

Billy didn't have a background in anything that had to do with law enforcement, but he had a good education and was always a valuable resource. He was a thinking man and couldn't help himself, asking about my investigations. He was as inquisitive as I was and would usually have more questions than I had answers for. If anything, he made me think harder.

He stood from the window and opened the door to outside. The warm, humid air slipped in, so he closed it again. "Don't remember the last time it got this hot so early in the season." He held his hand on the knob. "I have to get downstairs. But if you want a table to work on, let me know. You're too old to be hunched over the floor like that, sitting like some college kid doing a report. I have an extra high-top—a pub table—in the back room downstairs, if you want to come down and get it. Or I can ask one of the dishwashers to help after the lunch rush." He opened the door and started to walk out.

I got up from the chair. "Billy?"

He turned before he pulled the door closed.

"Thanks," I said.

He gave me a nod with a half smile, and walked out, pulling the door closed behind him.

Chapter 8

THE BELL OVER THE glass door jingled when I stepped into the pottery place in Murray Hill. A sulfur-like odor hung in the air; the heads of at least a dozen women turned to gawk at me, seated at round, wooden tables, with what looked like clumps of clay in front of them.

I looked around for the person in charge, and a woman with long, gray hair, tied in a ponytail, leaned over the shoulder of another woman seated at the table. She straightened up, looking at me, then excused herself and started my way.

The place was bright inside, the white walls aligned with wooden shelves filled with pottery, like mugs and cups and a lot of bowls. Some appeared to be unfinished and maybe even in bad shape, including the bowls, too warped to hold anything inside. Or maybe they were made that way on purpose.

The woman with the gray hair stood facing me. She wore a green smock with a Jacksonville Pottery Studio logo printed in white on the front. "Are you here for the class?"

I almost laughed. "Not today." I recognized her from the photos I found online, although she appeared older than she did when they were taken. Maybe it was just the hair. "Are you Sherry?"

She stared at me, somewhat suspicious, a cheerful expression dropping from her face as she nodded. "Can I help you with something?"

I looked at the other women, working like preschool kids, with all the focus and joy adults didn't normally experience in life anymore. "Maybe this is a bad time," I said. "But I'd like to talk to you, ask a few questions."

"I guess it depends what it's about," she said.

I pulled my business card from my pocket and handed it to her, pausing as she looked it over.

She raised her gaze from the card. "A private investigator?" Her mouth opened slightly, like she was about to say something else.

"It's about Stuart Graves."

She took a quick look over her shoulder at the women seated at the tables, paying us little attention. She kept her voice hushed. "We can step outside." She turned to the women, raising her voice: "Ladies, I need to step outside for a moment."

They all looked up and nodded, smiling, and went right back to their projects.

I followed Sherry outside, and we stood on the sidewalk on Edgewood Avenue, a few feet from her door.

Her hands were tucked into the pockets of her smock. "Who are you working for?"

"A relative of Stuart's."

Sherry Carter stood still, not saying a word, at first. "I... I don't understand." She tried to hide her nervous swallow. "He doesn't have many relatives who would…" She paused. "Was it Jane?"

"His sister?" I shook my head. "No, ma'am."

She stared back at me, expecting an answer. But I let it hang for a moment.

I said, "Did he ever tell you about his daughter?"

Her eyes opened wide. Sherry swallowed hard again and looked away.

"By your reaction, I'll assume you didn't know?"

She shook her head. "No, I didn't. But, I… It just made me think of something else. I'm sorry, I—"

"Something else?" I waited, and I could tell by her expression she was thinking something through.

"Stuart had a girlfriend a long time ago, before he and I got together. She was killed in an accident."

"I didn't know that," I said. "I'm sorry to hear, but…" It was a surprising piece of information, but I wasn't clear what the connection was.

Sherry's eyes were fixated on the ground. "Her name was Elizabeth. She was pregnant when she was killed."

"You knew her?" I said.

"We all did."

I didn't know yet who she meant by "all," but I'd soon find out.

Sherry said, "Stuart believed he was the father."

"He didn't know for sure?"

Sherry shook her head. "And it was determined, after they recovered her body, that it was a little girl."

I hesitated a moment, at a loss for words. "I'm sorry. I mean, that's hard to hear. Do they know how it happened?"

Sherry nodded. "They believe she might've taken her own life."

That was something I felt Trish needed to know right away.

Sherry said, "So, no, I didn't know he had a daughter. I mean, besides..." She closed her eyes. "Stuart died not knowing if she would've been his or not. The whole thing was just so sad."

"I'm surprised he didn't mention anything to you about it," I said. "I mean, his daughter. Her name's Trish. Trish Williams."

"We had an odd relationship the last couple of years before he was killed," Sherry said. "We hardly spoke, even though he was living in my house."

I thought about Trish and knew what I'd just learned wasn't something that could wait. "You know what?" I said. "Do you mind if I come back later? I actually have to run. I'm sorry, but I'll be in touch." I jogged across Edgewood to where I'd parked the Jeep, jumped inside, and headed for Trish's hotel.

·········

I walked across the white marble floor inside the lobby of the Marriott Hotel in downtown Jax, looking at my phone every few moments to see if Trish had tried to call. I'd already been there waiting for twenty-five minutes, assuming when she said she'd meet me in the lobby that she was up in her room.

I hadn't told her when I called why we needed to meet, only that I had some information she needed to hear.

Throughout the fifteen-minute drive from Murray Hill to downtown, I wondered about being the first to tell her there was a chance the woman who was killed in a car accident may have been carrying Trish's unborn sister.

I had very little information. There was a chance I was jumping the gun, but the story struck me in a strange way. I wasn't even sure Sherry Carter wanted to tell me, even though she did.

I turned when I heard my name.

"Henry?"

Trish's voice echoed off the concrete walls and high ceiling of the busy lobby.

She walked toward me after stepping off the elevator, then gave me a hug I wasn't expecting. She smelled nice, like something sweet. Her hair felt wet against my face.

"I'm sorry I made you wait," she said. "I went for a swim in the pool, then went to my room to get cleaned up."

I shook my head, trying to force a smile when I knew what I had to tell her wasn't something she'd be expecting.

"Did you talk to my father's ex?" she said.

I nodded, thinking through what I was about to share. "I just left her pottery studio. But she was in the middle of holding a class, so we didn't get to talk for long."

"Oh," she said, nodding toward an empty hotel bar. "Do you want to go sit?" She rubbed her bare arms up and down. "It's cold in here, the air conditioner's always on full blast."

That was the thing in Jacksonville, or any part of the South. It would get too hot and humid to ever go outside, so most buildings were often frigid from the air-conditioning.

We sat across from each other in red-padded-leather chairs, with a small glass table between us.

It took me a moment to speak, deep in my own thoughts.

"Is something wrong?" she said.

"Stuart's ex-girlfriend, Sherry Carter, told me something that... I just thought you should know right away. I didn't even finish questioning her."

Trish waited. "What are you going to tell me?"

"There was a woman who was killed in an accident. She was pregnant. It was a girl. It turns out there's a chance Stuart Graves was the father."

Trish's expression didn't change. She stared back at me. I couldn't tell if it was shock or something else. "That's what she told you?"

I nodded, and she looked away, toward the lobby.

"Sherry said nobody knew for sure. But your father claimed the baby would've been his."

"I... I don't understand. Nobody knows?"

"Someone probably does," I said.

"Do you think it has anything to do with him being killed?"

I didn't answer. I didn't know.

Trish appeared somewhat shocked. Or maybe sad. She seemed hard to read.

"I'm sorry," I said. "I came right over to tell you. I thought it was important you knew."

She got up without a word and left. She walked across the lobby, her flip-flops slapping the cold marble until she made it to the sliding door at the entrance, and stepped outside.

I followed her into the hot sun, but she walked at a good pace ahead of me, continuing on the sidewalk, along the front of the hotel, until she stopped at the end, before a parking lot.

"Trish," I said, halting a few feet behind her. "Are you okay?"

She kept her back to me, silent for another moment or two. "It was bad enough knowing I had a father I never had a chance to meet. And now"—she faced me—"you're telling me there's a chance I could've had... I could've had a sister?" A tear slid down her face. I knew she'd be surprised but didn't fully expect her reaction. I should've known better. "I'm sorry. But I think I just need to be alone for a little while." She brushed past me and headed toward the hotel's entrance.

"Trish," I said.

She didn't stop, stepping through the entrance, into the hotel.

I didn't follow.

Chapter 9

Trish hadn't answered my calls, so rather than wait around to talk to her again, I headed over Mathews Bridge into Arlington.

I hadn't been in that part of Jax since before Alex sold her house and decided to take a spin by.

I stopped in front of the small two-story and stared at the porch where Alex and I spent so many days and nights. I didn't know who the new owner was, but with a shiny new Tesla and BMW in the driveway, I had to assume it was someone with money. Or maybe someone with a lot of debt.

I grabbed my phone and sent Alex a text:

I'm in Arlington, in front of your old house.

I waited for a response, but I didn't get one right away. I started to pull away but stopped when my phone buzzed. I pulled over and looked at the phone's screen.

Alex had replied:

I'm sorry. So busy, in the middle of something. I'll call soon!

I was glad I heard back from her but looked forward to having an actual conversation with her one day. It'd been a while.

I drove away and continued toward the eastbound ramp onto the Arlington Expressway, turning onto Kernan Boulevard in East Arlington.

The newer suburban neighborhood had mostly one-story stucco houses, all with the same overall design, including a fancy-looking portico in front, a two-car, side-entry garage, and a couple of large trees the builder hadn't cut down.

I wasn't exactly sure what a logistics consultant did, but Rick Lilly seemed to do all right for himself. The garage door was open with a black Mercedes parked inside. I parked behind it and made my way along the stone walkway to the door.

When I got to the steps, an older gentleman had already opened the door, his white hair slicked back, wearing a tight T-shirt that showed off a fit physique. "Can I help you?" he said, leaning out through the door's opening. "I saw you drive up, and..."

"My name's Henry Walsh," I said.

"Henry Walsh?" he said, narrowing his eyes. "Why's that name sound familiar?"

I didn't know and didn't answer. "I'm here to ask you a few questions about Stuart Graves."

"Stuart?" The man stepped outside and let the glass storm door close behind him. "What about?"

"I'm investigating his murder."

"His murder? Now? Are you with the sheriff's office?"

"I'm a private investigator."

Rick Lilly cocked his head and crossed his arms. "Are you serious?"

"Yes, sir, I am."

He sighed, looking out at his perfect, green lawn. "It's just that, it's been such a long time. Now, out of the blue, some private investigator shows up at my door asking about my old friend?"

"It's never too late to solve a crime," I said, giving him a grin.

He looked at his watch. "I don't have much time."

"I'll try to make it quick and painless," I said.

He seemed hesitant, then nodded, and opened the door, holding it for me to go in ahead of him. "Come on in," he said calmly.

I stepped into a good-sized foyer, with what looked like red Spanish tiles on the floor and large, potted tropical plants of various sizes, spread around the area. There was one tall enough, it looked like it'd overgrown the space, like a tree, coming close to the chandelier, high up, over our heads. A gurgling sound came from a rock water fountain almost hidden between the plants.

"I guess you like your plants?" I said. "Friend of mine has them all over his place."

"They're good for us," Rick said. "Cleans the toxins from the air."

A fact I knew but maybe didn't appreciate enough. Although living on a boat, I had plenty of fresh air around.

Rick walked ahead of me, down a hall, toward the back of the house. "I'm interested in hearing why, after all these years, someone's showing up at my door to talk about Stu."

I followed him turning right, down another hall, before stepping into an office. He sat behind the desk and pointed at the two chairs across from him. "Have a seat," he said, his fingers steepled, watching me. "Would you like a drink?"

"No, thank you."

"Okay, before you get started with whatever it is you've got in mind, I'd appreciate it if you'd get to the part where you tell me who hired you?"

"Are you aware Stuart Graves had a daughter? From New York?"

Rick's eyes opened wide. "Are you serious?" He laughed, shaking his head. "Leave it to Stu."

"So he never said anything to you about her?" I said.

Rick shook his head.

"But before I get into more about her, can I ask you what you know about Elizabeth Sutton?"

"Elizabeth?" He shrugged. "Like what?"

"I understand she was pregnant when she was killed, and Stuart Graves may've been the father?"

Rick was quiet at first, then nodded. "I guess nobody really knew for sure, one way or the other. Guess it could've been, since they were together for a short time."

"A short time?" I said.

Rick shrugged. "Listen, I don't know much about what went on between those two. I mean, of course, it was a shock when Elizabeth died."

"So you knew her?"

"Yeah, we all did. She'd hung around this bar we used to go to. But, I wouldn't say any of us knew her well. Like I said, Stu had a short fling with her, that's all I know of. Guess that's what led him to believe he could've been the father. I guess anything's possible, but I don't know what you want me to tell you about it, or what it has to do with."

"You were friends with Stuart Graves, weren't you?"

He nodded. "Of course I was. I'm going to assume you knew that already, or you wouldn't be here."

Rick leaned back in the chair, staring at me. "Now, what's the story with this supposed daughter of his, from New York? She's the one who hired you?"

I didn't want to give him too many details about her, but told him what I thought he needed to know.

Rick said, "What's Elizabeth's accident got to do with her?"

"If her father was the father of the unborn child…"

"Oh, I see. But I'm still trying to wrap my arms around the fact Stuart knew he had a daughter up there and never mentioned her to me. And you said Sherry didn't know about her either?"

I nodded. "That's what she claims."

"Sherry's a fairly honest woman. If she knows something, there's a good chance she's going to tell you." He paused. "Maybe Stu just wanted to keep it to himself. That's kind of how he was, anyway."

"You mean he kept things to himself?" I said.

"Yeah, I'd say so."

"And you'd consider him a good friend? Good enough to tell you something like this?"

"Yeah, of course he was a good friend. Good enough, at least. I mean, like I said, he kept to himself. Kind of one of those creative, introverted types, you know what I'm saying? He liked to do his thing, would even disappear without anyone knowing where he was or what he was up to. Then he'd show up again out of nowhere, like it was normal. Man didn't even ever own a cell phone. That's just how he was."

I looked around the home office. "I'm surprised you were friends with him."

"Why's that? Because we're opposites?"

"For the most part, yeah. You're a businessman," I said. "Stuart, from what I've heard, was somewhat of a hermit. A recluse. At least, it seems he was."

"Oh, he was. For sure. But, I don't know. I liked the man. He did what he wanted to do. Didn't give a damn about money. It was the last thing on his mind." Rick grinned. "Me? I wake up in the morning thinking about it."

"Money?" I said.

He nodded. "Gotta have it, you want to get anywhere in this world."

"If he wasn't into money, why would he get into real estate?"

"Because the man was broke. He needed to eat." Rick laughed. "I'm the one who convinced him to go get his license, thought maybe it'd be something he could do, without having to go sit at a desk, or take some kind of demeaning job." Rick shook his head. "I still feel guilty to this day, just for putting him in that situation."

I said, "So how does an introvert sell real estate?"

Rick smiled. "Stu still had a good personality, even though he preferred to keep to himself. Most people can't survive on their talents alone, if you know what I mean. Stu was the textbook definition of a starving artist. I appreciate being creative and all that, but a man's gotta eat. So I tried to help him, even sent some clients his way. He didn't have to do much, other than show someone a house. He didn't get involved in selling; that wasn't his thing. But he did all right, to be honest. Made a few bucks, even though he hated the fact he was in real estate."

The gray walls in the office were covered with plenty of framed artwork and photos.

Rick pointed at a painting of a farmer with two cows next to him. "He painted that one, you know. It was a gift, because my daddy was a farmer." He huffed out a quick laugh. "I remember when Stu gave it to me. Funny thing is, he got to a point he didn't want to paint anymore. Too bad, because he was good at it. He'd started writing, from what he told me. I don't know much about what he was up to, but took off on a trip to the West Coast, like some crazy kid, chasing a silly dream."

"Silly?" I said. "Do you know what it was about?"

"Not really. I guess it was some kind of movie he'd written. Maybe he thought it was something special, but..."

"You don't think so?" I said.

Rick shrugged. "I never actually read it. I'm just saying, he landed back here, didn't he? Came back more broke than when he left, had to move in with his old girlfriend 'cause he had nowhere else to go."

This man wanted me to believe he was a friend of Stuart Graves, but the way he came across, I wasn't exactly sure he was.

"Are you married?" I said.

"What's that got to do with anything?"

"I'm just asking a question."

He took a moment before he replied. "I was. Twice."

"You have kids?"

"They're older, off and married now, kids of their own."

We both sat quiet for a couple of moments.

I said, "I read through your interview, when the police questioned you after Stuart's murder."

Rick stared back, waiting for more. "That was a difficult time for a lot of us," he said. "My own friend, murdered in my house. Of course, as I'm sure you might've read, the cops didn't have any suspects. So, for one reason or another, they came down on me. They had nothing else." He got up from his chair. "You know what it's like having the cops try to pin a friend's murder on you?"

Rick walked to a window on the other side of the room, standing with his back to me, looking out.

"Are you surprised they never found the killer?" I said.

He shrugged without looking back. "I don't know if I'd say I was ever surprised. I was the only person who knew Stu was in that house. I mean, besides whoever it was killed him," he said.

"Was that house your primary residence at the time?" I said.

"It was an investment property, was hoping to unload before the market crashed." He turned from the window. "Took a lot longer to get it off my books once word got out someone'd been murdered inside it."

"And he never mentioned a name to anyone? From what I read, nobody knew who it was. But he called you, made sure you were out of there before he met the person?"

"Yeah, he called. Left me a message. I'd been separated from my wife at the time, and was actually spending my nights there, sleeping on the damn floor. I didn't speak with Stu directly, like I said. I wish I had, of course. Maybe he'd still be here. Or we'd at least know who killed him."

Chapter 10

I stepped down from the Jeep at the marina and walked toward my boat. I saw a figure standing in the darkness, almost as if hiding in the shadows, away from the lamps along the dock.

I suspected it was Trish, and when she came toward me, I saw I was right.

"Hey," she said, her head held in an almost shy, childlike way. "I'm sorry about the way I acted earlier."

"I don't blame you," I said. "One surprise after another. And that was a big one."

She smiled, lips tight together. "It was just a strange thing to hear. Kind of caught me off guard."

"Me too," I said. "But, I hope I made it clear nobody knows for sure whether or not he was the father. You may never know one way or the other."

Trish stopped. "Someone must know the truth," she said. "Just like with what happened to my father. Whoever killed him..."

"I can't say with any certainty the two are connected in any way." I pulled the ladder down on my boat. "I was at Rick

63

Lilly's house earlier. He didn't seem to know much about it. He also didn't know anything about you, that Stuart Graves had a daughter."

"I thought they were friends," Trish said. "He never told him about me?"

I shook my head. "Apparently not. It seems your father kept a lot to himself. Rick was surprised to hear about you."

I went up onto the boat and grabbed the two lawn chairs.

Trish stood at the edge of the dock, gazing toward the river.

"Are you all right?" I said, bringing the two chairs down the ladder. I sat in one and opened the other a few feet from me.

Trish stepped from the edge of the dock. "I need to know."

"You need to know *what*?" I said.

"I want to know if that woman was carrying his baby."

I'd realized I made a mistake telling her about the accident. I should have at least waited until I had more information, although I'm not sure there was more information to be had.

"Like I said, the answer may not exist. Maybe if it hadn't happened so long ago, it'd be a different story. But at this stage..." I shook my head. "I'm sorry. I think we'd be better off focusing on what happened to your father, which presents its own challenges as it is."

"Can't you do both?"

"Both?" I said. "Not alone, I can't. I try to stick with one case at a time, especially one that involves a murder. And now that I'm a one-man show... maybe if Alex was still around, it'd be an option, but..."

"What if they're connected?" She sat in the chair and pulled it so she was facing me. "How do you know for sure they're not?"

"I *don't* know for sure."

She reached out and put her hand on my knee. "Can't you at least look into it? I'm not looking for any charity. I'm looking for your help. I can't imagine my life, not knowing…" She paused, leaning back in her chair. "I lived my whole life thinking I had a normal upbringing. And now, here I am—I find out my whole life has been a lie."

"Did you talk to your dad?" I said. "In New York?"

"I called him from the hotel," she said. "I told him what you told me, and that I needed to know."

"What did he say?"

She shrugged. "He told me not to let my emotions drive my decisions. That was something he always said, because that's always been what I'd do. I can't help it if my emotions take over." She showed me a small grin. "It's why I'm here."

"I don't think there's anything wrong with that," I said. "It's not always about logic."

"He asked about you, you know. He wanted to make sure you were someone I could trust."

"And what'd you tell him?"

"That the jury's still out." She gave me a teasing look. "I told him I could tell the moment I met you, you were someone I could trust." She edged her chair a little closer. "I'm glad you tell it like it is. Some people might not like that, but I don't like it any other way." She stood from the chair and reached out for me with both hands, helping me from my chair.

I wasn't sure, at first, what she was doing.

Maybe I was, but I might've pretended in my own mind I wasn't.

We both stood, facing each other. She stepped closer and kissed me.

I was about to pull back from her. It would have been the right thing to do. She'd already told me she was emotional, and I didn't want to see either of us make a mistake we could regret.

The kissing didn't stop. With our arms wrapped around each other, we fell against the boat, then worked our way toward the ladder. She went first, holding my hand, pulling me after her.

Neither of us spoke, as if a force we couldn't control led us below to the cabin, in darkness.

··•·•····

I climbed out of my bed, feeling around the floor for my jeans I slipped on as I stepped to the window. I pulled aside the curtain and looked out at the dark sky with an orange glow to the clouds, the sun starting to rise.

Trish was naked under the sheets and at first looked to be asleep. But she rolled over. "What are you doing?" She looked around and sat up, holding the sheet up over her chest. "What time is it?"

"Almost six." I sat on the edge of the bed. "I'd make you a coffee, but I don't think that went over too well the first time."

She yawned. "I could use the caffeine, but I think I'll just wait to get some on the way back to the hotel." She swung her feet off the bed, her bare back to me, trying to hold the sheet around her as she bent over and picked up her clothes.

"I'll give you some space," I said. I went up onto the deck.

The air was nice outside, with less humidity than there had been. The sun was still making its way up, but the orange in the clouds had already started to fade.

I sat on the cushioned bench, the vinyl cool and damp. The smell of breakfast—bacon, to be specific—came from Jed's and filled the morning air. It made me realize how hungry I was.

Trish came up onto the deck, dressed but carrying her shoes. She sat next to me and leaned over, giving me a kiss on the cheek. "I had a nice time."

"Me too," I said, although feeling a little guilty about what had happened, for a number of reasons.

"Do you always wake up this early?" she said, unsuccessfully trying to cover another yawn.

"I like the morning, especially when everyone else is asleep."

She moved a little closer to me and put her hand on my leg. "Oh, well then, I hope I'm not ruining the atmosphere for you by being here?" She smiled, biting her lower lip.

I cleared my throat. "Listen," I said. "I've never done this before, with a client. I'm afraid... It was kind of a rule of mine that I—"

"I had a feeling you were going to say something like that." The smile changed to a frown, and she stood from the bench.

I reached for her arm before she could walk away. "It's not that I didn't want to. It's just that when something like this gets personal, it changes the dynamics of the relationship. Obviously."

"Sorry I took advantage of you," she said, a sly smile on her face. "But it already happened. So, now what? Are you going to fire me as your client?"

I pulled her back down to the bench, next to me. "You're my only client. I can't. But, I think maybe we should hold off. Maybe wait until we—"

"You're serious?" she said, the smile again leaving her face.

I thought for a moment. "I don't know."

She stood again, but this time I didn't stop her. "Then get to work," she said, climbing down the ladder, onto the dock.

"It'll take some restraint," I said. "But rules are rules. And I don't like to break them."

Trish looked up at me as she held onto the boat, slipping each shoe on her feet. "Why do I have a hard time believing you?" She didn't wait for an answer and started toward the parking lot.

"Where are you going?" I said.

"Up to Georgia."

I jumped from the seat. "Are you serious?"

She stopped and turned to me, nodding. "I'm going to visit Jane Ryan. My father's sister."

I climbed down onto the dock. "I don't know if that's a good idea," I said. "You need to be careful."

"I doubt she killed her own brother," she said, making light of it with her smile.

"That's beside the point," I said. "If whoever killed Stuart is still around, and you're snooping around..."

Trish said, "I'm not snooping around. I want to meet her. She's my aunt." She stood near her car, waiting as I approached her. She pulled me close and kissed me. "Don't worry. I'll call you after I talk to her."

She opened the driver's-side door.

"What if I go with you?" I said.

"She doesn't know I'm down here to find my father's killer, and showing up with a PI would be a dead giveaway."

Chapter 11

Sherry Carter stood at the entrance outside her studio with her back to the street. She appeared to be unlocking the door, a set of keys in her hand.

I walked up behind her, and said, "I'm back."

She jumped, startled, with her hand held to her chest. "You shouldn't sneak up on someone like that."

I held open the door for her as she removed her key from the lock. "I'm sorry. I didn't mean to scare you."

She walked in ahead of me with a deep and heavy-looking canvas bag hung over her shoulder, flipping on the studio's lights. The fluorescent lights above buzzed.

"I have a class starting in twenty minutes," she said, "so..."

I followed her to the back of the studio and stood in the doorway of an office no bigger than a small walk-in closet. She placed the bag on the floor next to her desk and walked back out, past me.

"Would you like a coffee?" she said.

"If you have some, sure."

She stopped at the kiln and pressed a couple of buttons, then turned a dial. A burning metallic odor filled the air. I noticed the duct coming out and up the back of it, vented through the wall.

She continued over to a kitchen-like area in the studio, which was nothing more than a granite counter with blue cabinets above and below. It looked like a kitchen display from Ikea, with nothing but a toaster and a coffee maker on top.

"You took off in quite a hurry yesterday," she said. "Was it because of what I told you, about Elizabeth Sutton?"

"You could say that was part of it," I said. "But I had to run. I hope my coming by this morning isn't inconvenient. I know you're busy."

She shook her head and dumped a bag of coffee beans into a grinder, pressing down on the top. The grinder buzzed and crackled, the beans popping around inside it. It was too loud to talk until it quieted down.

Once it stopped, she dumped the freshly ground beans into the coffee maker.

"This is a lot fancier than the stuff I make at home," I said. "Thank you."

"Life's too short to drink bad coffee," she said.

I nodded, and watched her finish her long process. I certainly appreciated it, although I didn't have the time or patience to go through those steps each morning. But that's why nobody ever drank the coffee I'd make.

"I spoke with Rick Lilly," I said.

"Oh yeah?" She wiped down the area with a paper towel. "How's Ricky doing?"

"Is that what you call him? Ricky?"

She shrugged. "I don't know. We used to. Maybe it was more appropriate when he was younger."

"I asked him about Elizabeth Sutton."

She stopped what she was doing and glanced my way. "And what did he say?"

"Not much. He doesn't know if Stuart could've been that unborn child's father or not," I said. "But, on the other hand, he said Stuart kept to himself."

Sherry smiled, nodding. "He sure did. As you can see, with this daughter of his. I still find it hard to believe he never mentioned her to me, even if our relationship wasn't what it used to be. But it also makes me wonder if what you're telling me is even true."

"Which part?" I said, although I think I knew.

"How do you know this young woman is telling the truth?"

"Would she have a reason to make something like this up?" I said.

Sherry shrugged. "I don't know. Maybe. Maybe not. You're the private investigator, I guess."

Sherry seemed to be a nice enough woman but had a little bit of a bite to her. Her Southern hospitality was apparent, but maybe she was hiding something else.

"Just so you understand, I wasn't around at the same time Elizabeth Sutton was hanging around. It all happened before my time, so there's not much I can add to the story. He did tell me once, after he'd had a few drinks, that he'd slept with her, and there was a good chance the baby was his. He didn't go into any details or anything, but it really seemed to bother him."

"Did he say anything else?"

Sherry just shrugged and started toward her office. "It was a long time ago."

I followed her, and leaned, watching her from the doorway. The smell of freshly brewed coffee was in the air, and I started to think she forgot about it.

She turned on her computer, leaning on her desk, and wiggled the mouse until the screen lit up. "I have to place some orders before the next class." She started to type but then straightened up. "The coffee!" She walked past me from the office and back to the kitchen area, filling two mugs, each with Jacksonville Pottery Studio printed on the side.

Sherry seemed to be a little bit all over the place. I wouldn't say she was flaky or anything, but maybe just a busy woman, trying to do too many things at once.

She handed me the mug, steam rising from the top of it. "I'm sorry, but I don't have any dairy or sugar."

I took a sip. "No need. It's good." And it really was.

She poured herself a cup, and I followed her to one of the tables, where we sat across from each other.

"Is there anything else Stuart told you? About Elizabeth?"

Sherry shook her head. "Not really. It seemed to me she didn't want much to do with him. That's how he made it sound. So I don't think there was ever much of a relationship there." She tilted her head a bit. "I'm not sure I understand why you're asking about her, or whatever happened. Are you trying to say there's some connection?"

I took another sip of coffee. "I don't know if there is or not. And without knowing a lot about Stuart's background, I'm trying to dig up whatever I can. You never know where something might lead."

She nodded, looking down into her mug, raising her gaze after a moment or two. "Don't you think it's possible it could've just been some random crime?"

"Graves' murder?" I said, nodding. "Anything's possible, although murders committed by strangers are rare. More than most people are led to believe."

"I didn't know that," she said, holding her mug on the table with both hands.

I said, "Maybe one out of ten homicides are committed by a stranger. Don't quote me on that figure."

She sipped her coffee, a look in her eyes, like she was thinking it through.

"So, what can you tell me about this trip he made out to the West Coast?"

"What about it?" she said. "We weren't really together at that point. Not until he came back, and needed somewhere to stay. But even then…"

"You weren't together?"

Sherry shook her head. "To be honest, we were on-again, off-again for most of the time we'd been dating, even before he made that trip. He came back; it was a year before his murder, almost to the day, and needed a place to stay. He'd really bottomed out. I think that's why Ricky convinced him to get his real estate license. Just to try and make some money."

I said, "So, that trip he made, it had something to do with a movie he was writing?"

Sherry only nodded.

"So he moved in with you, but there was nothing going on between you? Was it supposed to be temporary, until he got settled?"

"Settled?" Sherry laughed. "Stu was never settled."

"But, I mean, nothing ever happened, romantically?"

She looked at me funny, like she didn't like the question. "Are you asking if we were sleeping together?" She sipped her coffee, looking at me over the rim. He shrugged. "Maybe once or twice, out of convenience."

"What about his sister?" I said. "How well do you know her?"

"Jane?" Sherry rolled her eyes. "You'd think she and Stu were from separate mothers. They couldn't have been any more different."

"Did they get along?"

"Not really," she said. "I don't think she killed him, if that's what you're asking?"

"Can you tell me what their relationship was like?"

Sherry paused, glancing at the front door. "I don't know. I guess she never had much respect for him. She treated him like a loser, would even tell him so, because he never got a real job. But that's not what Stu was all about. He didn't care about money the way she did. He just wanted to make things. That's all that mattered to him."

"Did she ever feel any remorse?" I said. "After he was dead?"

"I doubt it."

I sipped my coffee, thinking about Trish going up there to meet the woman, knowing nothing about her.

"What about the rest of his family?" I said.

"There's nobody left, that I know of," she said. "His parents both died fairly young, not long after he was out of college. He lived with Jane for a while, but that didn't work out so well."

"Do you know her husband?" I said.

"Steve?" She nodded. "I don't know if he's still around. He was older than Jane by a few years. I'd guess he's in his eighties by now." Sherry looked at her watch and stood up from the table. "I'm sorry, I have to get to work."

"One last question," I said. "I'd started asking you about that movie he wanted to make?"

"The screenplay? I don't know much about it, to be honest."

"Did you read it?"

She shook her head. "No."

I stood as well. "Do you know where it is?"

She again shook her head. "I don't."

I said, "But wasn't he living with you when he was killed?"

"I guess the script must've been at my house," she said. "But I don't know what happened to it. I couldn't even find his computer."

"His computer disappeared too?"

"It was a laptop, so he'd take it wherever he went. He might've had it with him the day of his murder. I don't know. The cops never found it either."

"Is there anyone else who might know where it is?"

She smiled, but she had a look of doubt or maybe confusion on her face. "I don't know why you want to know about it. That's why he went out to Los Angeles, to sell it to someone. But he came back, so..."

"You're saying it wasn't any good?"

She shrugged. "I told you I never read it. But I'm just saying nobody wanted to make it into a movie, so who knows what he did with it after that. I'm not trying to tell you how to do your job, but I'm not sure there's any significance to it."

I nodded, like I understood. But something didn't seem right. I just didn't know what it was.

"I'm sorry, Mr. Walsh, I—"

"Call me Henry."

"Oh, okay. Henry, I have to get to work. I have a class soon, and—"

"Your husband was a good friend of Stuart's? Is that true?" We both started walking toward the door.

"Yes, they were friends. That's how I met Stu in the first place." She laughed. "I think Jack just wanted me out of his hair. We were married for fifteen years." She got a faraway look in her eye, like she was reminiscing. "We married so young. And Jack didn't like being tied down."

I reached for the door and looked back before opening it. "You were never involved with him again at any point?"

She swallowed, and I could tell she was holding something back. "Not before Stu was killed. Even though we weren't together anymore as a couple—me and Stu—it was an emotional time for me. And Jack was there. We were both feeling the same way when Stu was gone."

I think I understood what she was saying.

"It was just for a short time we started seeing each other again. But we quickly realized it was a mistake."

There was a knock on the door, and Sherry reached past me to open it.

I stepped back from a herd of women filing into the place, at least twenty of them, laughing and talking loud as they filled the empty benches around the tables.

"Good morning, ladies," Sherry said. She hadn't yet closed the door but nodded toward it. "I'm sorry, but my class will be starting." She looked at her watch and sighed. "I never placed my supply order."

Chapter 12

My phone vibrated in my pocket as I walked across the parking lot at Billy's Place. I thought I knew who it was and answered without even looking at the number. "Trish?"

There was a brief pause, and the voice I recognized too well said from the other end, "Who's Trish?"

I looked at the screen and couldn't stop the smile from forming on my face.

It was Alex.

"She's my new client," I said, trying to play it cool. "She's the only one who'd been returning my calls."

Alex laughed. "Is that supposed to be a dig, because I haven't called you back?"

"It might be," I said, after a long pause. "It's good to hear your voice. Mike tells me you're doing well."

"Mike?" she said. "I keep forgetting to call him back. I've just been so busy."

"Seriously? He said you call him all the time."

"You think you're the only person I've been ignoring? I just wish I had time to make some calls."

We were both quiet for a brief moment, like neither knew what to say next.

"So things're good?" I said.

"Uh... yeah, I think so. I mean... yeah, it's all good. I haven't really had time to think about it, to be honest. You'd think a small town like this, I'd have a chance to breathe. It's nonstop. And then, by the time I get home, whenever that is, I'm too exhausted to talk to anyone. And that's if I haven't brought home a case or two to work on. So, please don't take it personally."

"How many other detectives are there?" I said.

"It's really just me and Brett Hogan. He's the detective who was supposed to retire last year. I was hired to take his place, but then there was this murder, and, well, he's not retiring just yet. I don't know what I'll do when he does."

"Can't they just hire more detectives?"

"There were budget cuts recently, and..." She was quiet on the other end. "I'm sorry. Tell me how you're doing."

I had to think about how much I wanted to tell her. Ideally, she'd be by my side, making my job a whole lot easier.

"I renewed my private investigator's license," I said. "I guess that's news."

"I assumed so, when you said you have a client. That's good, isn't it?"

"I don't know. Is it?" I laughed. "I guess so. It wasn't until I got this call, from my latest client, that I made the decision."

I went ahead and told her a little about the investigation, at least what I knew at that point.

The heat was starting to get to me, wiping the sweat from my face with my arm.

"Where are you now?" Alex said.

"In the parking lot at Billy's. I'm actually going to be using the old office again."

"Really?" she said. "I thought you were going to work off the boat?"

"It's too hot," I said.

"You just realized that? One thing I don't miss being up there is the Florida heat and humidity. Not that it doesn't get hot up here, but..."

"Maybe I'll come up to visit one of these days," I said.

She didn't respond, which I admit bothered me a bit.

I said, "So, you think it's good that I'm sticking with the PI business?"

"Of course I do," she said. "I know you could never work for a police force or anywhere you might need to actually follow some rules. And you're good at it. As good as anyone. You know that."

"Am I?" I said, and wanted to tell her I wasn't half as good a detective without her around to help me. But there was no need to get sappy like that, even though it was true. "I just wonder how long this midlife crisis is going to last. I'm always wondering what I'm really supposed to be doing with my life. It gets old thinking about it."

Alex laughed. "I think you're not that different from most people. But you like to talk about it a lot more."

The line again went quiet.

"You actually sound pretty happy," she said. "I thought maybe you'd miss me being around."

I looked up the stairs, leading to the second story above the restaurant. "It's different. That's for sure."

I heard a two-way radio in the background. It sounded like a call from dispatch.

Alex said, "Henry, I have to go. Let's talk again soon, okay?"

"I hope so."

Alex hung up without another word. I don't remember the last time—if ever—I felt so distant from her. I knew it would eventually happen when she left, that we'd go our separate ways, and things between us would never be the same. I just didn't expect it to happen as quickly as it did. The part that might've bothered me the most was I was the one who persuaded her to take the job up there in North Carolina in the first place.

I went up the stairs to the office and slipped the key inside the lock. I opened the door and was surprised to see all the furniture inside.

There was a desk and chair, a tall wood bookcase with empty shelves, and a couch I recognized from Billy's house. There was a landline phone on the desk, but the wire was tied up in a knot and hanging off the side. I probably wouldn't need it anyway.

I sat on the couch and checked my phone to see if I'd missed a call. But there was nothing. I thought I would've heard from Trish, but there was no such luck. The only thing I could think of was she was still at Stuart Graves' sister's house. Maybe they were bonding in some way, if that was possible.

On the other hand, I was getting a little worried. Why wouldn't she have answered my calls? Or sent a text to tell me she's all right? The chance was still there, if word got out she was trying to find the person who murdered her father, that she could end up putting herself in danger. Especially if she planned to keep snooping around, rather than letting me do my job for her.

I tried not to worry, but I didn't want to keep calling like a worried old mother either.

There was a knock at the door, and Billy walked in. "Almost looks like a real office," he said.

I stood from the couch. "You didn't have to bring all this stuff up here." I glanced around the room that suddenly looked somewhat like a real office, thanks to Billy. "How much do I owe you for it?"

Billy flipped the back of his hand, waving me off. "Nah, it's all from my house. I've been wanting to get some new furniture anyway, so I went ahead and ordered it. Hired a couple of guys to rent a U-haul and drive this stuff over for you."

"You didn't have to," I said. "What do I owe you?"

He waved his hand at me. "You don't owe me anything. I told you, way back, when you were first starting your business, I'd help you out. And now I just want to make sure you land on your feet again, like you did the first time. Not that you *need* my help, but..."

"I appreciate it," I said, reaching out to shake his hand. "Really."

"You all right?" he said. "You look a little..."

"I'm fine." But I could tell by his eyes he wasn't buying it.

Billy was always good at reading people's emotions. It was like a special power.

"You're *fine*? That doesn't sound too convincing."

I looked at my phone and shrugged. "Trish Williams, my client, went up to Georgia to meet Stuart Graves' sister. I'm sure it's fine, but—"

Billy stared at me, his eyes on mine, his head slightly cocked. "You didn't."

"I didn't *what*?"

He folded his arms. "You *did*. You slept with her. I can see it in your face. And now you're worried that—"

"No! Of course not."

The problem was, no matter what I tried to say, Billy, like Alex, could see right through me whenever I tried to keep something to myself. I wasn't that good of a liar. At least not when it came to my friends.

He let out a sigh. "What happened to your rules? Or was the no-sleeping-with-clients an *Alex* rule?"

I walked to the new desk and sat on the edge of it, throwing up my hands. "I didn't mean for it to happen. I swear, it wasn't me. She's the one who came on to me, and—"

"I'm sure you really fought her off." He gave me a stern look, like a father might. "See, the problem now is it makes whatever you do personal. And you said it yourself, that it can be dangerous in your business."

I looked at the floor. "I know. But it's too late. What's done is done."

"Is it?" He huffed out a slight laugh and reached for the door. "I gotta get back downstairs. Busiest lunch rush we've had in a while."

Chapter 13

I pulled off Route 95, jumped onto Philips Highway, and followed it to Fortune Parkway, finally turning into the parking lot along the front of a long brick commercial building, with at least twenty or so businesses and offices listed on the large sign out front. Carter Photography was down the far end of the building, where I found a space in front of the glass-doored entrance. I parked next to a white van with a Carter Photography logo painted on the side.

A young woman sat behind the reception desk, smiling when I walked across the lobby.

"Good afternoon," she said, glancing at the clock on the wall as if she were making sure she had the time right. "May I help you?"

"Maybe," I said. "Is Jack Carter here?"

She looked at the computer screen in front of her, nodding. "He's in the middle of a session right now, but he should be done in a few minutes. Do you have an appointment?"

I shook my head. "No."

"Are you interested in his photography services, or—"

"I just need to talk to him about something. It's personal."
I looked behind me, on the other side of the lobby, where a
half-dozen modern-looking, plastic chairs with chrome legs,
every other one a different bright color, were lined up against
the wall. "I'll just wait over there, if that's all right?"

"Sure. I can give Jack your name, if you'd like?"

"No, thanks," I said. "He won't know who I am anyway."
I walked over to the chairs and stopped at a long, rectangular
coffee table that looked like it'd been cut straight from a tree.
Magazines were spread out on top of it, fanned like playing
cards. I picked up *Boating* magazine and sat in one of the chairs
with it.

The chair was more comfortable than I'd expected, for being
trendy and plastic.

I flipped through the pages, and wondered how many people
would actually subscribe to a magazine about boats. Looking
toward the reception desk, I said, "So, what do you do here?" I
held up the magazine. "I mean, what does Jack do? Is he a boat
photographer?"

The young woman nodded but had a look like she was
confused why I'd even have to ask. "He's one of the best in
Florida," she said.

I nodded toward the entrance. "Hard to get a boat through
that door, no?"

She smiled, humoring me with a quiet laugh. "We actually
have a garage door behind the studio, if he happens to be
shooting on-site."

I said, "Is that all he does? Boats?"

"Mostly. He used to do all kinds of commercial work. Still does, once in a while." She looked around the large reception area.

I followed her eyes to some of the poster-size, framed images. There were buildings, skyscrapers. I recognized some of the photos and walked up to look them over. "He took this photo? It's the Versace mansion, isn't it? I mean, it *was...*"

She nodded, staring at the photograph. "The Villa Casa Casuarina. I remember when he shot it, he took me with him to South Beach. I'd just started working for him."

"He took you with him to South Beach, huh?" I probably could have done a better job hiding my curiosity, wondering how old she could have been. And if there was some kind of story behind her joining him on a trip to South Beach."

But I moved away from the photo and looked at another. At first, I wasn't sure what it was, turning toward her, and pointing at the framed image. "Is this some kind of abstract work?"

She laughed. "That's a piece of machinery. He used to do work like that."

"Machinery?"

"Commercial equipment. Printing presses. That's from back when he would do catalog work. Mostly for dealers."

I looked at the other framed photos on the walls. It was impressive, although I wasn't sure how much skill it took to take a photo. But I guessed Jack Carter did all right for himself.

"His focus is on boats now," she said.

A door opened, and a tall, thin man, with a potbelly sticking out from under his Hawaiian-style buttoned shirt, walked into the lobby. With a bald head and a thick and bushy, white beard, he looked like a sea captain more than anything. I knew from the photos I found online he was Jack Carter.

Another man, younger and clean-shaven, with his dark hair slicked back, walked out the same door, behind him.

Jack shook the man's hand and patted him on the shoulder at the same time. "I think you'll like what we've got," he said. "We'll be in touch to schedule the viewing, in a few weeks."

The young man thanked him, walked to the door, and left through the entrance.

I rose from the chair, and the woman behind the desk said, "Jack? You have a visitor."

He looked at me, like he was surprised and hadn't even noticed me sitting there. He stepped toward me, extending his hand. "Jack Carter," he said, squinting one eye, like he was taking the bearded captain look a little too far.

"Henry Walsh," I said, shaking his hand.

"What can I help you with?"

"Is there somewhere we can talk?" I said. "I'd just like a few minutes of your time to discuss, uh…" I looked at the young woman, unsure she needed to know the reason I was there. "It's a personal matter."

Carter looked a bit suspicious, then glanced at the clock on the wall behind the reception area. "I have a meeting in forty-five minutes, off the site." He waved for me to follow him and walked through the same door he'd just come from. "I have a few minutes."

I followed him down a hall and past a door on the left with a sign that said, STUDIO, but he continued straight ahead. He walked through an open doorway and into a big office, with a good-sized desk and dozens of large, framed photos on the walls, mostly of boats and planes and a few landscapes.

I looked closer at one I recognized. "Was that taken from Trout River Marina, by any chance?" I pointed at a framed, black-and-white photo of water and a boat, with the sun setting behind it. It was a nice photo, something you'd see in a magazine.

He looked at it, nodding. "Good eye," he said. "I had a client, had his boat over there. You a boat man?"

"A boat man?" I'd never been referred to as such. "I live on my boat, at the marina."

"Yeah? I've thought about doing that one day myself—live on a boat. Not on the St. Johns, necessarily, but maybe down the coast somewhere. Or Costa Rica." He smiled and sat behind the desk, picked up a camera he had in front of him and looked it over. "You ever want to photograph that boat of yours..."

I sat in one of two chairs across from him, in front of the big desk that looked more like a table he used as a desk or maybe a workbench of some sort. "Oh, it's not the kind of boat you'd take pictures of. Just a place to rest my head, be out in the fresh air."

Jack placed the camera down and leaned back in the big leather chair. "So, you don't look like a salesman."

"I'm not," I said. "I'm actually here to ask about someone who I'm told was a good friend of yours."

"Was?" Jack squinted his eyes, like he had earlier. I got the feeling it was a look he'd practiced.

"I'm here to talk about Stuart Graves," I said.

Carter looked surprised. "Stu?" He ran his hand over his bald head. "You with the sheriff's office?"

"No, sir," I said, taking a business card from my pocket. I slid it across the desk, and he picked it up, giving it a quick look.

"A private investigator, huh? So, this is about what happened to Stu?"

I nodded. "You knew him pretty well?"

"Well enough I let him sleep with my ex-wife." He laughed. "Did us both a favor, at the time."

"I spoke to her, your ex-wife, earlier," I said.

Jack rolled his eyes. "She's always gotta drag me into something, doesn't she?" He picked up the camera again, acted like something on it needed to be fixed, but I had a feeling it was just for show. "I knew Stu, back when we were both into the art scene down here at the time. A bunch of us used to spend a lot of time together. We partied a lot back then, at this bar called The Crow. You may or may not've heard of it, down on Park Street in Five Points. But this was back when nobody tried so hard to be trendy, the way they do now over there."

I wasn't familiar with the bar he was talking about. "So it's still around?"

"The Crow?" Jack nodded. "But I'm not even sure Lenny's still there anymore, been so long since I stepped in the place."

"Lenny? Is he the owner?"

"Yeah. Lenny Coolidge. I suppose he still is, but I hear his kid took over the place. He makes a lot more money, from what it sounds like. But not the crowd it used to be when we were hanging around."

"So he must've known Stuart? Lenny?"

"Yeah, Coolidge knew him, all right. Lenny wasn't into the art scene like the rest of us, but he could pour a good drink without asking you to pay an arm and a leg. Again, this was back in the day. It wasn't always about making so much money as it was giving people a place to go, hang with their friends. You know what I mean?"

"I think I do," I said.

"One thing about Lenny was he appreciated what we all did. As artists, I mean. In fact, he had most of our work hanging in the place, would even let us do our own showings there... whoever wanted to."

I tried to remember the last time I was down in the Five Points area. It had been a while.

"So, for the most part, your friendship with Stuart Graves took place in a bar?"

"I guess," he said. "I mean, that's where we met. We were all artists, or, in Stu's case, he was more. He was a helluva painter, but all he talked about was wanting to be a writer. I don't know what it was; he had so much talent with the brush. He changed a bit, too, once he started writing more. We wouldn't see him as much. I'd say it'd been a year, maybe two, before he was killed, was the last time I saw him."

"Wasn't he out of town around that time?"

Jack nodded. "Yes, he was. Out in LA. Sherry would know better, but I'd say at least a year before he was killed, that's where he was."

That is what Sherry had told me.

I said, "What do you know about what happened with him, out in LA?"

"He didn't tell me much about it at all. I know it had something to do with some movie he was supposedly writing. But he didn't talk to me about it. I remember I'd asked him at one point about it, but he wouldn't talk. No idea why." Jack gave a weak smile. "I don't know if he thought someone was going to steal it from him or something else. He was always a little paranoid like that, afraid someone would steal his ideas."

I looked at the photos on the wall. "So what's the deal with you setting him up with your ex-wife?"

Jack laughed. "Sherry and I had already been divorced for quite a few years. But out of the blue, she starts calling me, wanting to talk, get together. It sounded to me like she was lonely." He shook his head. "I'd moved on, you know what I mean? But it got to a point she'd show up at places, no matter where it'd be. She started hanging around The Crow when I was there, trying to enjoy myself. I mean, she knew some of the other people there, but..." He shrugged. "I introduced her to Stu one evening, and they hit it off. They're both, or *were* both, quiet people. I knew I wouldn't have to deal with her anymore. They did all right for a little while, until he came up with this crazy idea to travel to LA."

We both sat quiet for a couple of moments.

"What about Elizabeth Sutton?" I said. "Were you around when she was dating Stuart?"

He picked up his camera again, looking it over. "Dating?" He shook his head. "I don't know if they had much of a relationship, to be honest. Stu sure acted like they had, but I was somewhat surprised he took it so hard."

"I understand she was pregnant?" I said.

Jack hesitated, then nodded. "I don't know much about that."

I said, "Stuart believed it was his?"

Jack swallowed, then nodded again. "You never knew what to believe with Stu. He was funny like that, like he'd get something in his head, and he wouldn't let it go, like he forced himself to believe it."

"Are you saying he was wrong?"

Jack held his gaze, quiet for a moment. "What's it matter now?"

"It was just a question," I said. Jack certainly wasn't the first to make the same comment, and I couldn't help but think there was something he knew, but wasn't about to tell me.

Chapter 14

I'D RECEIVED A TEXT from Trish, asking me to meet her at the marina. But when I pulled into the parking lot and saw her car, she wasn't inside it. I called her phone and she didn't answer. I climbed up on my boat, calling for her, peered below into the cabin, then stood up on the deck, looking back and forth on the dock and out toward the parking lot.

I knew she had to have been somewhere, but I couldn't find her. Why wasn't she answering her phone?

I sent a text:

I'm at my boat. Where are you?

After several minutes, there was still no response.

I started toward Jed's restaurant. There weren't many people outside around the boats. Maybe it was the heat. Glen Cooper, a man I'd known for as long as I'd been living at the marina, called out for me. I looked over at him, leaning on his boat's rail, bare-chested. His skin was dark and leatherlike from the sun.

"Hey, Henry. There was a woman here looking for you a little while ago." He smiled. "Good-looking one."

"How long ago?"

He shrugged. "I don't know. Ten, twenty minutes ago, I'd say?"

I lifted my sunglasses to just above my eyes. "Did you see where she went?"

"That's the thing," he said. "She was on her phone, over by that car." He pointed at the Taurus. "I was minding my own business, then looked over again, and she was gone. I can't say for sure, but it looked to me she got in another car."

"Another car? Are you sure you saw her get in it?"

He shook his head. "No, I'm not sure. I saw it over there, parked behind the car, where she'd been standing."

"You know what it was? What kind of car?"

Glen shrugged. "Maybe a Cadillac. I know it was a sedan, a black one. I don't pay much attention to what cars are out there nowadays." He grinned. "You know I've been driving the same pickup for twenty-three years."

I could feel my heart thumping in my chest. "You're sure you didn't see anyone?"

Glen shook his head. "I'm sorry, Henry. I wish I was a little more certain. I only looked when I heard the tires squeal. That's when I turned to look and watched it drive away. Left the parking lot in a hurry."

I looked down at the entrance to Jed's. "Maybe she went in the restaurant." I walked away, made it to the entrance at Jed's and opened the door. I looked inside, but the place was pretty much empty, other than a couple of stragglers at the bar.

I said to the two older men, and the young bartender standing with his eyes on the TV. "Anyone see a woman come in here? Early thirties?"

All I got were head shakes, like they couldn't be bothered.

I stepped outside and dialed Trish's number, heading along the dock toward my boat, Glen watched me as I hurried by, then I stopped to listen to the call. Her phone didn't even ring and went to her voicemail.

I left her a message: "Hey, it's Henry. I'm at the marina, but you're not here. I can see your car in the lot, right from where I'm standing, but you're not here. Call me." I hung up, picked up the pace, and ran to my boat. I thought about how I barely went all the way into the cabin, and maybe overlooked her on my bed. Maybe she was under the covers. Maybe she was taking a nap and didn't hear me. I guess I was being hopeful and maybe unrealistic.

I jumped up the ladder onto my boat and down to the cabin. There was nobody in my bed. The bed was empty.

She wasn't there.

I went back up onto the deck and looked around the marina, for as far as I could see. I glanced out at Trout River Drive, then dialed her number again.

But the call, like it did moments before, went right to voicemail. I hung up without leaving a message this time, jumped onto the dock and rushed over to the Taurus. I tried the driver's-side door and was surprised to see it unlocked. I leaned inside, into the unbearable heat, and reached around the steering column, thinking the keys might be in the ignition. They weren't.

· · · • · • · · ·

I went back to my office, pacing back and forth, unsure what to do. I tried not to panic or worry that something had happened to Trish. But I couldn't help myself.

Billy walked in, wearing his apron. He had a concerned look on his face, watching me as he eased the door closed behind him.

"Are you okay?" he said. "I saw you come flying through the parking lot; I thought maybe something was wrong?"

"Sorry about that," I said, looking through the files from the sheriff's office. "It's Trish. I don't know where she is. She was at the marina, parked in the lot. You know Glen Cooper? He's the one who saw her, said he thinks she left in someone else's car."

"Where's her car now?" Billy said.

"It's the rental. It's still there at the marina where she left it. The door was open, but the keys were gone."

"You're sure she left with someone else? You checked Jed's?"

I nodded. "Yeah, I looked. I looked everywhere." My heart raced and pumped so hard, it was uncomfortable. "I called her, left a message."

"You don't look good," Billy said. "Your face... you're white."

"I think I'm just freaking out," I said.

"I've never seen you like this, losing your cool."

I felt my forehead. I almost felt feverish, and clammy. "I'm worried. I should have kept an eye on her."

"Is that what you were hired to do? Protect her?"

I shrugged. "If someone's out there, and maybe doesn't like her plans..."

Billy had a look on his face, like he was thinking of what to say. "When was the last time you heard from her?"

I tapped the screen of my phone and showed him the last text. "She wanted to meet me at the marina."

"That's it?" he said. "A text? Did you talk to her?"

"No. I called her at least four, five times. She never answered. I haven't heard from her since this morning, when she left the marina and headed up to Georgia."

Billy sat on the couch, leaning forward on the front edge of the cushion. "Was she up there all day? You sure you're not just overreacting?"

"I'm not overreacting!" But as soon as the words left my mouth, I knew I needed to get my mind under control. "I'm sorry," I said calmly. "It's... I'm sure... I know something's wrong."

Billy stood from the couch, then walked toward me. "I didn't mean to say—"

"No, it's fine," I said. "You're right. I need to relax. I need to think this through."

Billy stepped to my desk, looking over the files I had spread out. "Why don't you call the sister, see if she knows anything?"

"Stuart Graves' sister?" I wasn't sure I wanted to. "That's just the thing," I said. "Trish had something to tell me. It could've been something either Jane told her, or maybe she figured something out." I ran my hands flat over my face. "Christ, I need a drink."

"I'm not sure that'll help," Billy said.

"Probably not." I flipped through the files on my desk, but I wasn't even sure what I was looking for.

My phone buzzed with a call coming in. I took a quick glance at the screen and saw it was Glen, from the marina.

I answered, "Glen? Are you still at your boat? Did you see anything?"

"I'm here now, but I just wanted to let you know that car, the Ford Taurus... It's gone."

"Gone? Did you see where it went? Or who was driving it?" I said. "Was it Trish? I mean, was it the same woman you saw earlier?"

Glen was quiet. "I'm sorry again, Henry. I... I wasn't watching. I came out onto the dock and the car was gone. I'm sorry. I really am."

I dropped my chin, shaking my head. "It's not your fault. I didn't ask you to sit around watching the parking lot all night." I paused, thinking. "Thanks for the call. If you see anything else, let me know." I hung up and dialed Trish's number right away, hoping this time she'd answer. I took a deep breath, waiting for the first ring.

But, as it had the two previous times, the call went straight to voicemail. I left another message: "Trish, it's Henry. Listen, you have to call me as soon as you get this. Your rental car's not in the lot at the marina anymore. I just hope you're all right." I hung up and looked over at Billy.

He said, "What do you think about calling Mike Stone?"

"Tell him *what*? My client's car was at the marina, and now it's not? And she's not answering my calls? You know how he is."

"But you said Glen saw another car, and she might've been in it, right? Why not just tell him the whole story? You really think he won't help?"

I shook my head. "You don't know Mike the way I do," I said, heading for the door. "I'm going back to the marina, see if anybody else saw anything."

"You want me to go with you?" Billy said.

I thought about it, then shook my head. "Thanks. But I'm not sure where I'll go from there. I'll let you know if I figure it out."

Chapter 15

It was dark by the time I got back to the marina, Glen standing on the dock in front of his boat, watching me walk toward him.

"I'm real sorry I didn't keep a better eye out," he said.

"It's not something you're responsible for, Glen," I said. "Like I said on the phone, I didn't ask or expect you to sit around watching that car. I should have waited here myself." I looked left at the boats tied up to the dock, then to my right, my gaze moving along to see anyone who might've been around to possibly see Trish, or whoever took off in the rental car, if by chance it wasn't her. I turned back to Glen. "Anyone else around, who could've seen something?"

"I don't know," he said. "You want me to ask around?"

I didn't answer but instead walked three boats down to where a couple I hadn't gotten to know very well, were sitting on their boat's deck having cocktails. They'd only recently started renting their slip at the marina. I introduced myself and pulled up my phone with a picture of Trish on it. I turned the screen so they could see it. "Any chance you saw this woman around here today? Or, perhaps driving a Ford Taurus?" I pointed toward the space where it was parked earlier. "It was right over there."

The man, white haired and older than the woman who looked to be half his age, stood up and leaned over the stainless rail, reaching for the phone. He stepped back and looked it over, shaking his head. "We were out on the river for a good part of the day. Just docked about half an hour ago." He showed the photo to the woman and she shook her head.

"Sorry," she said, smiling. "She's pretty."

I took the phone back and moved to the next boat where two men looked to be doing late-evening work on the engine. I knew the man who owned the boat, but didn't recognize either of the two on it. I guess they were mechanics. "Excuse me," I said, climbing onto the boat. "Have you two gentlemen been here for a while?"

They both nodded.

The shorter, heavier of the two, said, "We just got here, maybe twenty minutes ago."

I showed them the photo of Trish. "You happen to see this woman at any point this evening?"

They both stood side by side and looked at the phone, still in my hand. Neither answered right away.

The shorter one shook his head. "I would've noticed some-one like that."

The other man, tall and skinny, maybe somewhere in his early twenties, smiled, like he couldn't take his eyes off her picture. "Sorry, didn't see her. I wish I had." He laughed.

I didn't.

I clenched my fist, ready to let out a day's fill of frustration, building inside me.

But I knew better.

"There was a Ford Taurus parked over there," I said, pointing toward the space in the lot. "Either of you happen to see it?"

The younger one said, "I saw a gray Taurus leaving when we drove in the lot."

I pointed at my phone. "And you didn't notice her behind the wheel?"

The man nodded. "Had sunglasses on, wore a baseball cap. I noticed because it was getting dark, wondered what someone'd be wearing sunglasses for in the evening."

That wasn't much help, other than the fact Trish wasn't behind the wheel.

I said, "You see anyone else with this person? And are you sure it was a Ford Taurus?"

"There might've been someone with him, but I didn't get a good enough look." He turned to the shorter gentleman. "You see anything?"

He just shook his head. "Sorry."

"And you're sure it was a Taurus?"

The young man nodded. "My brother's got a Taurus. A little darker than that one. That might be why it caught my eye. Guy was going fast."

"Okay," I said, and started to climb down off the boat. "Either of you have a business card, in case I have any other questions?"

The two men exchanged a look.

The short man said, "Mind if I ask what this is all about?"

"The woman I'm looking for... she may be missing."

"You a cop?" he said.

"No." I kept walking, got in my Jeep and left the marina.

·········

I walked up to the front desk at the Marriott Hotel downtown and asked the uniformed man behind it for Trish Williams.

"Is she a guest?" he said.

I stared back at him, wondering why else I'd be asking him. "Yes, she's a guest."

He tapped the keys on the computer and looked up from the screen. "Patricia? Or Trish?"

"I don't know. I guess go ahead and try both," I said.

He stared back at me and cleared his throat, shifting his gaze to the computer in front of him. "We had a Miss Patricia Williams staying with us. But she's already checked out."

"Checked out?" I said. "Are you sure?"

His eyes were back on the screen in front of him. "Yes, I'm sure. She checked out earlier this afternoon."

"What time?" I said.

The man furrowed his eyebrows. "Sir?"

I said, "What, you're not allowed to tell me?"

He let out a sigh and tapped the keyboard. "She checked out at four forty-six this afternoon."

I looked at her earlier text to see the time she'd sent me the message. It was sent at five o'clock. Five-oh-three, to be exact. I couldn't understand why she would've checked out before texting me, and showing up at the marina.

"Thank you," I said, and walked across the lobby. I went outside and called Mike Stone.

He answered on the second ring, acting—as he always did—like he didn't know it was me. "Detective Stone."

I wasn't in the mood for playing along. "Where are you?"

"*Where am I?*" He laughed. Of course, he knew it was me. "What business is it of yours where I am?"

"No, I don't mean... Listen, Mike. I need to talk to you right away."

"Isn't that what you're doing right now?"

"I'm serious," I said. "No screwing around, Mike. Something's going on. I... I need your help."

"What'd you screw up now?" he said.

"Mike, please. Just tell me where you are, so I can come meet you. Hopefully you have a few minutes." I looked inside the lobby when the door slid open, and a group of well-dressed women walked outside into the night, laughing, looking like they were ready to take on the town.

Mike sighed into the phone. "Kind of late," he said. "But I'm out. I'm on a case, over in San Marco," he said. "I'm about to grab something to eat. I'm thinking about barbecue, if you want to meet me. I'll be at a place called the Bearded Pig."

"Where is it?" I said.

"King's Ave. But get over here now. I don't have much time."

I couldn't help but think those were the first words out of everyone's mouth lately. 'I don't have much time." Was everyone really busier than people were twenty years ago?

"I'm on my way," I said, and hung up, looking at the screen to make sure I hadn't missed another text or call. Especially one from Trish. I hurried for the Jeep, jogging across the lot while tapping her number one more time.

This time, it rang. In fact, it rang three times, and somebody picked it up, without saying a word.

"Hello?" I said. "Trish? Is that you?" I listened but couldn't tell if anyone was actually on the line. "Hello? Who is this?"

The line was quiet, but the call was still live. Whoever was on the other end was there, waiting. Listening. There was nothing but dead silence.

"Are you there?" I said. "Trish?"

I looked at my screen, and the person on the other end had hung up. I tapped her number and called right back. But this time, it went directly to voicemail.

Chapter 16

Mike was already in the booth at the restaurant, eating, when I walked through the entrance and past the line of people waiting to order at the counter.

His mouth was full, watching me as he took another bite from the sandwich he held with both hands. Dark-red sauce dripped down the back of his hand. "So, what's the problem?" he said.

"The woman, my client, the one who came down here from New York... Something's happened to her."

Mike wiped his hand and mouth. "You talking about the Stuart Graves' case? The daughter?"

"Yes. She's disappeared. She came to see me at the marina, but when I got there, she was gone. Someone from the marina, this guy I know, he thinks he saw her get into another car."

"So you think she's missing? Because she left with someone else?"

"She told me to meet her there. Why would she leave on her own? But now her car's not even there. The rental... a Ford Taurus."

Mike said, "You check her hotel?"

"Of course. That's the other thing so far. She allegedly checked out right before she sent me a text."

"Checked out?" he said, shrugging. "Sounds to me like she's bailing on you, no?"

I shook my head "She's not answering my calls, like her phone is off. Only one time, someone answered, but didn't say a word."

Mike took another bite of his sandwich, hunched over the table, watching me, nodding his head. He finished chewing what was in his mouth, picked up his drink and took a sip through a long straw. He shrugged. "Honestly, it doesn't sound like you should be alarmed."

"Are you serious?"

He took another bite from his sandwich, chewed and swallowed, chasing it with a sip from his drink. "Who's to say she didn't leave with someone, then went back and you weren't there, so she left?"

"You're not listening," I said. "She called me, told me she'd meet me there. And now she's not answering her phone. There were two guys working on a boat there; one of 'em thinks he saw someone driving her car."

"The rental?"

I nodded. Mike was acting like he was in his own world, or had little interest believing anything I'd told him.

I said, "She texted me, told me to meet her at the marina. She showed up before I got there, then possibly got into someone else's car. Next thing, her car's leaving the parking lot, tires squealing, with someone else driving it. What makes you think any of this sounds normal?"

Mike finished what was in his mouth, took another sip of his drink, and wiped his face with the napkin. "All right," he said. "When was the last time you spoke to her? Besides the text."

"This morning. I left her a couple of voicemails, sent her a number of texts."

"And they told you at the hotel that she'd checked out?" he said.

"Right before she drove to the marina." I pulled out my phone and showed him what she'd said.

Mike leaned back and picked something from his teeth, examining whatever piece he'd removed. "I wouldn't be so quick to assume she's in danger."

"Why's that?"

"She checked out of the hotel, and you didn't know anything about it. Am I right?"

"So what? Just because she checked out and didn't tell me beforehand doesn't mean she's not in trouble. Who knows why she did. One thing I can tell you is it doesn't make any sense." I leaned back in the booth, thinking through the different scenarios. I said, "What if it was someone else?"

"Someone else *what*?"

"Who checked her out," I said.

Mike gave me a look, like I was nothing but a fool, tossing ideas out that made little sense. Maybe he was right. "Do you have reason to believe someone else would've checked her out? And why someone might do that?" He took another bite of his sandwich, stuffing whatever was left of it into his mouth. He pointed toward the counter, his mouth full. "You gonna eat?"

I shook my head. My stomach was hungry, but I had too much on my mind to think about food. "Her father was murdered. I knew I should've warned her about being careful who she spoke to."

"Like who?" he said. "Who'd she talk to?"

"As far as I know, Stuart Graves' sister. She lives up in Georgia. In Kingsland. I can only guess she must've learned something when she was up there."

Mike said, "Did you call her?"

"The sister?"

"Yeah, I would think that's a good place to start."

I held my gaze on Mike. "You're seriously not going to do anything?"

"I didn't say that. I just want to make sure we have all the facts straight first. Is that all right with you?" He rolled the waxed foil from his sandwich into a ball, got up, and tossed it in a nearby trash can. "I have to get going," he said, reaching for his drink from the table.

"Why aren't you taking this seriously?" I said, following him toward the door.

He walked outside ahead of me, pulled a cigarette from his pack. "Let me be honest here. I'm still a bit suspicious of the whole ordeal. The fact this strange woman shows up out of the blue from New York, asking you to investigate the eleven-year-old murder of a man she'd never met, who she happens to believe is her father?"

"You don't believe it?"

Mike walked toward his Crown Vic, parked under one of the streetlamps in the parking lot. "I think you should start with figuring out who this woman really is. You never know who's on the up-and-up and who's not these days; you know what I'm saying?" He gave me a look from inside the car, pulled the door closed, and started the engine. He opened the window. "You find out what you can. In the meantime, I'll see what I can do on my end."

He had started backing the car out from the parking space, but put his foot on the brake, looking out at me through the window. "You have a recent picture?"

"Of Trish?"

"No, of you." Stone rolled his eyes. "Who else?"

I took my phone from my pocket and showed him the photo I had of her.

"Attractive," he said. "No wonder you took a case you'll probably never solve." He gave me a nod. "Text that to me. I'll see if I can get someone moving on it. I can't make any promises." He hit the gas and whipped the back end or his car around, the Crown Vic's engine roaring as he took off toward the street, then disappeared into the late-night traffic.

·····•·••··

After driving around aimlessly for a couple of hours, I had started back for the marina but decided to swing by the Marriott. I knew I wouldn't find Trish there but had some questions I hadn't thought of until that point.

I pulled the Jeep up to the front of the hotel and parked under the porte cochère, leaving my hazard lights flashing.

The hotel lobby was empty, each step I took echoing off the marble floor. The woman behind the desk smiled, watching me as I approached her.

"Good evening," she said. "Are you checking in?"

"No," I said, resting my arms on top of the counter. "I have a question about a friend of mine who checked out of here earlier." I looked at the clock on the wall behind her. It was well past midnight. "I guess she checked out yesterday, technically. Later in the afternoon, which I assume is late for a checkout. So, I was wondering if perhaps she cut her reservation short? Considering check-out time must be, what, ten or eleven in the morning?"

The woman nodded. "Eleven." She stared back at me, appearing somewhat suspicious of me. "You said this is a friend of yours?"

"Yes. Her name's Trish Williams. She checked out a little after four in the afternoon. Yesterday."

She seemed hesitant to do anything for me. "I'm not sure sharing the information of our guests is something we—"

"She's a friend," I said. "Actually, she's a friend who's disappeared. I can't find her anywhere. And what's telling me, whether or not she had a reservation beyond today, going to do? That's all I'm asking."

"She's missing?" she said, her eyes widened. "Do you mean she's—"

"Nobody knows where she is. Cops are involved," I said, nodding. "And, like I said, she checked out of here yesterday, but I don't believe that was her plan."

The woman still appeared hesitant. "I'm going to have to check with my manager," she said. "To make sure I'm allowed to share this information with you." She shook her head. "I don't believe I—"

"Can you please check with him, then?" I said. "Or... her?"

"I'm sorry, but the manager is not here right now. Not until morning."

"It's not a big deal," I said, looking at the computer in front of her. "Come on, please? This could be a matter of life or death. I'm serious."

"If someone from the sheriff's office came in here, then it would be a different story. But I can't just—"

"I'm a private investigator," I said, handing her one of my cards. I don't know why people treated them like a badge without realizing anyone could make a business card online for fifty bucks. But it always seemed to give me the credibility I needed. At least most of the time. "I told you the sheriff's office is involved. They're out there looking for her right now. But I was just driving by, and I just thought I'd get some details. I'm not asking any personal information." I folded my hands together, as if in prayer. "*Please?*" I thought about bribing the woman, but I wasn't sure I had more than a couple of dollars in my pocket.

She swallowed, looked around, and turned to the computer to her left. "What did you say the guest's name was?"

"Trish Williams," I said. "Actually, it's under Patricia. Patricia Williams."

She typed on the keyboard, nodding, squinting as she looked at the screen in front of her. After a few moments of quiet, she looked up from the computer. "Her reservation was for two more weeks."

It didn't make sense. "Is it possible someone else could have checked out for her?"

The woman stared back, like she was thinking it through. "Yes, I suppose so. But why would—"

"Thank you," I said, turning from the desk. I rushed for the doors, leaving the hotel and standing out on the sidewalk out front, thinking things through. I looked to my right, toward the parking lot at the far end of the building where Trish had walked when I first told her about the possibility of Elizabeth Sutton being pregnant with Stuart's child. She took it harder than I'd expected.

I headed for the Jeep, looking around the lot as if I was going to see the Taurus, or some random clue that would lead me toward some kind of answer. But there was nothing anywhere. I was left wondering what exactly I'd gotten myself into. And what could've possibly happened to Trish.

Chapter 17

I HADN'T SPENT MORE than an hour sleeping, if that, and was up well before the sun showed I was on my way to Georgia for an unannounced visit to Stuart's sister's home in Kingsland.

I had two large coffees and a Danish I grabbed from a 7-Eleven to get me across the state line, and ended up rolling into Jane Ryan's neighborhood a few minutes before seven in the morning.

I continued past a sign at the entrance that read "A John Dawson Luxury Homes Community." I was familiar with this particular builder because it was all over the Southeast, somehow maintaining the perception—with the gold, signature-like logo at the entrance to every neighborhood they'd built—that it was some guy in charge, a local builder who carried his hammer wherever he went. The truth was it'd become another corporate behemoth charging rich people big money so everyone, at least those in their closed-off communities, would know that they'd made it.

After a few turns and one into a cul-de-sac, I made a right up the long driveway of a two-story brick home. It sat on a hill, with at least a half acre of lawn surrounding the home, most of it excessively green, from whatever chemicals the landscaper sprayed on it.

I rang the doorbell and turned to look around the neighborhood of nearly identical brick homes, as the sun was coming up over the roof across the street. The neighborhood was quiet enough, although I could hear the sound of tennis balls from a court somewhere nearby.

I faced the door when I heard the clicking locks.

An older man with skin that looked artificially tan stood looking out at me, his hand on the door. I couldn't tell if it was a toupée on his head or if his hair was dyed an unnaturally dark color. He was dressed like he was ready for a morning on the golf course, with a bright red Polo shirt tucked into his pants.

"Yes?" was all he said, looking out at me in virtual confusion, likely wondering why someone was at his door so early in the morning.

"Mr. Ryan?"

He didn't answer right away but looked me up and down. "Who're you?"

"Henry Walsh."

"What do you want?"

"I'm sorry, I know it's kind of early, but I'd like to speak with your wife—both of you, actually—if she's available?"

"What about?" he said, the man clearly lacking the Southern hospitality Georgians were known for. He looked past me, toward the driveway, where my Jeep was parked.

"I'd like to talk to her about Stuart Graves," I said. "And, a woman who visited here yesterday."

He quickly glanced over his shoulder and into the house. After a pause, he shook his head. "I'm sorry, but I don't believe

Jane wants to get into another discussion about Stuart." He looked me over. "What business is it of yours?"

"I'm a private investigator."

"A *what*? Private investigator?"

"Yes, sir," I said.

"And you're here about her brother?" He shook his head. "I'm sorry, but neither of us are interested in rehashing the past or anything that has to do with Stu, at this point." He had his hand on the edge of the door, as if he was getting ready to close it.

"I'm investigating his murder. And now there's a missing woman I'm looking for, and—"

"What missing woman?" he said.

"His daughter. As far as I know, she was here yesterday."

The man appeared to be caught off guard.

A woman's voice called out from somewhere in the house. "Steve? Who is it?"

He said, "Nothing, Jane. It's nothing."

"Are you Steve?" I said.

After a moment, he nodded, about to say something else when a short woman, a bit pudgy with glasses on the edge of her nose, stepped into view. She stood next to Steve, her husband, and opened the door wider, so they both could fit in the doorway.

"Mrs. Ryan?" I said. "My name's Henry Walsh. I'm a private investigator, and—"

"Did I hear you say something about Stu?" she said.

"Yes. But more importantly, I need to know if Trish Williams was here yesterday?"

"Yes, she was. Not for very long, but..."

"All right," Steve said, nudging his wife away from the door. He started to close it. "We don't have time for whatever it is you're here for."

"Mrs. Ryan," I said. "Trish Williams is missing. Since yesterday. I don't know what happened when she was here, but—"

"Nothing happened," Steve said. "She showed up, as you have today, looking for information about Stu. She had no proof she's his daughter, so—"

Jane Ryan appeared concerned. "What do you mean she's missing? She was a nice woman. I'd hate to think something happened to her."

Steve held up his hand as if to stop me from responding. "Hold up," he said. "Do you have some kind of identification?"

I pulled out one of my business cards and handed it to him. I always had one ready in my pocket.

He glanced at it, front and back, and handed it to Mrs. Ryan. She looked the card over and handed it back to me.

"You can keep it," I said. "Now, can we talk about yesterday?"

Jane shrugged. "She came here, introduced herself, and might've only been here, oh, maybe a half hour. I invited her inside, but she didn't seem very comfortable with the whole thing."

"Being in your house?" I said, unsure of what she meant.

"I don't know. I guess, Stu being her father. Me being her aunt, if she is who she says she is."

"You don't believe her?" I said.

The two exchanged a glance.

Mr. Ryan looked me in the eye. "How do you know, without question, Stu was her father? Did she bring some kind of records that prove it?"

I stared back and didn't answer.

"She asked so many personal questions," Jane said. "It made me a little uncomfortable."

"About your brother?" I said.

She shrugged, then nodded. "About him. About me. I just didn't like the idea of it."

Mr. Ryan said, "I'm sorry that young woman is missing, and I hope you find her. But we're not interested in discussing this any further."

I said, "Steve, is it? Or would you prefer I be more formal?"

"I don't care what you call me." He looked at his watch. "I have an eight o'clock tee time."

"Steve, I'm not here to cause you or your wife any trouble. But I find it a little troubling a woman who was here at your home is now missing. And you don't seem to be the least bit concerned."

Mr. Ryan said, "What are you implying?"

"I'm not implying anything. All I'm asking for is a little cooperation."

"Can't we have him in?" Jane said, gazing at her husband.

"I just told you, I have to get to the course."

Jane pushed the door open. "You can come inside. I don't know how much we can help you, but..."

The husband's face turned beet red, his teeth clenched, like he didn't appreciate his wife's decision to invite me in.

I walked through the door and followed Jane down a long hall, toward the back of the house. Mr. Ryan followed.

We walked into a large, open-concept kitchen, which included a room with a huge TV on the wall, and two matching leather chairs and a sofa.

A round glass table was tucked into a breakfast nook with four chairs around it. There was a newspaper folded over, two coffee cups, and a couple of dirty plates.

The windows went from floor to ceiling, almost like the entire back wall of the house was entirely glass. Outside was a stone patio and with an in-ground pool down the steps, off the patio.

Jane cleared the two plates from the counter and carried them to the sink. "Can I get you a coffee?" she said.

"No, thank you. I'm fine." The two coffees I had on the ride up were likely going to need to come out at some point. Having another would push me right over the edge.

Mr. Ryan picked up one of the two coffee cups from the table, walked to the other side of the kitchen and filled it from their coffee maker. "So, you're a private investigator?" He leaned back against the counter and sipped his coffee. "Are you working for Miss Williams?"

I hesitated, then nodded. "She asked for my help, yes."

"To find whoever killed Stu?" Jane said. "I wonder why she didn't mention that to me?"

"I can't answer that," I said. "But right now I'm focused on finding her. Did she happen to tell you where she was going, after she left?"

Jane shook her head, stepping to the table. She pulled out one of the chairs. "Would you like a seat?" she said, then sat down and reached for the other cup on the table.

I stayed standing, with Jane to my left, and Mr. Ryan to my right. "Can either of you tell me anything specific about what you may've discussed?"

"With Trish?" Jane said, looking at her husband like she needed his approval to talk.

I watched him give her a look, like he was hoping she'd just stay quiet until he could find a way to get rid of me.

I crossed my arms. "You must've talked about something, no?"

The two remained quiet for a couple of moments.

Steve finally said, "I told her the same thing I told you: that we don't want to have to rehash whatever happened in the past, and weren't interested in talking about that man."

I said to Steve, "I get the feeling you didn't like him?"

But Jane answered for him. "He just thinks Stu was irresponsible, that it was his own fault he got himself in trouble."

"By getting himself in trouble, do you mean, getting killed?" I said.

Steve said, "He was always screwing something up. That woman, I don't know how old she is, but she shows up after all these years. She has no idea who that man really was. If she did, she wouldn't be wasting her time down here."

"Is that what you told her?" I said.

Jane said, "Steve works hard. He thinks everyone should be like him."

"Stu had a lot of problems," Steve said. "And he brought most of them on himself. Like I told that young woman, not everyone was shocked to hear he'd gotten himself killed."

"What's that supposed to mean?" I said.

"He burned bridges," he said. "Borrowed money, never paid people back. Fooled around with married women…"

"Did he borrow money from you?" I said, looking from Steve to Mrs. Ryan.

Steve gave a quick nod. "He borrowed from whoever was foolish enough to trust he'd ever pay them back. I'm telling you, the man never grew up."

"I wish you would be nice," Jane said, giving her husband a look, like she was finally trying to stick up for her brother.

"I didn't see anything in any of the reports about him owing anyone money," I said. "Is this something you shared with the sheriff's office at the time?"

"It was a long time ago," Jane said, her eyes toward the floor.

I said, "Is there anything else you shared with Trish? Besides trying to convince her that her father was no good?" I couldn't help but think there was something they weren't telling me. But whatever it was, could it have been enough to drive Trish to leave the area? Is it possible she simply left to go back to New York?

I didn't know.

"I don't know what else you're expecting from us, but I don't think there's anything else to say. If you don't mind…" Steve straightened from the counter and looked toward the hall. "I think we've said all we need to."

I glanced at Mrs. Ryan, with a look on her face like she was holding something back.

Steve waved for me to follow him. "Let's go."

I looked at Jane, but she now had her back to me, looking at the backyard through the window.

I hadn't yet moved or followed her husband out. I said to Jane, "Is there something you're not telling me?"

"Don't make me call the cops," Mr. Ryan said, reaching for my arm. "I want you out of this house."

I looked back at Jane Ryan as I headed for the door, expecting she'd look my way as her husband led me to the door, but she never did.

Chapter 18

I left Mike Stone a message after I left Georgia, hoping I'd hear back from him with some kind of news. Trying to be somewhat hopeful in my own mind, I considered the fact Trish could've changed her mind about the investigation after speaking to Jane and her husband. Maybe she decided to leave Jacksonville altogether but didn't have it in her to tell me she wasn't going to continue with the investigation.

But nothing else that happened made any sense, with far more questions than answers bouncing around my head. Nothing could explain why she wouldn't return my calls, why she wouldn't just shoot me a text—and who answered her phone when I called. Without saying a word.

I wasn't exactly the type of person who relied on hope, and in this case, being hopeful was almost impossible, unless I chose to ignore the facts.

I took the exit for Route 17 and drove into a Sunoco gas station in Becker, a few miles north of Yulee. I decided it was time I called Trish's father. The one up in New York. All I knew about him was he was a physician in New Rochelle. I Googled Dr. Ken Williams, and found him listed, practicing at a place called New Rochelle Medical Associates. I found a residential listing for a Dr. Ken Williams with a street address but no phone number.

My first attempt to reach him was at the medical office. After the phone rang twice, an automated messaging system picked up, giving me the option to speak with someone about an appointment. So that's what I chose, and waited on hold for another five minutes until a woman finally answered.

"New Rochelle Medical Associates."

I was tempted to use my real name, but at the last second, I decided to go with something else, considering Trish had already told him about me. I didn't want to give him a chance to avoid me or come up with some kind of story to hide something. I said, "Hello, this is Dr. Hank Rollins..." I looked at my screen at the search listings. Starland Medical was listed in the same search results as Dr. Williams, so I gave it a shot. "I'm calling from Starland Medical, and I need to speak with Dr. Williams right away."

"I'm sorry," the woman said. "Dr. Williams is not available today. But I can put you through to the nurse practitioner?"

"No," I said. "It's important I speak with him directly. I have a critical situation, that could be life or death."

The last part was true.

"As I said, Doctor, he's not available. He'll be out of the office for the rest of the week."

"On vacation?" I said.

There was silence for a moment on the other end.

"I'm not at liberty to say," she said. "But I can take a message and see to it that he gets it. Or, like I said, if you need to discuss a medical situation, I can put you through to the nurse practitioner, or another physician?"

"No. That's all right. I need to reach Dr. Williams," I said.

There was a pause, and she might have sighed into the phone before telling me to hold.

Music came through the phone while I waited.

The music stopped, and the woman picked up the line. "Doctor? If you give me your number, we will see to it that he calls you back."

"Today?" I said.

"Most likely, yes. We'll do our best to get him the message as soon as possible. Dr. Williams is out of town."

My phone beeped, and I looked at the screen. It was Mike Stone, and I wasn't going to miss his call. "I'm sorry," I said to the woman. "I have to call you back." I hung up and answered Mike's call. "Mike? You got something?"

There was a pause, his voice a bit hushed and almost somber. "Yeah, I actually do have something," he said. It was one of the few times I asked a simple question and didn't get Mike's typical sarcasm or some kind of insult to make himself feel good. And I knew it wasn't good. He cleared his throat. "Listen. We have officers pulling a car out of the St. Johns right now, near the fishing pier at Dames Point Park."

"What kind of car?" I said. My heart was starting to race before he said another word. I already knew where he was about to go.

"A gray Ford," he said, hesitantly. "It looks like it could be a Taurus, but I don't have official confirmation yet. A couple of fishermen clipped it, ripped a hole in their boat's hull."

I'd already started the Jeep and pulled back out onto 17, heading south. My heart was pounding so hard in my chest, I thought I was going to bust a rib. Harder than it ever had before. I felt a weakness coming over me, combined with a light-headedness I wasn't sure I'd experienced before, whether it was the caffeine from the two coffees, or the fact I couldn't remember the last time I'd eaten, other than the Danish from 7-Eleven.

"You there?" Mike said.

I slammed my foot on the gas pedal, swerving in and out of traffic in either lane. "Yeah, I'm here. I'm on my way." I was about to hang up, but said, "Mike? Was there anyone inside?"

"They're pulling the car out. I'm on my way there now."

I was still at least a half hour away. "I'll see you there." I hung up and decided not to call Dr. Williams' office back. Not yet.

· · · · ● · ● · · ·

By the time I was on Dames Point Road, before the bridge, the area around the fishing pier at the park had two rescue vehicles, two fire engines, and at least six or seven sheriff's vehicles, making it hard for me to get close enough to the scene.

My heart was still pounding hard in my chest. My ears were burning and ringing so loud, I could hardly hear the sounds around me. I was nauseous and felt bad enough I wasn't certain I could walk. I wasn't even sure how I drove there. That, too, was a blur.

Mike's Crown Vic was parked near the pier, by one of the rescue vehicles. I could see him on the other side of the yellow tape, standing near the shore.

I jumped from the Jeep and started running toward the gray Ford. The chains were still attached, with all four doors and the trunk wide open.

My fingers tingled, like pins and needles that moved through my wrists. My left arm ached. I tried to shake off the feeling coming over me, but it only got worse. I started to call out Mike's name, but my throat had become so dry, it was hard to find my voice. I cleared my throat and called again, watching him at the backside of the car, over the trunk, raising his gaze toward me.

I stopped at the yellow tape. My heart thumped so hard and fast, I felt it in my ears. The ringing got louder.

Mike walked toward me, pulling the white rubber gloves off his hands. He stood on the other side of the tape, looking at me. "Jesus, Walsh. Are you all right?"

I nodded, trying again to clear my throat, looking for something to hold on to.

"Walsh?"

The pain had taken over my body.

"You want to sit down?" he said, showing uncharacteristic concern.

I shook my head, running my tongue along my dry lips. "Is it her?" I looked through the blur in my eyes, at the car.

"Victim's a female. No ID. But the car's a rental."

I started to duck under the tape, but my knee hit the ground and I stumbled. I caught myself, but stayed kneeling, trying to catch my breath.

"Walsh?" Mike reached down to help me, lifting me to my feet. He yelled out for a medic.

"No, I'm all right." I pulled my arm from his grasp, and collapsed to the wet ground. I tried to speak, but my mouth wouldn't move. *Nothing* would move. I looked up at Mike, watched him screaming at or toward someone, waving his arms. The ringing was too loud for me to hear anything outside of my body, other than the sound of my own heart, pumping in my ears. Then it turned to silence, and I felt my eyes close.

Chapter 19

Apparently, I'd died. At least that's what I heard the doctor say when they were rolling me into my room after two hours of surgery to repair my mitral valve. Supposedly, I owed the paramedics for keeping me alive on the ride to Baptist Medical Center when my ticker stopped working for at least a handful of seconds.

I couldn't believe it. Early forties. In decent shape, I thought cardiac arrest was something that only happened to fat, old people. Apparently that wasn't the case at all.

Luckily, I didn't have to deal with open-heart surgery. Crazy to hear, but they did it all through my groin. I didn't know exactly what the mitral valve did, or why it caused my heart to stop, but the doctor claimed it was something that'd been brewing in there for a while.

I guess if I'd gone to the doctor once in a while, maybe they would have figured something out. I mentioned a few black-outs I'd had a couple of years back—where the hack doctor I went to at the time found nothing wrong with me—and this doc agreed the valve issue was the likely cause.

I was alone in the room, looking at a maple-colored wardrobe I guessed had my belongings. But I was told not to get out of bed until the nurse showed up, which wasn't much of an option anyway with the electrodes taped to my chest. I wanted to rip them off and leave, like the tough guy would do in the movies, but I didn't feel like I could move a muscle, even if I wanted to.

I think I might've dozed off for an hour or so, woke up and thought about Trish. I needed answers and reached for the button to call the nurse.

A middle-aged woman immediately rushed in, looking me over. "Can I get you something?"

I nodded, tried to talk, and realized my throat was just about locked, it was so parched. I reached for a cup of water on the table next to me and took a sip. "Does someone have my phone?"

She opened the wardrobe and crouched down for my clothes, stuffed in a plastic bag. She looked it over and handed it to me. "I don't see a phone in here."

I could barely lift my head, feeling around inside the bag. I looked around the room. "I need a phone. It's urgent."

The nurse reached somewhere behind me and placed a landline phone on the cart next to me, pushing it closer. "Here you go," she said.

I picked up the receiver and rested it on my chest. I didn't know Mike's number offhand. I didn't know anyone's number offhand, other than my parents'. Another downside to relying on so-called "smart" phones for every single thing we do.

I asked the nurse if she could get me the number to the sheriff's office, but she glanced at the door. "There were two or three officers outside your room a little while ago. You want me to go see if they're still here?"

"Both in uniform?" I said. "The guy I'm looking for is dressed in plain clothes. He's a detective."

"There was a man talking to the officers. He looked like a detective. Tall, maybe a little older?" she said.

I nodded. "His name's Mike Stone. Detective Stone. Can you see if he's still here?"

"Let me just check your vitals," she said, grabbing the clipboard off the end of the bed.

"Just get him!" I snapped. The pace of the beeps on the heart monitor somewhere behind me started going faster.

The woman looked at me, eyes wide open. She didn't seem the type to take to demands too kindly. "Mr. Walsh, I—"

"I'm sorry," I said. "Please. I need to talk to him."

She nodded, placed the clipboard back on the foot of the bed, and left the room.

A moment later, she was back, with Mike behind her. She gave me a look, like she wanted another apology. She said, "You need to relax, Mr. Walsh." She gave Mike a grin and left the room.

Mike waited, then closed the door, stepping to the side of the bed as he cleared his throat. "So, bad ticker, huh? You almost died on the ride over." He handed me my phone. "You dropped this."

"I heard I was dead." I looked at the cracked screen. I hadn't received any calls. I said, "So, are you going to tell me?"

Mike swallowed. He seemed hesitant, and cleared his throat. "It was her," he said. "The body in the trunk. It was Patricia Williams."

I kept my eyes on him, but he looked away, walking to the window across the room. With his back to me, he stared out into the night, the lights shining down over the parking lot. "I'm sorry."

I didn't know how to react. In fact, I just stared at the stained ceiling tile above my bed for what seemed like ten minutes. My emotions were a bit out of whack with whatever drug I had inside me. Aside from whatever they used to sedate me, the pain meds had me pretty juiced up. My eyelids were heavy. I fought off any tears that might've been coming.

Mike walked over and stood at the foot of my bed. "Did you know the father was down here? Dr. Williams, from New York?"

I stared at him, slowly shaking my head. "You sure?"

"Am I sure?" Mike nodded. "Yes, I'm sure. It took us a little while to track him down, but turned out he was at some kind of medical conference in St. Augustine."

To say I was surprised would be an understatement. "I called his office this morning," I said. I looked around the room, feeling somewhat confused. "It was this morning, wasn't it?"

"Still the same day," Mike said.

I had no sense of time, other than seeing the darkness outside.

"Do you find it strange at all," I said, "that he was an hour away from here when his daughter was killed?"

"Strange?" Mike paused, like he was thinking it through. "We haven't questioned him, yet, but... I'm not ready to assume he had something to do with what happened to her, if that's what you're getting at?"

"No, I'm not."

I wasn't sure what I was saying. Or thinking. I reached for the cup of water on the cart with the phone and took a sip. "Any clues yet?"

"We've got officers on it as we speak," he said.

"Suspects?"

"Walsh, knock it off. We're working on it. I know what you're thinking. I should've moved faster. But you have my word; We'd already started before we got the call."

I believed him. At least, I wanted to. But if there was anyone to blame, I thought it was me.

"How did they do it?" I said.

Mike took a slow, deep breath and exhaled. "She was shot twice in the back." He glanced at the floor, then raised his gaze. "Don't worry, Walsh. We'll find whoever did this."

Mike knew better than to think I was going to sit around, waiting for the sheriff's office to make some headway. Of course, I trusted Mike. But I knew how slow things could move in cases like these.

"I tried to tell her to be careful," I said. "I knew there was a chance someone was out there—whoever killed her father—and wouldn't want her snooping around." I closed my eyes for a moment.

"Who'd she talk to?" Mike said.

"I don't know. The only person I'm aware of is the aunt, Stuart Graves' sister. But I don't know who else. She was gone the whole afternoon. And I have no idea where she was before she showed up at the marina. Someone obviously knew she'd gone there to meet me."

Mike said, "You said someone saw her rental car leaving, didn't you? I'd like to talk to whoever it was that told you."

"A couple of mechanics. I have their numbers. But why would someone go back to the marina and take the rental car? Just to have somewhere to put her body?"

Mike didn't respond, and we were both quiet.

There was a knock at the door, and Mike went and opened it.

I couldn't see who it was and didn't have the energy or strength to turn and look.

From the doorway, Mike said, "Good evening, Detective."

I pushed myself up as best I could and looked toward the door.

It was Alex. She stepped toward me, tears in her eyes. She leaned over and kissed me on the forehead, then gave me a hug, her face against mine.

Billy walked in behind her and walked around to the other side of the bed.

"What are you doing here?" I said, holding Alex's hand.

She wiped a tear from her cheek. "What do you mean what am I doing here? What do you think?"

"I mean, how'd you get here so fast? Why aren't you in North Carolina?"

"Stop asking questions," she said, forcing out a grin. She squeezed my hand. "Are you okay?"

I nodded, clearing my throat. I fought back tears of my own.

Billy said, "When Mike called and said you were here in the hospital, I was sure you'd gotten shot again."

"I wish I had," I said, putting my hand on my heart. "But I guess at least I don't have to deal with being dead." I looked back at Alex. She appeared tired. But still as good as ever. "If I knew this is what it'd take to get you down for a visit…"

She and Billy laughed. Mike was looking at his phone.

Billy said, "Doctor said this is something you must've had going on for a long time? That it could be something hereditary?"

"I guess," I said. "Remember those blackouts a couple of years ago?"

"You mean when you never went back to the doctor," Alex said. "Remember? They wanted to do an MRI?"

"Well, now we know," I said.

I looked past Alex at Mike. "Mike? Do they know?"

He looked up from his phone and shook his head.

"Know *what*?" Alex said.

"My client was killed," I said.

Alex's eyes opened wide. "The new client? The one you told me about?"

I nodded.

Billy put his hand on my shoulder. "I'm sorry, Henry."

Alex tilted her head with a look of suspicion or confusion, maybe at the way Billy had reacted, consoling me.

But I wasn't going to give her the details. Not right then. She didn't need to know Trish wasn't just a client. Or that finding her killer would become personal.

Chapter 20

AFTER ONE NIGHT IN the hospital, I was ready to leave, the doctor telling me in the past I'd be stuck there for at least a week, maybe more. But with the new technology they used on me, patients were out the door in twenty-four hours.

I was already out of bed and sitting in a recliner tucked in the corner, next to the window, waiting for Alex and Billy to show up to give me a ride home.

I actually felt decent. Better than I had in a while. I couldn't say I felt normal, because I don't think I knew for sure what that felt like. But knowing whatever was going on inside me could have killed me if I weren't in the right place at the right time, I realized there was a bit of luck involved in my survival. But the circumstances didn't make me feel any better about why I'd driven to the pier in the first place, surrounded by paramedics.

I was looking out the window and turned when a well-dressed older man, I didn't recognize, walked into my room.

He stopped a few feet from where I sat in the recliner. "Henry Walsh?"

It took a moment, but it hit me who he was. I stood from the chair. "Dr. Williams?"

I reached out and shook his hand. "I'm so sorry."

"How do you know who I am?" he said.

"I saw your photo online. I actually... I tried to get in touch with you yesterday." I didn't mention I'd used a different name, although he likely never received the message, since I never called back.

The doctor's eyes were red, lids heavy. It was obvious he'd been crying. "I should have never let her come down here," he said. "I knew it was a bad idea from the start. But she's not a little girl anymore." He closed his eyes and dropped his chin. He said nothing for a few moments. "Trish always did what she wanted to do. And nobody would bother trying to stop her."

"How'd you know I was here?" I said.

He looked up. "A detective told me."

"Mike Stone?"

He nodded. "I think that was his name."

"You were in St. Augustine?" I said. "Did Trish know?"

He shook his head. "It was a last-minute trip."

I still found it a bit odd; the man was an hour away. But then he explained:

"She called me yesterday, somewhat upset about meeting Mr. Graves' sister."

"She called you? After she went there?"

"Apparently, they were somewhat hostile to the idea she was his daughter. It sounded to me like they weren't convinced she was telling the truth."

I thought about meeting Jane and her husband, recalling their skepticism. I said, "Did she tell you where she was? In the afternoon?"

He paused, clearing his throat before he spoke. "She was going to drive down to meet me. In St. Augustine."

"She was?" I said.

"I had also reserved a room for her in my hotel. I thought it would be good for her to come stay with me. She was upset."

I said, "Is that why she checked out of her hotel?"

"I... I don't know. I suppose so. I knew she wanted to get back to Jacksonville, but..." He shrugged, shaking his head. "I can't answer that."

It was the only answer I had, and likely the only one that made sense.

He smiled, slightly, through his apparent pain. "I told her I'd take her to a nice dinner, so she could forget about this craziness she refused to let go of."

"Craziness?"

"Trying to find out who killed Stuart Graves." He rubbed the back of his neck, moving it around like he was trying to get rid of a kink. "Did Trish pay you?"

"Pay me? For what? I didn't do anything. And I don't ask for a deposit. At least, most of the time."

"She spoke highly of you," he said.

I didn't respond, because I wasn't sure what I was supposed to say.

He reached his hand into his pocket and pulled out a roll of bills. "How much do we owe you?" he said.

I shook my head, confused. "You don't owe me anything. Please. No."

He pushed a slight smile through a hurt-filled expression. "I know you were doing the work. You were helping her. The detective, uh, Stone, was it? He told me you were at the scene, when you... " He pulled bills from the roll he'd taken from his pocket and counted them out before handing them to me.

I put my hands up. "No, you don't owe me anything."

He kept his hand in position, waiting for me to reach for the money. "I realize whatever you would normally make from a case like this would've been much more. Trish mentioned your fee was two hundred and fifty dollars a day. This should cover the work you did, with a little extra."

Ordinarily, I'd be happy to be paid for whatever time I'd put into a case, even when it didn't work out. There were never guarantees. At least I never gave them. But I still needed to get paid for my work.

But this time was different.

I felt weak and sat back down in the chair. "Please, put your money away."

He waited another few seconds, then finally lowered his hand. He tucked the money back into the roll and slipped it in his pocket.

"Can you tell me what else she told you?" I said. "Do you know where she went after she left Georgia?"

Dr. Williams took a deep breath and slowly exhaled, like he was trying to maintain the calmness he'd portrayed. "I just wanted to come by and take care of the payment, for your time. I lost my daughter, Mr. Walsh. And I've already answered a lot of questions. I hope you understand."

I stared back at him. "I want to help find the person who did this."

"I don't want any conflicts," he said.

"Conflicts? There are no conflicts."

"I mean, with the sheriff's office. It doesn't make sense to me to have you—"

"I can move faster. I'm already steps ahead of them," I said.

The doctor said, "It's funny. We hired a private investigator, back when Trish's mother wanted to find Stuart."

"She didn't tell me that," I said.

"She didn't know. Remember, this was going back quite a few years. Trish was young. And Joyce—"

"Trish's mom?" I said.

"Yes. My wife. I'm sure Trish told you she passed away a couple of months ago?"

"Of course. Yes," I said, still thinking about the private investigator, and where the doctor was going with it. "So, you hired a PI? And he found Stuart?"

"Not exactly. The best he could do was Stuart's sister. Joyce had never met her, so it was all a bit of a surprise when she called her."

"You mean, when your wife called Jane Ryan?"

He nodded. "She wasn't helpful at all. It was kind of strange, to be honest."

"Your wife didn't mention Trish to her at the time?"

Dr. Williams shook his head. "Joyce didn't feel it was up to her to tell the sister."

He hadn't really gotten to his point, and I thought maybe he was saying he didn't like private investigators, especially if the guy didn't do a decent enough job. "Do you have this guy's name? The PI?"

"Why?"

"Maybe he knows something."

Trish's dad stared back at me, like he wasn't exactly sure what he wanted to say. "Knows something about *what*?"

"I don't know," I said. "I'm sure you understand this wasn't some random act. What happened to Trish has to be connected to what happened to Stuart Graves."

Dr. Williams nodded, like he understood. "All he did—the private investigator—was help track down the sister. He was fairly useless. You'd be wasting your time. Besides, I wouldn't even remember his name." He again glimpsed at the door. "I'm going to go now," he said.

I stood from the chair. "Was that a payoff?" I said.

"Excuse me?"

"Were you offering me that money so I don't get involved? Is that what you want?"

He tucked his hands into his pockets. "I told you, I'd like to believe the sheriff's office will find who did this."

"What makes you so sure?" I said. "And there's a good chance Mike—Detective Stone—will be asking for my help."

He started for the door. "How about I let you know if I decide I'd like to hire you?"

"I'm not asking you to hire me," I said. "But, I just want to be clear. Whether you like it or not, I'm going to find whoever did this to her."

Dr. Williams was still for a moment, finally nodding as he started toward the door. "I wish you luck in your recovery," he said, then walked out of the room.

Chapter 21

ALL I WANTED TO do was sleep in my own bed. But as we walked across the parking lot of the marina with Billy and Alex, Billy tried to convince me to spend a couple of days at his house.

"The doctor told you to rest," Alex said. "And what if you need something? I don't think it makes sense to be here, on your boat by yourself."

"Suit yourself," Billy said. "I know how much you hate sleeping at someone else's place, but you're welcome to it."

"I'll be fine," I said, doing my best to reassure my friends I didn't need anyone's help. "Honestly, I feel good. Better than in a long time." I stepped onto the dock, up the ladder and onto the boat. "And here I was, thinking it was the booze making me feel like crap."

"I doubt the drinking helped," Billy said.

Even though he made his money off people buying booze at his restaurant, he hadn't had a drink himself in years.

I opened three chairs on the boat's deck, under the overhead cover I'd installed. But even with the shade, the humidity we'd been dealing with was excessive. And it came earlier in the spring than normally would.

I watched Alex sit in one of the chairs, a look on her face where I could tell something was bothering her. "When do you have to go back?" I said.

She crossed one leg over the other, a sly smile on her face. "Why? Have you already had enough of me?"

I laughed, but didn't bother answering.

She said, "I have a few days before I have to go back. But I brought plenty of work with me, so I can't escape completely." She looked away, out toward the river, and stayed quiet for a couple of moments.

"Are you all right?" I said.

She turned back, and I noticed a tear come out from under her sunglasses. "When Mike first called, he didn't know if you were going to make it."

The three of us were quiet.

"I'm fine now," I said.

Billy said, "You were lucky. I was told if you hadn't been seen to by those paramedics, you probably wouldn't have survived. Most people who go into cardiac arrest..."

"It's crazy to think about, isn't it?" I said.

Alex pulled off her sunglasses and wiped her eyes. "I prefer not to think about it."

Billy reached over and put his hand on Alex's shoulder. "Henry, you were telling us about your client's dad. The doctor from New York. You sure he doesn't want you involved in finding out what happened to his daughter? It doesn't make sense."

"No, it doesn't," I said. "And as I mentioned, it was after he tried to pay me for the work I did. So, on one hand he's paying me for a job I didn't finish. On the other, he's coming across like he trusts the sheriff's office and would prefer I steer clear of the investigation."

"Did he say why?" Alex said.

I shook my head, and told them about the first time he and his wife hired a PI to find Stuart Graves, without much luck.

Billy said, "Maybe something about working with the guy left a bad taste in his mouth."

Alex rose from her chair. "Do you think maybe your client told him something? Gave him a reason that'd make him not want you involved."

"Like what?"

She paused, with a slight shrug. "I don't know. Was the case going as expected?"

"Clearly not," I said, almost confused by her question. "Or she'd still be here, wouldn't she?"

Alex stared back at me, holding her gaze, but I couldn't see her eyes behind the sunglasses. She clearly didn't like my response. "That's not what I meant," she said. "You don't have to get snippy. I'm asking if maybe there was something about it she didn't like? Did something happen between the two of you?"

Billy and I both looked at each other. I feared Alex was about to dig a little deeper into the situation between me and Trish.

The truth was, however, that whatever happened with me and Trish didn't matter. At least, I didn't think so. But I wasn't about to get into it with Alex.

"She never answered my calls," I said. "I left her a couple of messages that afternoon. I sent a couple of texts. The only response I got from her was that she'd meet me at the marina. But then it turned out, at least according to Dr. Williams, she was going to St. Augustine to spend time with him. Maybe just to get away from it. I don't know if that's why she wanted to see me, to tell me she was leaving for a few days? It still doesn't make sense. And doesn't explain where she was for the afternoon, before she checked out of the hotel."

"Mike said he was still waiting on forensics," Alex said. "And he'd hoped to get fingerprints from the car. Hopefully there's something there."

"Can you still get fingerprints after a car's been in the water?" Billy said.

Alex nodded. "The vehicle hadn't been in there long, so it's possible they can find something. A couple of weeks in the water, and it's a different story."

I was surprised Alex seemed to have discussed the case with Mike, more than I'd realized. And she asked a lot of questions, as she always did. But something was different about her, and I couldn't pinpoint what it was.

Billy said, "What's the story with the sister? You said the husband was there? What's his deal?"

"I don't know yet. He didn't seem to be very sympathetic to what happened to his brother-in-law or what happened to Trish. He was more interested in getting me out of there. Something doesn't add up."

I faced Alex. "I'm talking about Stuart Graves' sister."

She said, "You don't have to explain it to me, like I don't understand what's going on."

"Sorry," I said, putting my hands up in front of me. I wasn't sure why she took it the way she had, being defensive. "I was just making sure we were all on the same page."

I knew she was aware of most of what was going on, and I could see her point. But there was something else going on with her. Something else was bothering her, and I couldn't figure it out.

The truth was, something felt very different between us. It was an almost uncomfortable feeling. Maybe I was overthinking. Or maybe we were both just tired and worn out.

The one thing I wondered about was if perhaps she didn't see us as on the same level because she was a member of law enforcement. Alex wasn't the type to let something like that go to her head, but maybe it was hard to avoid. She was a detective now. Maybe, like Mike, and most of his buddies at the sheriff's office, she saw a private investigator as the lower rung on the ladder of success.

I couldn't imagine it was the case with her, but I thought about it.

Billy wanted to know more about Jane and Steve Ryan. "What did they tell Trish? Doesn't it seem like she must've come away from there with some kind of information? Maybe sent her off in some direction that perhaps got her in trouble?"

"Like I said, he was more interested in getting me out of there. He claims they just didn't want to be involved, that they'd already dealt with so much. On the other hand, I'm not sure they were convinced Trish was really Stuart Graves' daughter."

"Did they say that?" Alex said.

I nodded.

"What's their deal?" Billy said. "I mean, their lifestyle, I guess. Where do they live?"

"Kingsland."

"I know that. I mean, what's their situation? What's the house like? Do they have money?" he said.

I wasn't sure of the significance, but Billy always had a good enough reason for asking a question. "Big house. Cookie-cutter, McMansion neighborhood near a golf course. I heard balls bouncing... tennis courts. Does that paint a clear enough picture?"

"What's the husband do for a living?" he said.

"I think he's retired now. I wished I had a chance to ask more questions, but they hustled me out of there. From what I was able to find, before I went to see them, the husband owned some kind of leasing company he recently sold. Commercial equipment leasing. It appears he did pretty well for himself."

Chapter 22

ALEX WAS AT MY desk in the office and picked up a copy of the police report from Stuart Graves' murder case. "Did you talk to this detective yet? Allen Holt?"

I was on the couch with my laptop. "No, not yet."

"Did Mike say anything about him?"

"Not much, other than he retired soon after that case," I said.

"So who was in charge of the case, after he retired?"

"I didn't ask."

She gave me a quizzical look, like she wasn't sure why I hadn't.

"I was planning to talk to Holt myself," I said. "I don't know what kind of answers he'd have, but I figured it wouldn't hurt." I looked at my watch. "Maybe we should go over there now. He lives out by Herlong Recreational Airport."

"You said, 'we'?" She had her own laptop out on my desk and looked up. "Just because I came back to the office to look through some of these files doesn't mean I can get involved, Henry. I mean, I can help a little, but there's no way I can't put myself out there with you. I'll jeopardize my job."

"Okay, sure," I said. "I get it."

I couldn't help but feel we were back together, like old times.

"Do you?" she said. "Because I'm serious. If word ever got back to Selma I was somehow involved in something like this. As far as they know, I came to visit a friend who almost died."

She got up and walked over to the couch, standing in front of me, with her arms crossed. "Can I ask you something?"

"Can I say *no*?"

I could tell by the way she stood, staring back at me, I wasn't going to like whatever she was about to say.

"Was there something between you and your client? Between you and Patricia Williams? I know... I know it's none of my business. And I know we agreed that what happened between us before I left was something we both thought should be left in the past, but..."

"We agreed to leave it in the past so you could have the career you always wanted. So don't make it seem like I—"

"Okay," she snapped. "I'm sorry. I didn't mean to..." She turned from me, shaking her head. "Let's not get into all that again. It doesn't matter."

I said, "Then why are you asking about her, if it doesn't matter?"

She threw up her hands in frustration. "Stop trying to... I didn't mean that it didn't matter. I was—" She walked to the window and stared out, quiet for a couple of moments. "I'm sorry," she said. "Forget I even asked."

It was awkward, to say the least. I got up and started for the door. "I think now would be a good time for me to go talk to Allen Holt."

"Wait!" she said.

I had the door open. "Do you want me to drop you off at the hotel? I was going to ask Billy if I could use his car."

She shook her head. "Don't you want me to go with you?"

I closed my eyes and shook my head. Alex wasn't one to play games. Ever. But this time was different. "Will you make up your mind?"

She nodded, taking her time with a response. "It's... it's just been kind of weird coming back here. It hasn't even been that long since I left, but I feel like I'm completely removed from your life... and from this business. A business we built together."

I nodded, like I agreed. "I hear you," I said. "It is what it is. It's different. But we've both moved on. Haven't we?"

I watched her and waited for an answer. She didn't give me one.

"I'll go visit Holt with you," she said. "But only because the doctor said you're not supposed to drive for a few days."

"Did he?" I said. Although I knew he had.

• • • • • • • • • •

Allen Holt lived in the Naylor Mill Village mobile home park, off Normandy Boulevard, a mile past Herlong Recreational Airport. We drove down a long, paved road through the community, homes practically stacked on top of one another, with mostly woods behind them.

Holt lived at the very end of the road, where it ended abruptly a few feet before a chain-link fence with woods on the other side. I could see cars in the distance, through the trees.

Alex parked Billy's Lexus on the road, and I stepped out of the passenger side. I said, "Are you coming?"

She shook her head. "It's best I wait right here," she said. "Anyone asks, I'm only your driver."

I closed the door as a small plane flew overhead. There was a cigar smell in the air, and I followed the odor around the corner, behind the home. With the woods behind him, was the man I recognized from pictures as Allen Holt. He sat in a wooden Adirondack chair reading a newspaper, a cigar hanging from his mouth, and a cup of coffee on a wide, cut log he used as a side table.

"Mr. Holt?" I said. I had already called him before we left Billy's and let him know I'd be coming out, so there were no surprises.

He dropped the paper and looked up, nodding. He bit the cigar between his teeth. "You Henry?" He was a tall but thin man when he stood, folding the paper over as he rose to shake my hand. He had a strong grip for an old guy, probably someone you didn't mess with in his prime. "You want a coffee?"

"I'm okay for now," I said.

He stepped past me, and peered around the corner toward the driveway, where Alex was parked. "Nice car," he said. "You got someone waiting for you?"

"Just my driver."

He appeared unsure if I was being serious.

"So you said you're a PI, huh? I thought about doing something like that myself, when I first retired from the sheriff's office. But I'd already stayed in law enforcement long enough." He smiled, showing off the aged look of his teeth. "They had to force me into retirement. I was sixty-four at the time, oldest detective in the department."

I looked over the mobile home. "Do you live here alone?"

He nodded. "Wife died a few years back. We downsized during the last recession and bought this place, thought we'd both be able to relax, maybe travel a little." He puffed on his cigar, removed it from his mouth, and examined the ash on the tip. "Not a bad place, I guess."

Holt grabbed his mug from the stump and sat down at a picnic table that looked like it could collapse if we both sat at the same time.

I stayed standing across from him, my back to the wooded area, one foot up on the bench across from him. "As I told you on the phone, I was initially hired by a client to investigate a case you worked on."

"I got that part, but you didn't say what case," he said.

"I didn't want to get into a discussion about it over the phone. It's the Stuart Graves case, assuming you remember it?"

"Graves, huh? I remember. You don't forget, at least until the brain won't let you do otherwise. I'd love to say I batted a thousand, but it's just not reality. More like three hundred, is the way it is in reality. But that leaves two-thirds of the cases I worked on unsolved. The Graves case, of course, was a strikeout on my part."

I took my foot off the bench and straightened up. "Do you happen to know about the woman who was recently found in the trunk of a car in the St. Johns? Over at Dames Point Park?"

"Wasn't that yesterday?" he said. "I heard something about it on the news, but can't say I know much about it. Why do you ask?"

"The victim... She was my client. And the daughter of Stuart Graves."

His eyes opened wide. "A daughter? That's news to me. You sure?"

"I'd be lying if I said with one hundred percent certainty she was his daughter. She was born out of wedlock, a little over thirty years ago. She didn't know about him until recently. And he only found out about her shortly before he was murdered."

Detective Holt seemed to be more than just a little surprised. "And, she was killed?" He lowered his head, gazing at the grass, raising his head again after a brief pause. "What are they saying? I mean, the sheriff's office?" He had a look of concern on his face, perhaps like he felt a sense of responsibility, even though that couldn't have been further from the truth.

He said, "She hired you, for what? To find Graves' killer? After all these years?"

"Like I said, it was all new to her."

"And I assume you're thinking there's a chance she's dead because..." He squinted, like he was thinking. "She comes down here looking for her so-called father's killer, and gets herself in some kind of trouble? Is that what they're saying might've happened?"

"It's what I believe," I said. "That's why she hired me. And now she's dead. I believe that whatever happened to her... she must've either run into someone the afternoon she was killed, or dug something up that had to do with Graves' murder."

"But it sounds to me you're making some assumptions," Holt said. "You have a piece of evidence that's pointing you in that direction?"

"Mike Stone's involved in the case. Do you remember him, from the sheriff's office?"

Holt nodded. "Yeah, I remember Mike. A lot younger than me, but probably closer to retiring himself, than he was last time I saw him. Was also a bit of an arrogant son of a bitch. But he turned out to be a good detective."

"He's all right," I said.

Allen Holt sipped his coffee, made a bitter face, and tossed what was left of it to the ground. "He send you over here by any chance?"

"Detective Stone? No. I'm on my own. But the fact I believe this is connected to Graves' murder has me thinking whatever I can find out about what happened back then should open some doors for me. Or at least get me a little closer. I'm not sure Mike's taking the same approach."

Holt looked off into the woods. "Where's this woman from? The daughter?"

"New York."

Holt said, "And you're here because you're hoping there's something I might know about the case? To help you?"

"You know it's never that easy, but I'd appreciate hearing whatever you care to share with me."

"I imagine you've spoken to some other people?" he said.

"Mostly friends of his. I don't think he had many."

Holt shook his head. "No. But who does, once you hit middle age? I guess maybe you get a little more selective in the people you associate with." He cleared his throat and stuck the unlit cigar in his mouth. "He had a girl back then he was living with." He pulled at his chin. "Name escapes me, but she'd been married at one time to a friend of—"

"Sherry Carter?" I said.

He nodded. "That's right. Sherry Carter. Nice woman. Came up clean, although she never was too broken up when Graves was killed. Made us a little suspicious, but there was nothing else more to give us reason to believe she was a suspect."

"What about her ex, Jack Carter?" I said.

"The photographer?" he said. "Nothing on him either. The only real suspect, although we didn't have much of anything on him, was, uh... oh yeah: Rick Lilly."

"I spoke with him too," I said. "Was he only a suspect because it was his house where Graves was killed?"

Holt shrugged. "I guess so. There was just something about him. Like it never made sense to me how those two'd ever become friends. Not cut from the same cloth, that's for sure. But, yeah, I'd say for the most part, just a few things he'd said or done around the time of the murder. Of course, the fact it was in his home didn't help him either."

"He had an alibi?" I said.

"Yeah, he did. And no real motive that we could ever establish."

"I haven't looked at everything, but from what it looks like, there weren't any real suspects outside of his friends?"

Holt played with the wedding band on his finger, twisting it. He shook his head. "I wish I could give you some kind information that would help, but... you talk to the sister?" Holt said.

"I did. Both Jane and the husband. Trish Williams—Stuart's daughter—had gone up there earlier in the day, before they found her. But it doesn't look like either was ever a suspect in your investigation?"

"No reason for either to be," Holt said. "But, as with Sherry Carter, neither seemed to be too upset about the whole thing. I got that from a lot of people. It wasn't like he wasn't liked, but I didn't get the feeling he was ever missed by anyone either. He didn't appear to be a man with any real strong ties to any particular individual, which is what made the investigation somewhat of a challenge."

"Jane and Steve Ryan didn't want to talk about any of it," I said. "I found it odd, the way they acted."

"I think they both're a little bit odd," Holt said. "But that doesn't make one a killer. At least not most of the time."

I looked toward the front of the home, but couldn't see Alex in Billy's car from where I was standing. I was hopeful the detective would be able to shed some kind of light on the Graves' case, but he didn't seem to have much to add outside of what I already knew.

"Do you know anything about a missing laptop?" I said.

Holt shook his head. "Not that I recall. You mean something that had to do with Graves?"

I nodded. "Do you know anything about the trip he made to the West Coast? Had something to do with a movie he'd written."

"Yeah, I'm aware of it. Was long before his murder, and didn't seem to have anything to do with what happened to him."

"But the laptop—his laptop—apparently went missing. It just disappeared. It sounds like it's what he used for this movie he was working on."

He shrugged and shook his head. "I'm sorry, but I don't see the significance."

"Wouldn't you want to check a victim's computer for some kind of clues?"

He stared back at me, his pleasant expression dropping from his face. "I'm willing to discuss things with you, Mr. Walsh, but don't you show up at my home, pointing fingers, asking why I didn't—"

"I'm sorry," I said. "That's not what I meant. I was just curious. I just found it strange. And I assumed you must've searched Sherry Carter's house at the time?"

"Of course we did. But, like I told you, she was never any kind of suspect, so—"

"She's the one who told me it was missing. So I'm just surprised she never mentioned it to you."

Holt stood, quiet.

We both spun around when Alex walked around the corner, holding her phone. I could see by the look on her face something was wrong.

I introduced her to Detective Holt, but she acted as if he wasn't there. She seemed flustered.

"Mike's been trying to reach you," she said. "Stuart Graves' old girlfriend, Sherry Carter... She's dead."

Chapter 23

Alex and I both jumped from the Lexus as soon as she found a parking space, more than a block from Sherry Carter's studio. We ran down the sidewalk and stopped at the yellow police tape blocking access to the area around the entrance.

The door was held open as the medical examiner pushed the gurney out onto the sidewalk with Sherry Carter's covered body. I watched as he went past us, with an officer lifting the tape for the gurney to roll her under. The medical examiner's van was parked in the middle of the street, where he wheeled the gurney toward it and into the back.

Mike Stone walked out of the studio, holding a cloth over his mouth. He faced me and Alex, shaking his head, but didn't say a word, tossing the cloth inside a trash can on the sidewalk. He coughed, taking a moment before he spoke.

A strong odor came from inside the studio.

"What happened?" I said.

Mike coughed again. "Carbon monoxide poisoning that doesn't appear accidental. The vent to the kiln was blocked with towels stuffed inside the duct and covered with duct tape.

I slipped under the tape and started into the studio, but Mike grabbed me by the arm. "Where do you think you're going?"

I yanked my arm free. "To look around."

"You'll need a mask. But there's nothing to see anyway."

I looked through the doorway at the handful of officers inside, most with gas masks on their faces. A couple held cloths over their mouths, as Mike had done.

"Who found her?" I said.

Mike nodded his chin toward a middle-aged woman talking to two officers. "That woman, over there."

The woman wore the same green smock Sherry had on last time I saw her. She appeared to be upset, tears rolling down her cheeks.

Mike said, "She's her only employee. But there were a dozen women out front when we got here, but none had gone inside. They were here for a class. Lucky for them the door was locked."

I said, "Whoever did this knew Sherry goes in early and cranks up the kiln."

Mike looked at me with a hint of suspicion on his face. "How do you know?"

"Because I was here. I came to see her early, before her class, and watched her turn it on." I looked through the doorway again and into the studio, catching a glimpse of the kiln in the back corner, about four feet in height with a door in the front that was wide open. A door was propped open at the back of the studio with industrial-sized fans blowing outward to clear the CO_2. Sun shined from outside.

"No carbon monoxide detectors?" I said. "Isn't there some kind of code that—"

"She had them," Mike said. "But the batteries had been removed."

Alex said, "You think someone removed them?"

Mike looked at her but didn't answer. I could see on his face he had something else on his mind. He peered at me. "Do you know if Sherry Carter knew Trish Williams? Did they ever meet?"

"Not that I know of," I said. "But I can't say for sure. But even if they never met, it's hard to believe this isn't connected." I looked at the female employee talking to the officers. "Did anyone ask her?"

Mike nodded, and walked over to the two officers with the woman. Alex and I stood and watched, and Mike pulled out his phone, showing it to the woman. She looked at it, her face without expression, until she finally nodded. The two spoke for a couple of minutes, but we couldn't hear what they were saying.

Mike walked back over to us. "Trish Williams was here two times that afternoon, before she was killed," he said. "But the employee doesn't know if she ever spoke to Sherry."

"She doesn't know?" I said.

"Sherry Carter wasn't here either time Trish stopped by, looking for her."

Alex said, "Did she say what time?"

Mike nodded. "She said two o'clock, then came back soon after, but Sherry Carter hadn't returned."

I said, "Then she must've gone to the hotel from there, to check out. Then to the marina. She could've been followed from here."

"You're speculating," Mike said. "We have no idea who else she spoke to that afternoon."

The three of us stood quiet.

I said to Mike, "Have you talked to her father again? Don't you find the fact that she was checking out of her hotel, and allegedly going to St. Augustine, a little odd?"

"I don't," Alex said. "Maybe she just needed some comfort. You said yourself, she doesn't know anyone else around here. Why not go stay with her dad?"

I took a deep breath and exhaled.

Mike reached into his pocket and held out my keys. "Here, before I forget. You know where my condo is, don't you? Your Jeep's parked in back."

Alex reached out and grabbed the keys before I could take them. "He's not allowed to drive," she said. "So if it's all right, he may need to leave it there for a couple of days."

Mike said, "No, it's not all right. It's taking up space. I should've just sent it over to impound, but for some reason I thought I'd be a nice guy."

"I appreciate it," I said, giving him a small grin.

"Why can't you drive?" he said. He looked me over. "You look better than you did when your ticker stopped. Isn't it all fixed?"

Alex grabbed me by the arm and started to pull me away. "He's not driving. But we'll get out of your hair." She pulled me down the sidewalk toward the Lexus on the next block.

But Mike called out, "Hey, Walsh! Remember, if you're going to be talking to anyone, I need to know. We don't need you stepping on our toes, you understand?"

"You're the boss," I said, and continued along the sidewalk. But I stopped again as Mike was stepping through the doorway into the studio. "Hey, Mike!" I yelled.

He poked his head out the door and looked at me, waiting.

I said, "Has anyone told Jack Carter?"

"The ex-husband?" He shook his head, then disappeared through the door without another word.

··········

Alex was behind the wheel, quiet, with her eyes on the road for most of the ride.

"Are you going to tell me what's going on?" I said.

She gave me a quick glance. "What's going on?" She shrugged, and gave me a weak grin. "That poor woman was poisoned to death, not even knowing what was happening until it was too late."

"Someone really went out of their way to do it that way," I said. "You ask me, whoever did it knew what he was doing."

"He?" she said. "How do you know it's a he?"

"I'm just saying... He. She. I have no idea. Could've been more than one person. But I don't think it was just your average Joe who murders someone by blocking the carbon monoxide. And what if some of those women were in there?"

"So you think it was some kind of assassin?" Alex said.

I glanced out the passenger window, thinking. "Trish Williams was abducted by someone, shot and killed, stuffed in the trunk of a car they dumped in a river. That's not just your average murder."

Alex took her eyes from the road for a moment, nodding as she gazed at me. "I think you're right. If it's an individual who wants them dead, that's a lot to go through." Then Alex said, "I don't mean to be playing devil's advocate here, but don't you think there's still a chance they may not be related?"

"No way," I said. "How could they *not* be connected? In fact, I'd go so far as to say all four murders—"

"*Four* murders?"

"If you include Stuart Graves, then we go way back." I turned to Alex. "Elizabeth Sutton."

"The woman you told me about who drove off the bridge? Now you think that was a homicide?"

·········

It wasn't easy, but I convinced Alex to drop me off at Mike's condo so I could pick up the Jeep. I didn't see much of a problem with me driving, considering I felt as good as I had in a while. At least, physically. I followed Alex to Billy's Place to drop off his Lexus, then took her back to her hotel so she could catch up on whatever work she'd taken with her.

"Where are you going from here?" she said, stepping out of the Jeep at the entrance.

I hesitated, not sure if I should tell her or not. It was only something that had popped in my mind on the drive over to her hotel. "I was going to go down to Riverside."

"What's in Riverside?"

"Five Points."

She folded her arms and gave me a look, knowing I wasn't being completely clear. "Okay, what's in Five Points?"

That was the detail I wasn't sure I should tell her. "I just need to check something out down there. No big deal," I said, and shifted into gear.

She said, "You're not going to tell me?"

I thought about it for a moment, then shook my head. "Nah."

"Henry, what are you up to?" I felt like I was being spoken to by my mom, when I was a kid.

"Nothing. I'll call you in a little bit," I said.

She took a deep breath with an exaggerated exhale. "Do you have to play games like this?"

I paused at first. "I kind of do," I said. "You're on the other side now, with that badge of yours."

Her eyes opened wide. "The *other* side? Are you kidding me? Is that really what you think?"

"You and Mike are on the same team now. The two cops. And then there's me."

She rolled her eyes, shaking her head. "Why are you acting like a child?"

"Am I?" I shrugged. "I know Mike doesn't want me involved, but I'm not going to sit around and wait for him to give me the go-ahead. If either of you think I'm just going to sit and—"

"I'm not a fool," she said. "And Mike's not either. But I still think it makes sense to talk to him, let him know what you're doing. It's only fair, not to either of you, but to these victims. It makes no sense to step on each other's toes."

"Don't you mean that *I'm* not to step on *his* toes?"

"No," she said, shaking her head. "Why do you think I'm taking sides?"

She looked at the hotel's entrance, when a young couple walked outside, holding hands.

Alex waited for them to pass. "I was saying, it's not about taking sides, Henry. It's about having some kind of order to an investigation. I think you'd agree this one's a little more complicated. It's not just one victim here. It's not just about your client."

"It is for me," I said. But as soon as the words left my mouth, I wish they hadn't.

She dropped her arms by her sides, nodding with a crooked grin, like I'd revealed something she knew all along. "She wasn't just your client, was she?"

I didn't respond. "Why don't you call me when you're done doing whatever it is you have to do," I said. "I'll come back here, and..." My eyes searched the parking lot. "You didn't rent a car or anything?"

Alex shook her head. "I was planning on it. Billy picked me up from the airport, and we went right to the hospital to see you. I haven't had a chance."

I'd successfully changed the subject.

Alex looked in at me, holding her gaze before starting for the hotel's entrance. "I'll talk to you later." She stopped on the sidewalk, a few feet from the door, then turned around. "You don't have to tell me what you're doing. Just do me a favor and be careful."

Chapter 24

Most of Five Points had been redeveloped with trendy shops and new restaurants, but The Crow stood out as the one old-school bar left standing. It looked to be exactly what it was: an old bar in an old building.

Not a bad thing, in my opinion.

The bar inside was half full, a handful of tables taken up, but aside from the music, fairly quiet.

I grabbed a stool on one end, and the stocky, middle-aged man behind the bar came right over. "Good evening," he said, tossing the coaster like a Frisbee. It landed perfectly in front of me. "What'll it be?"

I didn't like the idea of taking up a stool and having a soda, considering no bartender comes to work for the tips he'd make from serving a two-dollar soda. But ordering a drink just so I didn't offend the man didn't make much sense.

I threw down a five-dollar bill. "Just a ginger ale, for now."

He didn't seem to mind. "Menu?"

"Yeah, that'll be good," I said.

I was hungry, even though I thought about holding off until Alex was done with whatever she was working on back at the hotel. It would've been nice if we could've gotten dinner, but I had no idea how long she'd be working. And I didn't know how much longer my stomach could go without food. The last meal I had was at the hospital, if you could even call it a meal.

The bartender poured the soda and placed the glass on the coaster. "Name's Mac," he said, and reached across to shake my hand.

"Henry," I said.

The man had a crushing grip.

"Let me know if you'd like to order some food," he said, walking toward the other end of the bar, where a group sat together, laughing, throwing back beers.

I looked over the menu. It wasn't the type of place you'd get a healthy meal. At least it didn't seem that way. But I figured eating a greasy burger with fries—which is what I really would've liked—probably wasn't on the list of foods the nurse had handed me at discharge.

It wasn't that I ate poorly. But I never really worried about it either. The truth was, what happened to my heart had nothing to do with my diet or anything else. At least that's the way I understood it. But it did make me think how I wasn't some twenty-five-year-old kid who could shovel whatever I wanted down my throat.

But I had hit the age where I'd stopped looking forward and spent more time looking back. I'm not sure when exactly that happens. But it does.

I'd just hoped my little episode—little, being subjective—was all I'd have to worry about for a while. I had no interest in dealing with health issues the closer I got to the back nine.

Of course, the reality was I had some things to worry about. I had Alzheimers in my family. Cancer. Diabetes. Who knew what else.

When I was in that hospital bed, I thought about everything I'd do when I was out. Eat better, for one. Maybe join a gym.

I looked around the L-shaped bar, and the area behind me, a mix of smaller round tables and pub-height high-tops. It wasn't a big place, a couple of TVs and a red brick-colored tile floor that looked like it'd been there since the place opened. Which, according to the sign, was 1978.

The Crow looked like the kind of place I could get comfortable in, hang around for a while. At least in my drinking days, I could.

Mac came back over, and I still hadn't found much of anything to eat. I looked up at him standing in front of me.

He said, "See something you like?"

I nodded. "Everything," I said. "But I'm trying to eat healthy. I just had a little bit of a health scare, and"—I held up the glass of ginger ale—"I'm also on the wagon."

Mac laughed, nodding. "I hear you, man." He looked to be in decent shape but patted his stomach. "I've been trying to do the same, knock off a good twenty pounds. No fun getting old."

Now, although the thought of calling myself old hadn't yet entered my mind, Mac triggered the thought in my head. Was I old? In my forties?

I folded over the menu. "You know what? I'll have a burger. Well done."

He laughed. "Good choice." He took the menu. "You want fries?"

I shrugged and cleared my throat. "Any chance I can get a salad?"

"Yeah, man. Of course. That'll level it all out for you." He laughed again, grabbed my glass, and topped it off with more soda, which I knew I shouldn't be drinking either. I was going to have to come up with a better alternative to booze.

He walked through a swinging door, came back out a moment later. "Be out in a few minutes." He started to head down the other end of the bar again.

I said, "Hey, Mac?"

He stopped and came back over. "What do you need?"

"I was wondering if Lenny still owns this place?"

Mac smiled, nodding. "He's my dad."

"Oh, no kidding? So, does that mean you're the owner now?"

"Sort of. He's not involved anymore. But he said it'll be his until someone puts him in the ground."

"He doesn't come around?"

He looked like he was about to answer, but didn't. "You mind I ask why you're asking?"

"I wanted to talk to him about something. About some of his old patrons, from back in the day."

"Yeah? You want to try me? I might know who you're talking about. I practically grew up in the place."

"Maybe," I said. I sipped my soda. "You remember a man, Stuart Graves?"

Mac cocked his head back. "Graves?" He nodded. "What about him?"

I pulled my business card out and pushed it across the bar.

Mac looked it over. "So, what, you're investigating Mr. Graves' murder? Kind of a long time ago, no?"

"It was," I said, but didn't offer much else. "So, how well did you know him and his buddies?"

"I knew most of those guys," Mac said. "We had a different crowd back then."

"In what way?"

He grabbed a glass and poured himself a splash of soda and drank it all. "What do you want to know?"

Someone yelled from the kitchen. "Mac, burger's up."

Mac put up his finger and went into the kitchen, came out with my burger on a plate in one hand and a bowl of salad in the other, placing them in front of me. He reached underneath the bar and came up with a bottle of ketchup.

"You must've known Jack Carter? And Rick Lilly?"

"I knew them all. I was younger, but I hung around enough to see what was going on."

"So, what *was* going on?"

He laughed. "Like any bar. Bunch of guys getting drunk."

"That's it?"

"Well, guys. Women, too. The women loved those guys. They weren't your typical barflies, you know what I mean? They were all artists, most of 'em. My dad liked that. He had respect for what they did."

I said, "Sherry Carter used to hang around here?"

He paused, like he was thinking. "Oh yeah. She was Stu's girlfriend. But I remember when she was married to Jack Carter. I never understood much of how that all worked, between the three of them. I asked my dad once; he told me to mind my own business."

"How about Elizabeth Sutton? You remember her?"

A smile left his face, and he nodded. "I didn't know her that well. You know she's dead, right? Drove her car off the bridge up in Yulee, into the Nassau River."

It struck me as odd, he mentioned Elizabeth Sutton's death, but it dawned on me he likely didn't know about Sherry Carter. "Did you know Sherry was found dead this morning? At her studio?"

Mac stopped what he was doing. "Sherry? She's dead?" He shook his head. "I had no idea."

"They don't know exactly what happened, but there's a good chance she was murdered."

Mac leaned on the bar with his hands, shaking his head. "I wasn't expecting to hear that."

"When was the last time you saw her?" I said.

"Oh, geez, I'm not even sure. A long time ago. I mean, way back. That whole crowd has been long gone for years. I don't know... Must've been fifteen years ago. Long before what'd happened to Mr. Graves."

"Any other women you remember who used to hang around back then? Maybe had something to do with Stuart Graves?"

Mac pulled at his chin. "I don't know. I guess there were some who would come and go. To be honest, it was hard to keep track of who was with who, and who was dating who. I don't know if they were all into orgies or something, but, again, my dad would just tell me to mind my business."

"You mean, besides Jack and Sherry and Stuart Graves?"

"Well, you already asked, but before that, there was Miss Sutton. That was while Jack and Sherry were still married."

"How old were you back then?"

He shrugged. "Early twenties, I guess."

I said, "Was she ever with anyone else? That you remember?"

Mac cracked a crooked smile. "Like I said, if I asked my dad about it, he'd tell me to mind my own business. He knew what was going on, but never talked about it. But, yeah, Elizabeth... She was beautiful. As good looking as any woman who ever came in here. It looked to me like every guy who walked in the place must've hit on her, tried to get with her, at one time or another."

"Did you know she was pregnant when she died?"

"Well, yeah. I'd heard it was Stu's baby. But nobody talked about it much after the news broke." He nodded at my burger. "You don't want your food to get cold."

I poured ketchup on my burger and took a bite. It was the best thing I'd ever eaten in my life. At least the first bite was. I followed it with another, and Mac started to walk away. I swallowed and wiped my mouth. "Mac, what about your dad?" I said. "Is there a chance I could talk to him?"

Mac nodded, and reached for the phone. "He's usually up late. He'd probably love to have a visitor."

Chapter 25

It was late when I knocked on the apartment door. Lenny Coolidge opened it within a few seconds, like he'd been waiting on the other side. "You Henry?" he said, holding the door wide open. "Come on in." He reached out with his thin, bony hand and shook mine. "Lenny Coolidge. Nice to meet you."

I stepped inside, and he closed the door behind me. The TV was on with the volume down in the small room adjacent to the kitchen. There was a strong cooked-fish odor in the apartment, and it looked like he'd been cooking something on the stove.

He grabbed the pan and spatula from it, placed them in the sink, and ran the faucet over them. "Friend of mine came by a little earlier, brought some wahoo he'd caught, fishin' off Amelia Island." He looked back at me from the sink. "You ever had wahoo?"

I shook my head. "I don't think so."

"Good fish. Mild. Nice round flakes." He cleaned the pan, wiped it down, and stuck it in one of the lower cabinets. He stuck the spatula in the dishwasher.

"I hope it's not too late for you," I said.

Lenny waved me off. "I've always been a night owl, owning the bar all those years. Even at my age now, I'm lucky I get to bed before midnight."

Mac had told me his father was seventy-seven years old. But I thought he looked younger. His hair was gray but not all of it. I could see the resemblance between the two, almost identical twins, if not for the twentysomething years in between them. Mac was bigger overall, but it probably wasn't always the case.

"Would you like a drink?" he said. "I mean, a soda or tea or... I don't have any booze in the place, so—"

"I'm fine," I said. "Thank you."

We went into the other room with the small TV in the far corner. Curtains were pulled closed over the only window in the room, centered on the opposite wall from where I stood.

He had one of those late-night news programs on, like *60 Minutes* but it was something else, showing wild horses running on a beach. I couldn't remember the last time I watched one of those shows. I wasn't even sure if *60 Minutes* was still on the air.

"Have a seat," he said, nodding toward the couch. He sat in a recliner across from it and picked up the remote from the side table next to him. He changed the channel and put on a baseball game. The Rays were playing the Yankees. He turned up the volume, but not too much. "You like baseball?"

I sat on the couch. "I don't watch it much anymore. Once they started making more in a game than I could in my whole life, I started to lose interest."

"I know what you're saying. All sports are like that now. And it's the little guys like us who pay the tab. Can't even get to a sporting event for under a hundred bucks."

I nodded, smiling. "I used to work for the Jacksonville Sharks, before they moved to Tennessee."

His eyes seemed to light up. "No kidding, huh? What'd you do there?"

"I ran security."

He appeared to be somewhat impressed, although I wasn't sure why. "So, you're a private investigator, huh? Mac didn't give me much detail, said it had something to do with what happened to Sherry Carter?"

"You're aware of what happened?"

Lenny nodded. "I got a call, old friend of mine, told me about it. Something about carbon monoxide poisoning?

"As far as they know that appears to be the cause of death. But how it happened is another story."

"What's that mean, how it happened?"

"It's under investigation, but it appears it wasn't an accident. There's evidence of foul play."

Lenny straightened up in his chair. "You don't mean she was murdered, do you?"

I leaned forward on the edge of the couch. "Your son didn't mention that?"

Lenny shook his head, a look on his face like he didn't know how to react. "Wow," he said, his eyes shifting toward the floor. "That's... It's hard to believe. Sherry was a good woman." He looked into the kitchen. "I think I have a bowl she made around here somewhere. I remember she dropped it off for me at the bar. Oh, I don't know if it was a bowl. Maybe a mug. It was a long time ago, I suppose." He turned back in his seat, his quiet gaze on the TV.

"I'm sorry," I said. "About Sherry."

He nodded, like he appreciated it. "I haven't been in touch with her or anyone else from that crowd in years. But…" He paused. "Why would anyone do such a thing? Kill a nice woman like her? This world's gone mad, I tell you."

Lenny sat there, quietly, like he was thinking through some things. I was surprised to see him take the news I shared as hard as he had. "Sherry had a boyfriend, used to hang around the bar. I don't know if you know this already, but he was killed a few years back. I'm not even sure how long it's been, but—"

"Stuart Graves," I said, nodding. "The only reason I met Sherry, just a couple of days ago, is because I'd been hired to investigate Mr. Graves' murder."

"Oh," he said. "I thought you were a friend of hers, the way Mac made it sound."

I went ahead and told him about Trish, how she'd hired me, and how she might've spoken to Sherry at some point that afternoon, and that it had to have had something to do with them both being killed.

Just like everyone else, Lenny was shocked to hear about Trish.

"And you're telling me this poor girl… She comes down here from New York because, for some reason, she wants to find out what happened to her old man? A father she'd never even met?" He squeezed his eyes shut and shook his head, like he was shaking off cobwebs. "And someone killed her? Boy, that's a lot to digest." Lenny stared at the TV. "I hope you or someone from the sheriff's office will catch the son of a bitch, whoever it is, before he harms someone else."

"I hope so too," I said.

We both looked at the TV when someone on the Yankees apparently hit a bases-clearing home run.

I said, "What about Elizabeth Sutton? What can you tell me about her?"

"Elizabeth? I'm not sure I..." He paused, slowly nodding his head. "Oh, right. Elizabeth Sutton. Now there's another name I haven't heard in years. You're not going to suggest what happened to her had something to do with the others, are you? That was so far back, I mean, when Elizabeth had the accident. I suppose she'd been drinking."

"She was pregnant," I said. "But nobody seems to know anything about who the father was."

"The rumor going around at the time, after it happened, was that Stu was the father. But I never got involved with any of it at the time. None of my business, if you know what I mean."

"You never heard anyone talk about it? Stuart, or any of his friends?"

"Sure, they all talked about it. But by the time word got out she'd been pregnant, I guess it was too late. You know what I'm saying?" Lenny stared back at me, his mouth slightly open, like he was going to say something but waited another moment. "Truth is, Stu was pretty upset about the whole thing."

"He told you that?"

Lenny nodded and cracked a slight smile. "Bartenders have two jobs: keep the drinks flowing, and listen to people whine about their problems."

"Did he say anything else about it? Or what happened?"

"Stu kept to himself. He was pretty reserved, for the most part. But you could tell he was always thinking. Observing."

"But you're telling me he was upset about Elizabeth? Was it more because she was dead? Or because she might've been carrying his baby?"

"Oh, I suppose both. No? I mean, it was a long time ago. It's not like I'd remember every conversation we might've had, word for word. We're talking, what, maybe fifteen years back? I don't even remember when it happened."

So I reminded him. Elizabeth was killed five years before the same fate struck Graves.

Lenny pushed himself up from his recliner. "You sure you don't want a drink? I have lemonade, or I can make some hot tea. No coffee. Don't drink the stuff anymore. All those years of drinking two or three pots of coffee for breakfast, beer for lunch, ate a hole right through my stomach." He walked into the kitchen and filled a kettle with water, placing it on the stove.

I followed him into the kitchen. "Did Graves ever talk to you about the movie he was working on?"

"The movie?" The look on his face said he had no idea what I was talking about. But then he nodded, and said, "Funny thing is, he used to sit at the bar with his laptop out, eyes on the screen, typing away like a madman. He never said a word about it to me, and I never asked what he was working on. None of my business, right? But one afternoon this woman came in the bar looking for him. That's the only time I ever heard him mention it—some movie he was working on. The way she was talking, she must've been in the business. I thought maybe Stu was going to make the big time."

"Any chance you know who she was?" I said.

Lenny chewed the inside of his cheek, shaking his head, appearing like he was trying to jump-start the memory once again. He finally said, "You know what? I do remember. Because she had a funny name, like her first and last name rhymed. I'm not sure I'll ever remember it though."

He had a blank stare, but then burst out, like a little kid who'd just won a prize. "It was May! May Lay!"

"Lay?" I said. "Like L-A-Y?"

"Yeah, I guess so. That sounds like it'd be right. If my memory serves me correctly, which sometimes it doesn't."

"And she met with Stuart? About his movie?"

"I think so. Like I said, I don't listen to customers' conversations, but sometimes you can't help it. I thought maybe she was some kind of agent, or—"

"A movie agent?" I said.

Lenny shrugged. "Ah, I don't know. I'm sorry. I hate to give you bad information."

"You never asked him about it?"

"No, no. If he wanted me, or anyone else to know about his business, he would've said something. He clearly wanted to keep it to himself for a reason, I guess. But it must've been at least a good six months he'd been working on that laptop. Funny, he'd only come in when it was slow, when none of his buddies were there. He'd peck away on that thing, one finger at a time, like the old sports writers used to do."

I said, "And you never saw this woman, May, any other time?"

He shook his head. "I think they met there maybe once or twice after, and that was it. In fact, most of Stu's other friends, like Jack and Rick and Sherry, and a few others, I'm not even sure I could tell you their names, they'd all stopped coming in around that time. It was sort of the end of it all, I'd say. You know? Like the band broke up. You know how that goes, right? People move on. Nothing lasts forever."

Chapter 27

I OPENED MY EYES and sat up on the edge of my bed. It took me a few seconds to realize I was in my own bed with the messy, tangled sheets rolled up in a ball behind me, like I'd wrestled with them all night. I'm not sure who won, but my T-shirt was soaked in sweat.

I didn't end up meeting Alex. She stayed in her hotel room and worked through the night. I wanted to see her, but I also needed sleep, even if it was only for a handful of hours.

My phone was on the floor, and when I picked it up, I saw it was only 5:23 in the morning. Looking out the porthole, I saw a hint of sunlight starting to leak into the lower part of the dark morning sky.

I made some coffee and sat on a stool in the galley. The coffee wasn't as bad as everyone always said it was, but all I could think about was that first time I met Trish, when she couldn't drink it. For me, it was all about getting caffeine. I always thought that was the purpose of coffee.

I was anxious to get over to the office to use my laptop. I did some brief research on my phone, trying to see if I could find the woman, May Lay, who Lenny had told me about.

But I had no luck at all. There were a few people, including both men and women, with similar names. There was even a rapper with the last name Maylay, although it turned out to be his stage name. There were also variations in spelling, a clothing store with the same name, and an actress with a different spelling.

I couldn't find a middle-aged woman, who at one time was involved with movies or scripts, or maybe was an agent, at any point.

All said and done, searching on the phone was useless.

By the time I got into the Jeep, it was a little before six o'clock. Other than some fishermen already on their boats, the marina was quiet and still, although it was just starting to come to life. The streetlamps over the parking lot shone down on whatever vehicles were still parked there.

I had one foot up in the Jeep when I stopped to look across the parking lot. I was almost certain I saw someone in the distance, on the other side from where I was parked. I stood up on the side step to get a better view but saw nothing. Maybe my eyes were playing tricks on me.

I slid into the driver's seat and took off across the lot, stopping before I pulled onto Trout River Drive. I looked back into the parking lot, seeing headlights in the distance. I assumed it was the person I thought I saw a couple of minutes earlier. At least I knew I wasn't losing my mind.

I turned onto the street and continued toward Billy's Place, and by the time I pulled into the parking lot, the sky had started to brighten. But it was still pretty dark outside. I parked near the stairs and looked up toward the second level. It appeared, at first, that lights were shining from one of the offices. I didn't remember leaving them on. In fact, I was almost certain I'd shut them off. There was also a chance Billy installed new lighting on the exterior walkway while I'd been away, and I just hadn't recognized the glow.

On my way up the stairs, I stopped on the top step where I could see the windows to my office. Sure enough, the light was coming from inside. Walking up to the door, I was about to reach for the knob and realized the door was cracked open. The door wasn't damaged in any way, so it was hard to tell if someone had broken in or if the door could've been left open.

I looked inside, through the glass on the door, but instead of going in unarmed, I ran for the stairs to my Jeep. I took a baseball bat out of my trunk and hurried back up. I tried to be light on my feet with each step I took.

When I got to the door, I raised the bat and used my foot to push it open. Stepping inside, I peeked behind the door, then back and forth and toward the back. There was only one entrance, and really nowhere to hide other than the bathroom or the storage closet.

I looked at my desk where I'd left the files Mike had given me from Stuart Graves' case. But they were gone. My desk was completely cleared, which wasn't how I'd left it.

Not only were the files missing, but so was my laptop.

I pulled open the drawers, hoping I'd simply forgotten that I'd put everything away, like I probably should have.

No such luck.

It was all gone. Everything.

I headed to the bathroom, the bat again raised, and flipped on the light switch. It was empty. I hurried down the short hall to the storage closet.

Other than my own breathing and the air blowing through the ceiling vents, it was pretty much total silence. I stood in front of the closet, raised the bat with one hand, and reached for the knob. Without a second of hesitation I turned the handle, ripped the door open and stepped back, holding my weapon up like I was in the batter's box.

But other than the barren built-in shelves, the closet was empty.

I wasn't going to call the cops just yet. And I certainly wasn't going to tell Mike the files he'd given me had disappeared. I knew how he'd react. I felt like a fool. It would've been one thing if I'd put them away, stored them somewhere out of sight. But it was another to think I left them out in the open. I hadn't even set the alarm when I'd left earlier in the day.

I turned off the lights and pulled the door closed, starting for the stairs. But I stopped before the top step and sent Alex a text.

Me: *Someone broke into the office.*

Alex: *I'll be right there.*

Me: *You have a car?*

Alex: *Yes.*

I didn't ask where she got the car but knew I'd find out soon enough.

I headed down the stairs, but I stopped when I thought I'd heard a voice. It was a man, hushed, talking to someone else, somewhere in the parking lot. The morning darkness was starting to lift, and I couldn't see anyone near my Jeep.

I had a firm grip on the bat and tried to be quiet going down the stairs. I stopped at the corner of the building and listened, but I could no longer hear the man. I poked my head around the corner, and there he was. A man wore a ski mask and was on the phone.

He noticed me right away and yelled into the phone, "It's him!" He reached his hand around his back and aimed a gun. I was already too close to turn away and run, so I charged him with the bat and took a hard swing. He screamed when I made contact with his hand, knocking the gun free and to the ground.

I took another swing, and he raised his arms to protect his face. I connected, and he fell to the asphalt. But the problem for me was he landed next to his gun. He grabbed it, and I threw the bat at him to give myself enough time to run away.

Just as I ducked behind the Jeep, he fired three or four consecutive shots, striking the hood. I hid behind the steering wheel, crouched down, and looked under the Jeep to the other side. He was on his feet and walking toward me, his long shadow stretched along the ground from the streetlight on the corner of the lot.

He was almost at the hood, coming toward me, when I heard tires squealing. I looked toward the street, and a black SUV jumped the curb and sped toward us. I stayed crouched down and looked underneath again, seeing the man's feet, running away, heading to the front of Billy's Place.

The SUV went right past me, skidding, going full speed toward the man.

He fired a shot and the SUV's brakes locked; the vehicle stopped before turning the corner toward the front.

The driver's-side door opened, and Alex stepped out, gun in her hand. She ducked behind the open door.

More shots fired, striking her windshield.

I ran toward her but stayed close to the building. She stayed low and ran from the SUV to where I stood, leaned against the building's brick exterior and had her gun up, ready to fire. Her breathing was heavy.

Alex looked out around the corner and more shots were fired. Headlights shone on the street, and Alex stepped out, firing back at the man. She took five or six shots, then took cover. "Do you know who it is?" she said.

I shook my head. "No idea."

We both waited. Cars could be heard off in the distance, but otherwise it was quiet.

She stuck her head out to look. "He's down," she said, waiting a couple of moments, then stepped away, gun raised. I followed her, unarmed.

The man was facedown, all the way on the other side of the front parking lot, almost near the road. I looked around for a vehicle. "Did you see those headlights?" I said.

The daylight was enough to see the man was lying in a pool of his own blood. He didn't move.

"Is he dead?"

We both stood over him.

There was a gun a few feet from him. Alex stepped over and kicked it farther away, then came back and crouched down next to him. She put her hand under his jaw. "Oh no," she said, almost under her breath. She stood up, but kept her gaze on the man, then leaned over, and pulled the ski mask from his face.

I didn't ask again but was pretty sure, by her expression, that the man was dead.

"This isn't good," she said. "I have to call Mike." She moved away from the body without saying anything else and ran toward the SUV.

Chapter 28

By the time Billy showed up at his restaurant, the parking lot had been taped off in front, with six sheriff's vehicles and one rescue vehicle parked near the road by the body. Billy drove past me and Alex, standing out front by the entrance to Billy's Place, and continued around to the back of the building.

A few moments later, he walked around the corner, talking on his phone, stopping a few feet from where Alex and I stood. He finished his call and came over to us. "This won't be good for business," he said, as if he were trying to make light of the fact a dead man's body was in his parking lot. He looked at the closed entrance. "Do the cops need to get inside?"

I shrugged. "They're up in the office right now."

Billy looked over at the cops, standing around the covered body. "Was he alone?"

"We think there was a car in the street waiting for him, but whoever was behind the wheel must've decided to take off."

Billy nodded, looking around. "You were here early, as usual?" he said. "You said it sounds like you surprised him?"

"Yes."

Alex was quiet and looked as concerned as she ever had.

We all turned when Mike walked over.

He gave me a nod with his chin. "You sure you've never seen this guy before?"

"I don't recognize him at all," I said. "But he knew who I was, as soon as I came down the stairs."

Mike didn't say much or react in any way. He took a toothpick from his shirt pocket and stuck it in his mouth, then reached for Alex. "Come on, let's go talk."

She gave me a quick glance as she walked away with him. They went over to where she'd left the SUV. Mike's Crown Victoria was behind it.

"So," Billy said, looking around the lot. "You left the alarm off?"

"A little late for that," I said, a bit snippy on my part. "It was a mistake. I thought I was coming back last night."

"I'm not trying to place blame on you," he said. "I was just asking."

I looked at the body and could feel Billy holding his gaze on me.

"They would've gotten it whether the alarm was set or not," I said. "They. He. Whoever it was. They got what they wanted."

Billy said, "Your laptop? What for?"

I didn't mention the files that were technically the property of the sheriff's office. "Maybe they thought I had something on there, someone's name. I don't really know, honestly."

Alex walked over to us, but Mike kept going, back over to the body and the other officers. "This isn't good for me," she said. "I should've just let the guy go. Or hit him with the—"

"He was shooting at us," I said. "What were you supposed to do?"

"I'm an off duty police detective. Do you know what that means? There's going to be an internal investigation. There will be repercussions. And like Mike just said, I'll likely be put on administrative leave while it's investigated."

Billy said, "Mike's taking the footage from the cameras we have outside. They'll clear this up in no time, don't you think?"

Alex looked at him but didn't answer, pushing her hair back from her face.

I said, "They covered the cameras in back. Maybe they didn't think they'd be in front," he said. "Or maybe they didn't see them."

We all watched the medical examiner and someone helping him lift the body onto the gurney.

Billy said to Alex, "When did you rent that SUV?"

"Last night. I got it from a local rental place, a couple of blocks from the hotel. Figured it was easier to have my own car to get around with." She started to walk away, toward the vehicle.

"Where're you going?" I said.

"Call my sergeant." She kept walking.

I followed her. "Wait!"

She opened the driver's-side door and stood, watching me, without getting in.

"You sure it runs?"

She slid onto the seat and turned the engine. It started without a problem. "Looks like it."

She was about to close the door, but I grabbed it to stop her.

"Listen," I said. "I'm sorry about all of this. You were right from the start. About not being involved. It's my fault that you—"

"That man was going to kill you. You didn't make me do anything." She pulled the door closed, looked out at me through the window with a cold grin, and drove away.

Mike yelled over, "Where's she going?"

"To call someone," I said.

He walked over, and we both stood and watched her pull out onto the street and take off, engine roaring.

I said, "What kind of trouble is this going to cause for her?"

"It depends on a lot of things," he said. "Of course, it'll be investigated, but..." He looked me over. "You should feel lucky, you know that? She always has your back, even when she knows it puts her in a bad spot." Mike walked away, heading toward the rear of the building. But he stopped and turned around. "You sure there wasn't anything else stolen from your office besides your laptop?"

"No, that was about it," I said. "Just the laptop." I hated to have to lie, but I knew how he'd react. And I didn't want to have to deal with it right then. I had expected him to ask me about the files, but for some reason he didn't. He continued away from me and disappeared around the other side of the building.

· · · · · · · · · ·

I sat at the bar inside the restaurant and used a yellow legal pad from Billy's office to take notes, doing my best to remember whatever I'd had on my laptop and whatever else I could think of I needed to keep track of.

Billy still hadn't opened the restaurant after deciding to hold off for a few hours while the scene was cleaned up outside, although most of the police were gone.

He seemed to be fine with being closed. He made a pot of coffee and turned up the jazz he played over the sound system. He almost seemed to be enjoying the break, giving himself a chance to relax a few hours at lunchtime, for the first time in quite a while. But I knew he was losing money, being closed. Maybe he didn't care.

"I'm sorry about all this," I said. I watched him come back from hanging a handwritten sign on the front door, to let people know the restaurant would open again at four o'clock.

"Why should you be sorry?" he said, going over to the coffee machine. He poured two cups and gave one to me, then walked around to my side of the bar. He sat three stools down from me and leaned back, one foot up on the stool closest to him. "I'm sure you'll figure out who's behind it."

I took a sip of coffee and stared straight ahead. "Don't repeat this to Alex, but I really wish we caught this guy alive."

"You sound like an ungrateful—" He cleared his throat and sat up straight on the stool, folding his arms. "From what it sounds like, you would've been dead if Alex hadn't shown up and saved your..."

"I didn't mean it to come off the way it sounded," I said. "I know what she did. She's always been there for me, no matter what." I looked at my watch. "I should go over to her hotel and talk to her, see if she's okay."

"I think you should just let her do what she has to do. This is serious for her. It's her career."

For a restaurant owner who spent most of his waking hours in his restaurant, Billy knew a lot more about the way things worked out in the real world than most people did. He was smart. He liked to talk to people. And he actually listened.

He looked at the pad in front of me. "What are you writing?"

"Just trying to keep everything together. Suspects. Witnesses. People who the sheriff's office questioned in the past..."

He reached over, picked up the pad and looked it over. "May Lay? Is that a real person?"

"She's someone who met with Stuart Graves, a long time ago. I came to the office early this morning to see if I could track her down, but no luck."

"The sheriff's office doesn't know where to find her?"

"I don't think they ever spoke to her. I'm not sure they would've had a reason to."

"So where'd you get her name?"

"You know that bar, The Crow? Down in Five Points? I spoke with the owner, Lenny."

"Lenny?" Billy smiled. "I don't know him personally. But he was a friend of my uncle's, back when my uncle owned this place."

"You ever been to his bar?"

Billy shook his head. "Not my crowd down there."

"Back when Graves and his buddies were hanging around there, it was mostly artists."

"It's an artsy area. Always has been."

I sipped my coffee. "Lenny knew Stuart Graves, and most of his friends."

Billy looked at the pad. "So what's the deal with May Lay? Strange name, isn't it?"

"I'm not even sure it's her name. I only searched on my phone last night, but didn't have any luck."

"Almost sounds like a stage name."

I told Billy what Lenny told me, how she'd met with Stuart and talked to him about the so-called movie script he was allegedly working on.

"And you think she had something to do with movies? Like an agent or something?"

I shrugged. "I wish I could answer that. Lenny wasn't even sure. If only I could find her somehow."

Billy looked confused. "Are you saying you think there's some kind of clue, has to do with this script he wrote?"

"I don't know. I find it odd that nobody knows where it is. And nobody ever saw it."

Billy walked to the front window and looked outside. "Do you really think solving this Graves' case is going to get you any closer to understanding what happened to Trish? It just seems like—"

"Stone doesn't want me involved right now, at least in the recent crimes. But he didn't say I couldn't dig into a cold case that nobody at that sheriff's office wanted anything to do with."

"I guess that makes sense; work your way around it from that angle. But I don't understand why Mike wouldn't want your help?"

I finished the coffee and stood. I grabbed the pad and looked over my notes.

Billy walked around the other side of the bar. "What kind of parent would give their kid a first name that rhymes with their surname?" He picked up his coffee and took a sip. "A name like May Lay, you'd think she wouldn't be that hard to find." He leaned with his hands wide on the bar. "Have you asked some of Graves' friends about her?"

"I'm not sure I want to bring up her name with any of them. Not yet."

Billy said, "Why, because you think one of them killed Graves?"

I shrugged and started for the door. "If it wasn't a friend, I have a good feeling it was at least an acquaintance."

Chapter 29

Jack Carter was seated at the front desk in the reception area of his photography studio and looked up from the computer when I walked in. He removed his glasses and watched me approach the desk.

"May I help you?" he said. He didn't appear to recognize me.

"Henry Walsh," I said. "I was here the other day, about your friend Stuart?"

He stood up from the chair, nodding. "Oh, right. I'm sorry, Henry, I... My receptionist called in sick. I'm doing double duty today." He grinned, walked around to the front of the desk, and shook my hand.

"I'm sorry about Sherry," I said. "It was a shock to hear."

Jack shook his head, eyes toward the floor. "A shock is an understatement." He raised his gaze to mine. "I'll be honest; it still hasn't sunk in. I mean, Sherry and I hadn't talked much lately, not in a while, but it's... it's been hard to swallow." He put his hand over his heart. "The cops came by my house last night. I didn't even know it'd happened. I don't pay much attention to the news anymore."

I glanced over at the colored plastic chairs in the waiting area. "What'd they say?"

"The cops?" Jack shrugged. "Asked me a lot of questions, wondering when was the last time I talked to her, where I was the morning it happened, if I knew anyone who'd want to do something like this to her..."

"And what'd you tell them?"

Jack gave me a funny look, his head cocked a bit. "Which part?"

I said, "How about, 'if you knew anyone who'd want to do something like this to her'?" I didn't want to put him on the spot or cause him to get defensive by starting off with a question that might indicate any suspicions.

He shook his head. "Sherry wasn't perfect. I mean, for me, I don't..." He cleared his throat, shaking his head. "I'm sorry. I didn't sleep last night. I can't even get the words to come out of my mouth. What I'm saying is, everyone liked Sherry. I loved her. It wasn't the same kind of love we had for each other back when we were young. But I can't imagine... I can't imagine anyone wanting to harm her. And for what reason?"

"Because she knew something about what happened to Stuart," I said.

He stared back at me without an immediate reply.

"I hope you're not implying I had something to do with it?" he said.

"I'm just saying, if she knew something about it, why'd she keep it secret all those years? Who was she trying to protect?"

Jack shook his head. "Listen, I know you're just trying to do your job. But I had nothing to do with it. I would never—"

"Where were you that morning?"

"That morning? You mean—"

"Before she got to work. I'm assuming it was sometime between midnight and sunrise. Whoever it was knew something about that kiln, and that she turns it on first thing in the morning. And that's it's vented outside."

"You don't think that's common knowledge?" Jack said.

"Common knowledge? How a kiln works?" I shrugged. "Any oven would have to vent outside."

He looked mad. "I'll tell you what I told the police. I was either here in the office, preparing for a shoot, or was all the way out at Harbortown Marina. Was out there and set up before sunrise, around five or so. Like I told the detective, go ahead and talk to anyone there. I gave them my client's number, and—"

"You don't have to explain," I said. "I believe you."

Whether I did or not, I still wasn't sure. But I didn't want the man becoming defensive, considering he'd already been questioned by Mike Stone.

I said, "Any chance you know a woman, name's May Lay?"

"May Lay?" he said, shaking his head. "Is that one word?"

"No."

"Is that her real name?" he said.

"I'm not exactly sure. Apparently, she somehow knew Graves."

Jack said, "I'd remember that name if I'd ever heard it before. How do you know she knew Stu?"

"That's not important," I said. "But I'd like to find her."

"Because she had something to do with what happened to Stu? Or—"

"She may know something," I said. I didn't need to go into details with him, assuming he was telling the truth that he didn't know who she was.

"You mean, with what happened to Stu? Or, do you mean Sherry, and that young woman?" He pulled at his chin. "You know, when I spoke to Sherry a few days back, she mentioned—"

"Didn't you just tell me you hadn't spoken to her—Sherry—in a long time?"

Jack's face turned red. He swallowed, trying to hide it. "What I meant was I hadn't had any kind of real conversation with Sherry in a long time, that's all. And that's the truth. I mean, she called me after you showed up asking her questions. She was just nervous, you know?"

I stared back at him until he walked around to the other side of the reception desk. "Listen, Mr. Walsh, I—"

"Did you tell the detective the same thing? That you hadn't talked to Sherry? Because they have ways of finding out. Just so you're aware. Even the smallest lies can get you in trouble. Trust me."

He took a moment before he answered. "Uh, well, I don't remember exactly what I said. But, besides that one phone call—couldn't have been more than five minutes—I really don't remember the last time I spoke to her. To be honest, I wish I *had* talked to her a little more. It's... it's hard to believe she's gone."

I wasn't sure I was ready to buy the guy's act. Something didn't smell right. On the other hand, innocent people could say some foolish things that raised suspicions. Maybe that was the case with Jack, but something was off with him. I just couldn't put my finger on it.

"Are you telling me the truth about May Lay? You've never heard the name?"

He shook his head without a second of hesitation. "I swear, I've never heard of her."

The glass door behind me opened, and a middle-aged couple walked in. One look, and I could tell they had money. Maybe it was just the way they dressed, the way their hair was fixed perfectly, their skin evenly tanned and stretched in an unnatural way over their faces in an attempt to hide their real age.

"Chuck. Laura," Jack said, stepping around from the reception desk to shake their hands. "You're just in time. You're going to love the photos." He reached out for my hand. "I'm sorry, Henry, but Mr. and Mrs. Dugal are here for their showing. We had a photo shoot on their yacht a few days ago. I'm sorry, but we'll have to continue this conversation some other day. Good luck."

• • • • • • • • • •

I headed over to Yellow Bluff Park, across from Blount Island, where Alex was staying at a Holiday Inn. She hadn't called me, although she did have a lot to deal with. And it was all my fault.

I parked next to the SUV she'd rented. I wouldn't have known it was hers if it weren't for the cracked windshield and bullet holes in the door. I knew she wasn't going to like me showing up. I thought maybe she wouldn't even want me around.

But I had to talk to her.

I tried calling her one more time as I walked up to the entrance and stood looking through the glass doors and into the lobby.

I was surprised, after one ring, she answered.

"Hey," she said. "I'm sorry I didn't call you back; I was just—"

"I'm outside your hotel," I said. "Can we talk?"

The line went quiet.

"Alex?"

She said, "Give me five minutes before you come up." Then she gave me her room number and hung up without another word. I looked at the time on my phone and walked through the entrance. There was a seating area, with a handful of padded chairs facing a TV on the wall. The news was on. I didn't understand why the news was always the go-to for public-facing televisions, like the ones in hotel lobbies. Why would a hotel guest want to start the day hearing about something else gone wrong in the world?

I was on my way back outside when my phone buzzed. I checked the screen before I answered. It was Mike Stone.

"Hello?"

"Walsh, it's me," he said. "We've got an ID on your dead friend. Man's name is Omar Flores. He's a wanted man, along with his brother. Turns out they were involved in a murder down in Miami three years ago. What we're hearing on the streets is they were hired for a job up here in Jacksonville. Nobody has the details, but—"

"You think this guy was hired? For me? Or—"

"We don't have the details yet. Could be you. Could be Miss Williams... Sherry Carter. The murder they're wanted for had to do with a man who'd hired them to kill his wife. He's down in Raiford, doing life. The two brothers he hired were never captured."

"You don't have any other information?" I said.

"Unless we can get the dead man to talk? No. The brother's most likely long gone."

I gazed around the parking lot. "But you don't know if the brother's gone or not."

"No."

The line between us went quiet.

I said, "Does Alex know?"

"Not yet. I haven't spoken to her yet. I need to consider the investigation surrounding what happened, so maybe you can share it with her. That way, there's no question my relationship with her might influence what happens."

"She's not going to lose her job over this, is she?"

Mike said, "Considering the man she killed is a wanted fugitive, I can't see it. But I can't answer for her department either. Every state, every police force, or agency handles these things a little differently."

I didn't mention to Mike I was standing outside Alex's hotel, waiting to go talk to her.

"Listen, Walsh. I gotta run. I hear anything else, I'll let you know."

He hung up, and I turned back to the hotel's entrance. Alex was standing there, watching me, then came out through the sliding glass door.

"I don't feel like hanging in my room," she said, continuing past me and into the parking lot.

"Where are you going?" I said.

She stopped at the edge of the sidewalk. "I don't know. Get a coffee. You want to go to Java Jazz? It's been a while since we were there."

I stood on the sidewalk and watched her walk ahead of me under the porte cochère and in the direction of our vehicles. I followed her, and all I could think of was a few days earlier, when Trish and I went to Java Jazz. Funny, at the time, all I could think about was all the time I'd spent there with Alex.

When I finally caught up, she was standing over the windshield of her rented SUV, touching the bullet holes in the glass. "I should probably swing by, tell them what happened."

"Who?" I said, studying the bullet holes on the door.

"The car rental agency." She pointed to the building next door. "It's right over there."

"I'm surprised they let you drive this back here," I said.

"Who, the sheriff's office? They got what they wanted from the scene. Mike said it would be okay if I took it back here."

Alex seemed more relaxed than I'd expected, although I wasn't sure if she was just putting it on for me, trying to show it wasn't a big deal. But it was. I was the one who wore my heart on my sleeve. If it was on my mind, I'd usually end up letting it out. Alex was better at keeping things in.

"Are you sure you're all right?" I said.

"Sure."

"Sure?" I said. "That doesn't sound convincing."

She shrugged. "I'm not even sure what I'm supposed to do. Or how I'm supposed to act. Mike thinks I'll probably need to stick around here, longer than originally planned. At least while they clear up the investigation."

"You're going to be cleared. And this'll all be behind you before you know it."

"Will it?" she said.

"That man you shot was a fugitive. Mike called me a couple of minutes ago. His name's..." I had to think. "I think his name's Omar Flores. A man hired him and his brother to kill his wife. So there's a good chance he was hired by someone to not only kill Sherry Carter and Trish Williams, but to take me out of the picture."

Alex had a confused and somewhat suspicious look on her face. "Why would Mike call you, instead of me?"

"I think he needs to stay neutral."

"Neutral?" she said, cocking her head back. "What's that mean?"

"I think he's waiting for word on where things stand with you and the internal investigation."

Alex had a somewhat blank stare on her face, her gaze toward the hotel. "Oh." She took in a deep breath, then exhaled. "So, if this man, Omar, was the one who broke into the office, then where were the files? And your laptop?"

"He's got a brother," I said.

"They don't know where he is?"

I shook my head.

"They're wanted for a murder? Where?"

"Miami."

"And they stuck around Florida? And nobody ever spotted them?"

Chapter 30

Java Jazz Café was busy, and the table where Alex and I had always sat in the back corner—the same one where Trish and I had sat—was taken by an older couple, sipping from their ceramic cups, appearing to be without conversation but comfortable in each other's silence.

Jazz music, of course, played in the background.

We stood in line at the counter and looked around at the tables. All were taken.

I noticed the line that had already formed behind us. "Why don't we get something to take with us, go for a walk?"

"A walk would be good," Alex said, smiling. She looked up at the menu with fancy yet legible handwriting on a black chalkboard. "I think you should get green tea instead of coffee. It's good for your heart."

"Are you telling me coffee's bad for me?"

She cracked a smile and shrugged. "I have no idea. That's what they say."

"'They?'" I said. "'They' know everything, but end up being proven wrong at some point by some other 'they.'"

She laughed, but I went ahead and took her advice anyway and ordered us each a green tea. I had the kid behind the counter add enough honey to mine to cover up the leafy flavor I'd never really gotten used to.

"Let's walk to the park," I said, handing Alex her tea in the to-go cup before holding open the door for her.

She walked ahead of me, heading down West Bay Street.

I slipped on my sunglasses, the bright sun shining between the shadows from the tall downtown buildings. At least it wasn't as hot as it'd been a few days earlier.

We walked without saying much at all for the first couple of blocks. It was like there was so much to say, neither of us knew where to begin. Turning left onto South Laura Street, I could see Riverfront Plaza ahead, the St. Johns beyond it.

Alex finally spoke first: "Did Mike say anything else about this guy's brother?"

"Like what?" I said, although I had a pretty good idea what she was thinking.

She stopped and faced me. "You know those men weren't at your office to take your laptop and a few files that didn't provide much information to begin with."

"I know that," I said.

She put her hand on my arm. "Then you need to be careful. Don't be foolish."

"Don't you think we *both* need to be careful at this point?"

She paused, nodding after a moment. "Of course."

We continued our walk, heading south along the sidewalk, and past the front entrance to a place called the River Club. It was a private club located inside the Wells Fargo Bank, where Jacksonville's elite would go to rub elbows and schmooze. I'd never once stepped foot in the place, and hadn't ever planned to. Although I'd been told the views of the river were supposed to be the best in the city.

Alex said, "Did Mike say what we're supposed to do?"

She seemed worried.

"About *what*?"

"The dead man's brother. What if he comes back?" she said.

I didn't have an answer, but the more I thought about it, the more I thought maybe we did need to worry.

We continued our walk all the way to Riverfront Plaza and the new Landing Park. "I used to like The Landing," I said. "Remember that case we had, with the singer?"

"It wasn't that long ago," she said.

I nodded and looked around the park. "It was right before they demolished The Landing," I said. "And turned it into this, whatever *it's* supposed to be."

"It's a park," she said. "You don't like it?"

I shrugged. "It's a lot of grass. A big open field of nothing."

"With a nice view of the river," she said.

"I have a nice view of the river from my boat."

She laughed, rolling her eyes, and walked ahead of me to a bench on the edge of the St. Johns.

I sat next to her, the water in front and the wide-open, grassy field behind us. We spent some time talking about some of our past cases we worked together on, reminiscing, like it was the good old days.

I wasn't sure all of them were.

"So, what are you going to do?" I said. "What if they suspend you? Or put you on extended leave?"

Alex stared straight ahead at the river, taking a couple of moments without a response. She slowly turned to me. "I have no idea. Even if I got back in the next day or so, there's a chance I'd have to come back here in the next couple of weeks."

"So why wouldn't you just stay?" I said.

She looked into my eyes and shrugged, without an answer ."There's a good chance legal counsel will be sent down here, depending on where the investigation stands with the sheriff's office."

I was hesitant to say what was already on my mind, but I couldn't help myself. "Is there a chance you'd be forced to resign? Or... what if you just quit? Before it got out of hand?"

She looked at me, head tilted. "What if I *quit*? Are you serious?"

I just stared back at her. I wasn't even sure why I said it, or what I was getting at.

She held her gaze but was quiet for a few seconds, looking at me like the most bizarre thing I'd ever said had just come out of my mouth. "I can't just quit," she said. "And then everything just goes away? That's not how it works."

"I know," I said. "I didn't mean to say... I'm just thinking out loud. I guess, what I meant, was..." I had to think it through before I said something else that made no sense. Sometimes I couldn't help myself. "What if you came back?"

There was a long pause, but she hadn't taken her gaze from mine. "Are you being serious? Because that's the most idiotic thing—"

"I was just throwing it out there," I said. "I wasn't sure if the job... I was thinking—or maybe I was hoping—maybe that detective job didn't turn out to be what you expected. And now, you're up against this, and..."

Sometimes I wished the words in my head just stayed there. Alex had told me, more than once, that I needed to filter my thoughts before they leaked from my mouth. She was right, but I couldn't always help it.

The truth was, in a selfish way, I hoped she'd go up to North Carolina and decide she missed Jacksonville. Or maybe she'd realize she'd made a mistake, and come back.

I'd also realized the whole time she was gone that *I* was the one who made a mistake, hiding how I felt about her for all those years, right up until the days before she left.

"I shot a man," she said. "I'm not going to walk away, as if I can't take the heat."

"I didn't mean... It's not about you not being able to take the heat," I said. "It's—"

"*You* were the one who convinced me to take the job," she said. I could tell she was upset. Maybe even a bit angry. "*You* said it was the best thing for me. And I believed you. Now you're telling me to give it all up? For what? Why are you doing this?"

I didn't answer.

She said, "We already know this didn't work."

"We know *what* didn't work?"

She leaned forward on the bench, elbows on her knees. "I'm sorry," she said. "I don't mean that it didn't work. It was more about—"

"We didn't think we could have both," I said.

Alex just looked at me. She knew what I meant.

"But we never tried," I said. "We never actually tried. And when we finally did, we gave it all up without putting much thought into it."

She straightened up, her eyes on mine. "Why are you doing this, Henry? Why *now*?"

"I'm sorry," I said.

"I'm not asking you to say you're sorry. I'm asking you to—"

"I'm just not very good without you," I said. "And I'm not just talking about being a private investigator."

She took my hand, her knees up against my thigh. "When I was trying to figure out if I should go, you told me I had to go. You said if I didn't take the chance, I'd always wonder if I should have. Now, you're trying to tell me you think I made a mistake?"

I thought about it for a moment. "*I* was the one who made a mistake, telling you to leave."

Alex closed her eyes and held them that way until she straightened in her seat to face the river, and leaned her head on my shoulder. We sat quiet, without another word.

Chapter 31

I DROVE OUT TO Rick Lilly's house while Mike Stone was wrapped up in a meeting with Alex and an attorney who had flown down from North Carolina to represent her. As luck would have it, Rick was at home, although he didn't seem too excited to see me at his door.

He stepped out, onto the landing. "I have to fly out to see a client, so I don't have much time." He didn't bother inviting me inside.

I stood on the walkway, looking up at him. "Where're you flying to?"

"Texas."

"Does the sheriff's office know?" I said.

"Does the sheriff's office know *what*?"

"That you're leaving town? I assume they spoke to you?"

I'm not sure what made me do it, but more than anything I wanted to get Lilly's reaction. There was something about him that bothered me from the moment I met him. Maybe it was because I couldn't get it out of my head he was the primary suspect in Graves' murder. Or maybe it was just that he rubbed me the wrong way.

"You talkin' about Sherry Carter and that young lady?" He gave me a nod. "A detective stopped by, asked me a couple of routine questions." He narrowed his eyes. "Are you trying to suggest I'm some kind of suspect?"

"They're in the early stages of their investigation. So I don't think anybody's been crossed off their list just yet."

"I barely knew Sherry Carter. And, like I told the detective, I knew nothing about that other girl. None of us ever knew Stu had a daughter. He never told anybody a word of it. Frankly, I don't see how any of this has anything at all to do with me, anyhow. Nobody can tell an innocent man he can't go somewhere. This is a free country."

"Of course," I said. "Do you mind me asking you about a woman I'm looking for?"

"What woman?"

"Her name's May Lay."

"May *who*? Is that really someone's name?"

"I can't say for sure. But she met with Stuart a long time ago. Nobody's heard of her, other than Lenny Coolidge."

"Lenny? You talked to him? I can't tell you the last time I saw that old man. It's been years. He must gettin' up there in age, huh?"

"I guess so," I said. "Are you telling me you've never heard of this woman? Or that Stuart never mentioned a name like that before?"

Rick shook his head. "She from around here?"

"I don't know," I said. "I haven't been able to find her." The truth was, I hadn't had a chance to dig as deep as I wanted to, although I'd come up empty, searching my phone. Nowadays, it was pretty easy to locate just about anyone with a basic search unless that person was trying to hide. And even then…

Rick looked at his watch. "Stu kept quiet about a lot of things. I'm not surprised he had a lady friend none of us knew about. That old dog was—"

"I don't think it was anything like that," I said. "I think it had something to do with that movie he was writing."

"The movie?" Rick rolled his eyes. "Who knows if there ever really was a movie. Stu was funny. You never really knew what he was up to. Wouldn't surprise me at all, he had nothing but a notebook full of ideas when he went out to LA."

"From what I understand, it did exist. And it was supposedly on his laptop, which disappeared around the same time he was killed."

"Yeah?" Rick shrugged. "You sure that's true? You take a look around Sherry's place? I mean, I know she's gone now, bless her soul, but how do you know she didn't have it?"

"She said she looked for it before she moved, and never found it."

"And what makes you think she was telling you the truth?"

I didn't have much of an answer. I guess I just felt she was an honest person. She seemed to be, at least.

Rick gave me a sly smile. "Maybe she thought it was going to be a big-time flick, took it after he died, and tried to cash in? Who knows what she might've done."

I thought about what Rick was saying, but I had no reason to believe Sherry was hiding much of anything.

"I hope you know I'm just making light of a bad situation," Rick said. His expression turned serious. "I don't know much about what their relationship was like, or how she felt about him, by the time he came back from his trip. I know he didn't have anyplace else to go, and she gave him a place to stay, even though they were no longer a couple."

I looked at Rick's house, big enough, from what I could tell, for a friend with no place to go. "You couldn't put your friend up? Looks like you have plenty of space to yourself."

Rick didn't seem to like that. "I was still married to my wife at the time. I think I told you that."

"But you were divorced before he was killed. Is that right?"

Rick shook his head. "We'd been separated. I think the divorce between me and my wife might've been finalized a few months after Stu was gone."

"Did she know him?"

"My ex?" He nodded. "Not well. They'd met a few times over the years."

"A good friend of yours, didn't know your wife?" I said, finding it somewhat odd.

"Stu never came around. And my wife, well... she didn't like to go out much. I spent a lot of time at the bar back then. Probably a mistake on my part, young bride at home, and I'm out hanging with the boys."

I looked when a car drove by, going slow at first, but then it sped up and took off around the corner. I didn't think much of it. "I guess I'll let you get back to whatever you were doing. If you can think of anyone else who might know something about this May Lay..."

"Why are you so hopped-up, trying to find her? You think she knows something about what might've happened to Stu? Sounds to me this might've been long before he went out to

LA, no? Which means it had to've been a year or two before he was killed, so..."

I didn't have much of an answer for him. "I just thought I should talk to her," I said, then started for the Jeep. But I stopped and turned around. "Hey, that woman who was killed, Elizabeth Sutton... anyone you know of, besides Stu, who could've been the father of that baby she was carrying?"

Rick shook his head without a second thought. "Sorry. Not something I would know."

··········

I parked at a meter on East Bay Street, outside the sheriff's office, waiting for Alex. She'd sent me a text an hour earlier to say she thought she'd be done soon. But I'd already been waiting for forty-five minutes.

I looked up the number to The Crow and dialed, letting it ring a few times before a woman finally answered:

"The Crow."

I could hear the crowd and some music in the background, and asked for Mac.

"Uh, he's a little busy right now," she said. "Can I take a message?"

I looked at the clock on the dash and hadn't even realized I was calling at one of the busiest times of day for most eating establishments. I knew that from hanging around Billy's Place.

"Can you tell him it's Henry Walsh?"

"Walsh?" she said. "Can I have him call you?"

I gave her my number. "Or I can try back later. I just wanted to ask him a quick question."

"Do you want me to see if he can talk?"

"If he's not too busy, that'd be great."

She huffed a laugh into the phone. "Oh, he's busy. But I'll ask."

The loud noise in the background became muffled, and the woman yelled out for Mac. She came back on the line. "He'll be right with you."

I waited, listening to laughing through the phone, cackling, and glasses clinking.

"This is Mac."

"Mac, hey, this is Henry Walsh, the private investigator. I was in there—"

"Yeah, Henry. What can I do for you?"

I said, "I know you're busy, but—"

"Go ahead. I've got it under control."

"Were you around enough, back when Stuart Graves was in there, to know who else Elizabeth Sutton might've been hanging around with?"

"Elizabeth Sutton?" He was quiet for a moment. "Hanging around? Or *fooling* around?"

"Whatever you want to call it. I'm just doing some think-ing."

"So, you want to know who she was sleeping with?" He laughed. "I'm surprised you didn't ask my dad."

"I guess what I'm wondering, is if someone else could've been the father of that child, when she went off the road."

"She was somewhat flirtatious, the few times I saw her around. I can't say for sure she meant anything by it. I know she liked a drink or two. I remember she drank vodka tonics. The cheap liquor too. She'd flirt with a guy, if it looked like he had money, just to get the more expensive stuff."

"There's nobody in particular you can think of? Besides Stuart Graves?"

"You're asking me to remember something from, what was it, fifteen, twenty years ago? That's a long time."

He was right. I was probably asking too much. "If you think of it, maybe you can give me a call?"

"What'd Stu's old buddies have to say? You talk to them about her?"

"A little," I said. But I really hadn't come right out and asked either of them. The truth was, I was a bit all over the place. I was starting to understand why the case had gone cold, and why nobody was able to make any kind of progress. "I haven't gotten much out of either one of them."

Mac paused on the other end. "Well, maybe that should tell you something."

I wasn't sure I understood what he meant. "Are you trying to say one of them could've been the father?"

"Me? No, that's not what I'm saying. I'm just thinking out loud here, but..." Mac was quiet, and I could hear the crowd noise getting louder through the phone. "Hey, I gotta run, Henry. Stop by for a drink one night."

Mac hung up.

I looked up the steps of the sheriff's office and saw Alex walking down with a middle-aged woman, dressed in a maroon suit. I could tell from a mile away she was a lawyer, maybe from the way she walked or the expression on her face.

I leaned with my arm out the window, watching them walk along the sidewalk toward my Jeep.

I was afraid to ask what happened, but by the look on Alex's face, it didn't look good.

"How'd it go?" I said, stepping out of the Jeep.

The hard-looking woman, holding a briefcase in one hand, looked me over. She glanced at Alex. "Is this him?"

Alex nodded and introduced us. "Henry, this is Connie Bouchard. The attorney from North Carolina."

"I would've never guessed," I said, reaching out to shake her hand.

Alex gave me one of her side-eye looks.

Connie Bouchard shook my hand and asked if I was available in the morning.

"Me?" I said. "For what?"

"To meet," she said. "To discuss Alex's case."

I had a feeling I'd have to be involved at some point. I was actually surprised they hadn't asked me to go to the meeting they'd just come out of. But I was glad not to be stuck in the sheriff's office for the past two hours.

"Whatever you need," I said. "Is everything going to be all right?"

Ms. Bouchard seemed to hesitate, then nodded. "I'd like to think this one's open-and-shut, but you never know. We'll know more tomorrow." She said to Alex, "Like I said, we're looking at maybe thirty days, max."

"Thirty days?" I said, raising my voice. "Jail time?"

The lawyer laughed. "Leave of absence. And it'll likely be paid." She looked at her watch, then shook Alex's hand. "We'll talk again in the morning." She handed me a business card.

"Call me tomorrow, first thing. I have a call at seven thirty, and should be done by eight. I'd love to meet before nine, if you can."

Chapter 32

ALEX AND I SAT on the dock outside my boat. She'd been quiet, having a couple of beers she drank faster than she normally would. She cracked open a third and stood up from the lawn chair, stepping to the edge of the dock. She had her back to me, looking at the river.

The moon's glow reflected off the surface, with a slight breeze blowing through her hair.

I walked up next to her. "Are you okay?"

She nodded, her gaze straight ahead. She paused, and said, "You have it all figured out."

I said, "Come again?"

She sipped her beer and looked up at the crescent moon, taking a moment before she finally shifted her glance, looking me in the eye. "Look at this. You have everything."

I laughed. "A *boat*?"

"You know what I mean. You have all you'll ever need."

I knew that wasn't the truth but thought I'd let her run with it, if that's what she wanted to do.

"Nobody's telling you what to do," she said, glancing past me at the boat. "Yeah, it's a boat. But it's more. It's who you are."

"Is there something in that beer?" I said. "You're getting a little deep on me here."

She cracked a grin. "You're always just you. You don't try to fool anyone. You say exactly what's on your mind. I've never even met anyone who says, 'I don't know' as much as you do."

"I *do*?" I had to think about it. I said, "I'm not sure I see how that's a good thing?"

"Most people are afraid to admit they don't know something. So they just make something up. Everyone's so full of shit." She lifted her bottle of beer and looked it over. "My sergeant does it. He won't admit when he doesn't know something. And it drives me crazy." She let out a slight laugh. "My dad used to say the two things you don't hear enough of in this world, which is 'I'm sorry,' and 'I don't know.'"

I waited to see where she was going with what she was saying, but she just stood quietly, like she was thinking it all through.

She turned and stared at me, the dim lights from the lamps along the dock reflecting off her brown eyes. "I thought I was doing the right thing."

"That man would've killed both of us if you hadn't fired back. There was no option."

She shook her head. "That's not what I mean. Of course, I really wish that didn't happen. But I'm talking about..." She took a deep breath, her eyes closed. She exhaled. "What I'm saying is all I ever do is worry. Everything is eating at me. I hardly sleep. Sometimes I can hardly think."

I watched her looking out over the water. "Is it the job?"

She shrugged, then nodded. "I worry about you too. All the time."

"Why would you worry about me?"

"Because I do. It was different, when I was close enough... when I saw you every day."

I waited. I didn't want to say the wrong thing, almost certain the shooting had affected her mindset more than she was prepared to admit. I said, "I'm the one who put you in this situation. I'm so sorry."

"Stop saying that," she said. "I already told you, it's not just the shooting. It's more than that. It's everything. All of it. Before I came back here, I was... I've been having a hard time. I haven't had a lot of good days up there."

"Are you serious?" I said. I was dumbfounded, wondering if the beers had simply gone to her head. She had to have been exhausted. But normally Alex could handle her drinks as well as anyone. A couple of beers, for her, was nothing.

We both stood, quiet, looking out into the river.

A good half minute must've gone by when Alex sat in the lawn chair again. "I've been thinking a lot about what you said."

I had to think. "What did I say?"

She didn't respond, and I wasn't sure she'd even heard me.

She said, "Maybe I'm not cut out for it."

"Not cut out for *what*?"

"Law enforcement. And everything that comes with it."

"Wait a minute," I said. "Are you saying I said you weren't cut out for it? Because I never—"

"You said you never once thought of going back after you left Rhode Island. I know you had your reasons, but..."

"I lied about that," I said. "And it wasn't exactly my choice, even if I wanted to go back."

"Even if everything had turned out differently for you, do you really think you would've ever been able to handle the red tape? The bureaucracy? The lack of autonomy?" She shook her head. "I don't think so."

"But what about you?" I said. "What is it, exactly, that's bothering you?"

She took a moment to answer, her eyes toward the water. "I guess I thought being a detective would be different. That I'd be treated differently."

I watched her, waiting.

She said, "You know why I didn't always call you back all those times? I'd send you a text instead? Because I'd hoped it would all get better. And sometimes, when you'd call, I didn't want to have to lie to you again, tell you everything was all right."

I didn't know what to say.

She took a swig from her beer, and it crossed my mind to go below and grab that unopened bottle of Jack.

She finished what was left in her bottle and reached into the cooler under her chair for another. She didn't open it right away, resting the wet bottle on her thigh. "Sometimes I wish I never left."

It was obvious where she was going by that point, but I still had a hard time believing she meant it. I said, "I think you always miss what you leave behind."

She appeared to think it through. "What if it was a mistake?"

I said, "The only mistake would've been not going. You had to go, or you'd be sitting here on the dock, wondering, just like you are now, if you made a mistake."

She cracked the cap off the bottle and sipped her beer. "But is it better knowing you've made a mistake?"

"I don't know."

Alex got up from the chair. "Would you mind giving me a ride back to the hotel?"

"What? You want to leave? Now?" I thought she wanted to talk more. But maybe she felt she'd already said more than she should have.

She walked to the edge of the dock and poured whatever was left in her bottle into the water. "We have to get up early."

"I know, but... How about going over to Jed's, grab something to eat?"

She started along the dock, walking ahead of me, toward the parking lot.

I didn't know if it was something I said. "Hey! Aren't you going to at least wait for me?" I folded both lawn chairs and put them up on the boat.

Alex stopped, then pivoted. "I've missed you, you know."

"You did?" I said. "I guess I wasn't sure." I stared at her. "The thing is, I miss you all the time. Every day. So... I'm glad you're—"

Alex charged toward me and jumped into my arms. She pulled me close and kissed me. We both almost stumbled off the dock and into the water.

I pushed her away. "What are we doing?"

She didn't answer, leaning in closer to kiss me again.

I pulled back. "Alex, we can't. Don't you think we should—"

She kissed me, then stopped, her arms still wrapped around my neck. "We should *what*?"

We gazed into each other's eyes, and I thought about what I was going to say. I had no idea what it was. At least, at first. But then something occurred to me, out of nowhere. It wasn't exactly out of nowhere. I'd thought of it hundreds of times before, going back to the first time I met her.

My mouth went dry, the thoughts in my head going in five hundred different directions. I almost couldn't get the words out of my mouth, but finally took her face in my hands, looking her in the eye. "We should get married."

Her eyes opened wide, her head cocked back, with a blank expression on her face. She froze, like she was unable to move. "Are you... are you serious?"

I nodded. "Of course, it would be better if I actually had a ring, but..." I got down on one knee and looked up at her. "Alex, will you marry me?"

She nodded through tears as I stood, and she jumped into my arms, squeezing me so tight, I almost couldn't breathe.

Her cheek was pressed against mine, and I whispered into her ear, "You didn't give me an answer."

And through her tears, she whispered back, nodding her head up and down. "Yes!"

Chapter 33

I ROLLED OVER IN my bed, expecting to see Alex asleep next to me. But she wasn't there. I sat up, threw on the T-shirt I picked up from the floor, and slipped on my shorts. I looked into the galley and at the door to the bathroom. "Alex?"

She didn't answer.

I went up the ladder and stood on the deck, looking over the boat's railing.

Alex stood alone on the dock, staring out at the water. The sky was still dark, but the orange sun had already started to crack the horizon. Wiggling lights from the boats underway sat inside the river's dark surface, a steady hum coming from the engines. There was a stillness each morning that only early risers ever got to experience.

I didn't say a word.

Alex had on one of my old Jacksonville Sharks sweatshirts with the well-worn logo on the front. With her hands tucked in the front pocket, she turned, as if she heard me. "Hey," she said, her voice hushed.

I stepped down onto the dock. "Everything all right?" I said, almost in a whisper. Just because I liked to be up early didn't mean all the other liveaboards did.

"I think so," she said, gazing back at the water.

"You think so?"

She paused, like she had to consider it. "Is this for real?" she said. "Are we really doing this?"

I had to think for a moment, make sure I had it right, about what she was referring to. "Is it the ring?" I said. "Because, I'm going to—"

With a crooked smile, she shook her head. "Henry. Please. You know that's not what I mean."

I stood next to her and looked straight toward the river with her. "I know there's a lot going on," I said. "There's a lot to figure out. But..." I nodded. "Yeah, we're doing this. Unless you don't want to?"

She took my hand and squeezed it, then dropped a quick kiss on my cheek. "I do."

I held her hand. It was cold. "We'll be okay," I said.

She didn't respond, and we both just stood quiet again, for at least a few moments.

If there had ever been a time I felt stranger around Alex than I did right then, I couldn't think of when it was. It was like I didn't know what to say next. I couldn't figure out what she was thinking, and she wasn't about to let me in on it either.

I had a feeling something else was bothering her, beyond everything she was going through. "Are you sure you're all right?" I said.

She nodded, but I could see in her eyes there was something more. She was holding something back.

I said, "I know we'll have a lot to talk about. We have a lot to figure out." I cleared my throat. "But, what if you're... what if they want you back right away? I mean, say if today the lawyer somehow clears everything up, and—"

"It's not going to happen that fast," she said. "But, yeah. I'll have to go back at some point soon, if that's what you're asking?"

I tried to hide my swallow. I don't know what I was expecting her to say. I guess a part of me hoped it would be easier, like she'd just decide to stay in Jax, make a quick call up to North Carolina and give notice.

That, of course, wasn't realistic.

"What about you?" she said.

"What *about* me?"

"Are you really planning on staying involved with this case? Mike's been pretty clear he doesn't want you in the way. And it's not like you're getting paid by anyone to—"

"I owe it to... I owe it to my client," I said. "She's dead, and I'm feeling pretty guilty about it. I could've protected her. I *should* have. But I don't think I did enough."

Alex folded her arms. "Is that all there is to it?"

"I'm not sure what you're asking."

"You want to stay involved, because you feel guilty? Or..." She waved her hand at me. "Never mind." She smiled. It seemed forced. "Can you just drive me back to the hotel?"

· · • · • · • · ·

230

It was a little before nine o'clock when I walked out to the parking lot at the Sheraton at the St. Johns Town Center. I'd just left the meeting with Alex's lawyer, Connie Bouchard, in one of the conference rooms. Her interview lasted a little more than an hour, but I got the feeling I didn't provide her with any further details than what she already had.

But Connie wouldn't go into any of the specifics about what Alex was up against, going forward. All she kept repeating was there was a procedure that had to be followed.

No matter what, I couldn't see any way she wouldn't be exonerated. Of course, it wasn't for me to decide. The facts were that Omar Flores had just about emptied his .45, firing at Alex, with seven rounds retrieved in and around her vehicle and one left in the chamber. I'd also watched a copy of the video from the cameras in front of Billy's Place, and although you couldn't see every angle, it was clear Alex was firing in self-defense.

As I told Ms. Bouchard, Alex saved my life.

And it wasn't the first time.

I stepped up into the Jeep and called Billy. He answered on the third ring.

"Hey," he said. "I was going to call you. I just picked up an old convertible I wanted to show you. You'll love it."

"A convertible? For what?" I said.

"What do you mean 'for what'? To drive." He laughed. "It's a Boxster I got on a deal from the auction."

"You really needed another car?" I said.

"I sold off a few over the past few months. I only have seven now."

Billy loved his cars. He purchased them, usually older classics or antiques, held them for a few years, or had them fixed up and would sell them after he'd played around with them. He had a cousin who was a U.S. Marshal, so he was always in on the deals, going to auction. That's how I'd ended up with the Jeep, and a few other cars he'd gotten me over the years.

"So what's the latest?" he said. "Any luck finding your laptop? Or the dead guy's brother?"

"Neither," I said. "But I haven't been looking hard enough either. But Mike's concerned the brother could try and retaliate."

"Against Alex?" Billy said.

"Yes. But right now she's meeting with the attorney they sent down from North Carolina. I just got out of there myself."

"Any word what's going to happen to her?"

"Alex? Yeah, we don't know yet. But it's pretty clear what happened in that parking lot."

Billy didn't respond, and the sound of wind coming through the phone seemed to get louder.

"Listen," I said. "I have some news I want to share with you. But you'll need to keep it between us for now."

"Good news?" Billy said. "Or bad?"

"It should be good. But it might be a little mixed, depending on who you ask."

"Uh-oh," he said.

I hesitated at first, then spilled the beans. "I asked Alex to marry me."

Billy had absolutely no response right away. I wondered if he heard me.

I said, "You there?"

After another moment of quiet, other than the wind, Billy responded, "Yeah, I'm here. I'm pulling off the road. I don't think I heard you correctly." The wind coming through the phone had stopped. "All right," he said. "Can you repeat that? I'm not even going to tell you what I thought you said."

"I think you heard *exactly* what I said. I asked Alex to marry me."

More silence.

"You're serious? You... you asked her to marry you?" He laughed.

"Glad you find it funny," I said.

"No, no. It's... this is the best thing I've ever heard come out of your mouth. But, I'm still trying to process the whole thing. What exactly does this mean? Isn't she in the middle of dealing with what happened? And you decided to—"

"I *didn't* think it through," I said. "I mean, no, that's not true. I've thought about it plenty. But it just came out of my mouth last night. And I rolled with it. The only thing I wish is that I'd planned something a little more special, but..."

"So, she said yes?"

"Luckily, she did. Although she'd had a couple of beers."

Billy laughed again.

I said, "I'll tell you all about it when I see you. We're going to keep it quiet for now. But I had to tell you. It's all feeling a bit surreal right now."

"So, what happens next? What about her job? What does this mean for you? I can't imagine a marriage would last living seven or eight hours away, so..."

"There's a lot to figure out," I said. "It's not something that has to happen right away, I guess."

"What are you going to do, one of those engagements that lasts six years? You're too old for that, aren't you?" He was still laughing, although not exactly out loud.

"I didn't even give her a ring yet," I said.

"What? No *ring*? What kind of crappy proposal *was* this?"

"I know, I know. I never said I was good at any of this stuff. Besides, there's a lot going on right now. I don't even know if she's... I wonder if she's in her hotel right now, trying to figure out how to get out of it."

Chapter 34

I SPENT A COUPLE of hours at the marina, mostly cleaning the boat while trying to think through everything I hadn't yet been able to make sense of. The thought of that movie script was still on my mind, especially since nobody seemed to know what could've happened to it.

I had waited for Alex to call me after her meeting, assuming she would have been done within a couple of hours. But I hadn't heard from her at all. Of course, I tried not to worry, but with Omar Flores's brother, Alejandro, still out there somewhere, the warning Mike had given Alex was fresh on my mind.

I finally dialed her number. She answered on the second ring. "Where are you?"

"At the boat," I said. "I thought you were going to call when you were done?"

"I was, but..." She paused on the other end. "I may have to fly back to North Carolina in the morning.

That wasn't what I wanted to hear. But, of course, I understood. And I'd expected it, after the way my meeting went with the attorney.

"But, it looks like I may be put on administrative leave for thirty days."

"That's good news," I said. "Isn't it?"

There was silence. I was afraid to bring up the fact I'd asked her to marry me, and that she said yes. I thought maybe she'd try to forget.

I was afraid to ask her for help. "Listen," I said. "I've been thinking about this movie script, and was just wondering if you'd be willing to help me. I know you don't even think I should be involved, but—"

"Actually, I was wrong," she said. "I know you can't just walk away from someone who came to you for help. No matter what might've happened between you two. I get it, Henry. When have you ever turned your back on a case?"

I held the phone to my ear, smiling.

"I want to find this woman May Lay. I can't help but think she knows something. Or at least can maybe help me find that script."

"You really think there's something to it?" Alex said.

"I don't know. But if there is, and I don't look into it..."

"According to the attorney, I'm not allowed to touch anything that has to do with any police work. She didn't mention anything about a private investigation."

The funny thing was, Alex actually sounded relieved. Maybe even relaxed, as strange as that might sound.

"So you want me to help find this May Lay woman?"

"If you wouldn't mind?" I said. "If she really exists, then she may be my only shot at getting my hands on that script."

"What about Graves' friends? None of them know anything about it?"

"They all claim to not've read it."

"Isn't that a little odd?" Alex said.

"Well, yeah. But it sounds like Graves was the one who might've been a little odd. Or maybe a *lot* odd. The fact he was hiding something, or wanting to rat someone out for something... and he writes a movie about it?"

Alex said, "He sounds like he might've had some sociopathic tendencies."

"Maybe," I said. "Find that script, and maybe we'll know for sure."

· · · · · ● · ● · · · ·

Alex was in the lounge at her hotel, having a beer, with the laptop open in front of her when I walked in. I hung my sunglasses on the neck of my T-shirt.

Alex turned the laptop so I could see the screen. "I think I might've found her."

I almost wanted to laugh. I wasn't surprised. I looked at the screen and saw she was on Twitter. And the image she showed me was of an attractive woman with hair so wild, it looked like it was taken from the eighties, arms crossed in a posed photo with WPJB Hits Radio in red across the top of it.

"Is that her?"

She didn't answer. "This woman's name is Margaret Langford."

"Margaret *who*?" I gazed at Alex, wondering how many beers she'd had. "May Lay is the woman I'm looking for."

Alex smiled, nodding. "Yeah, I know. Margaret Langford is her real name."

"May Lay isn't?" I said.

"May Leigh was her pen name. And it wasn't spelled L-A-Y. She spells it L-E-I-G-H. I'm not even sure you pronounce it *lay*. It's probably pronounced like *lee*."

"Okay, but what do you mean... Why does she have a pen name? She's an author?"

"For a short time," Alex said. "I kept digging a little deeper, and it turns out she wrote a book under that name. But I also found an old blog post where she was interviewed as an agent."

"An agent?"

"A writer's agent. Looks like she tried to sell herself as having media connections, including movie producers in Hollywood."

I stared at the woman's photo. You could tell by the clothes she was wearing, it was an old, outdated photo. "You sure about this?"

Alex nodded, an expression on her face like she didn't appreciate my doubt.

"Why would she use the same pen name to become an agent?" I said.

"I have no idea. But she was also fired from the radio station, and apparently it was big news at the time. Maybe she didn't want the stigma that came with being a fired entertainer."

I leaned back in the chair, rubbing the stubble on my face. "I wonder if she found him, or he contacted her somehow... or if someone used her, trying to get a look at his script?"

"For what?"

"I don't know." I had to think about it for a moment, because I wasn't sure the pieces of the puzzle were fitting together. "Whoever he was trying to bury with whatever it was he'd written."

Alex had a blank look on her face, like she did whenever her wheels were turning.

"What was that photo you showed me of her?"

"The one on Twitter? It was for some kind of anniversary of the station. Apparently, she was one of their first DJs."

"So maybe someone from the radio station knows where we can find her?"

Alex shrugged, without looking up from the screen. "It was twenty years ago."

I watched Alex's eyes move, reading whatever was on her screen. "Can you just explain how you made the connection? I'm not sure I follow how you figured out these two are the same person."

"Oh yeah. Of course." She tapped a few keys on the laptop and turned it my way, showing me an image of a business card. "Remember when digital business cards were all the rage? When they said the world would soon go paperless? And all printing would cease to exist? This was May Leigh's digital business card." She reached over and tapped the space bar, and a photo of the same woman from the Twitter post came alive for a few seconds.

"How'd you find this?" I said.

She shrugged. "I can't take full credit. I might've gotten lucky. Spelling her name the right way helped, but there still isn't much about May Lay, the agent. It looks to me like her career was short-lived."

I looked at the moving image on the business card. It was obviously an outdated technology, long before the days when everyone threw their faces up online anywhere and everywhere, for all to see.

Alex said, "I used IRBsearch and found the same number from the card registered under Margaret Langford. That's how I ended up finding her on Twitter. But her name's not Langford anymore. She's married. Last name's Jordan now."

I wasn't exactly sure how Alex pulled this all together. But it didn't matter. What did matter was the one person I could always turn to, to help me out, was right there in front of me.

"Didn't I tell you I'm not very good without you?"

She rolled her eyes. "Give me a break." She tapped the keys on her laptop, wrote on her pad, then tore the top sheet off and handed it to me. "Here's her address. She lives with her husband. In Atlantic Beach."

Chapter 35

We were on Atlantic Boulevard, on our way out to what we believed was the home of Margaret Jordan, maiden name Margaret Langdon aka May Leigh. I was still amazed Alex managed to connect Mrs. Jordan to May Leigh, the alleged writer's agent and one-time pen name of Margaret Langdon. The DJ.

We had just pulled onto Mayport Road when Alex's phone rang.

"It's Mike," she said, and answered. "Hey, Mike."

I took the turn for Selva Lakes Circle and started looking for the Jordans' townhouse. But a quick glance at Alex, and I noticed the look on her face, eyes wide open. She gave me a look, on the phone, nodding. "Yes. Yes. Okay. I'm not sure what you want me to say. I guess we'll keep an eye out?"

I stopped the Jeep and pulled over to the side of the road. The townhouse was up ahead, within view. "What's up?" I said.

Alex held up a finger toward me and said into the phone, "Do you really think it's true? I mean, if it's just something you got off the street." She listened, nodding some more. "Okay,

okay. Of course. Yeah, Mike. I hear you. I'll be careful." She was quiet, closing her eyes for a moment, nodding again. "Yeah, he's right here. I'll let him know."

She put the phone down and stayed quiet for a moment.

I was anxious to hear. "What'd he say?"

"The brother of the man I shot—"

"Alejandro Flores," I said. "They get him?"

She shook her head. "No, not at all. But he's around. Mike said the word on the street is he's looking for me. Maybe both you and me. He wants to avenge the death of his brother."

I tried to hide my swallow and not let my face show my concern. But it was hard to fake it. "What else did he say?"

"He wanted me to come over to the station."

"For what?"

"Protection, I guess."

I said, "What are you supposed to do, sleep there until they catch him?"

She tried to force a smile, but I could see right through it.

"Maybe you should listen to him."

She shook her head, feeling around her torso. "I'm not armed," she said. "I had to hand over my Glock as part of the investigation. And I didn't bring anything else with me."

I took off my seat belt and stepped out of the Jeep, went around to the back and dropped the tailgate. Lifting the rug and board, I reached my hand down inside the storage area and pulled out a toolbox, placing it to the side. I reached back into the storage opening again and grabbed the .45 I bought a year or so ago. I'd never used it or even taken it out since the day I got it.

I climbed back into the driver's seat and handed the .45 to Alex. "Here," I said. "What do you want to do? We can go back, or…"

"We're already here," she said. "Let's go meet Mrs. Jordan."

I pulled back onto the road and drove slowly past a handful of houses, turning into the driveway of number 315A. There was a 315B to the right of it, the driveways divided down the middle by a wooden planter about four feet high running the length of the short driveway, flowers and small flowering trees growing up out of it.

I turned off the engine. "Are you going to wait here?"

She shook her head and stepped out, tucking the .45 in the back of her pants. "Somebody's gotta watch your back."

I wanted to smile, but I didn't.

We continued toward the townhouse, the front of it almost all garage with the door tucked back at the end of a short walkway, on the left. I glanced up toward the picture window on the upper level and saw a woman looking down at us. She appeared to be on the phone.

"Did that look like her?" I said.

Alex gave me a look like she didn't know, and we continued toward the door.

I rang the bell and waited for a good minute until the locks clicked, and the same woman from the window above stood on the other side of the opened door.

She was just as attractive as she appeared online, but the photos were certainly from a long time ago. She'd aged quite a bit, of course, but showed off her fit body with a two-piece bathing suit and a short robe left open.

"Margaret?" I said.

She looked from me to Alex, taking a moment before she answered. "Can I help you?"

"My name's Henry Walsh." I pulled out my card and handed it to her. "I'm a private investigator, and I'd like to ask you some questions." I thought it was best I didn't introduce Alex, considering her name had already been on the news or what had happened. And Mrs. Jordan didn't ask.

"Is something wrong? Is it Nick?"

"Your husband?" I shook my head. "No. Not at all."

She appeared relieved and exhaled.

I said, "Would it be all right if we came in?"

She held her hand on the door, like she was getting ready to close it. "Can you first tell me why you're here?"

"We're actually here looking for May Leigh," I said. "Do you know her?"

She cleared her throat and cracked a slight smile. "I haven't heard that name in quite a long time."

"Are you her?" I said.

She paused, taking a moment before nodding. "How'd you find me? I thought I did everything I could to bury that name for good."

I glanced at Alex, but she wasn't looking for any credit. "We just connected some dots."

Mrs. Jordan said, "But why? What is this all about?"

"I'm hoping you can tell us," I said. "Do you remember the name Stuart Graves?"

She didn't answer right away, squinting like she was tapping into her memory. She nodded. "He was the writer, wasn't he? The one who was murdered?"

I nodded. "You met with him, more than once. Is that true?"

She swallowed and looked around outside, then backed away from the door. "Would you like to come inside?"

Alex and I walked in and followed Margaret up the carpeted stairs to the second level. The townhouse wasn't exactly modern, with mauve carpeting, and a white-tiled kitchen with old maple cabinets. It had a musty odor, covered up with what I guessed were plug-in air fresheners. But the place was clean and seemed to be in good shape. She had music playing, a song from the nineties I recognized but didn't know who or what it was.

"Please, have a seat," she said, pointing toward the adjacent living room. There was a white leather couch to the left of the big picture window. "Can I get you a drink?" She had a martini glass on the kitchen counter, half full.

Alex and I both shook our heads and sat on the couch, sinking in like the springs had passed their prime. We both leaned forward. Margaret grabbed the glass and sat across from us, on a red wingback chair.

I said, "Can you tell us how you met Stuart?"

She pinched her face, like she had to think hard about it. "It was so long ago," she said. "I'm kind of a bit shocked to have someone even asking about him. I barely remember meeting him."

"Do you remember how you met him?" I said, repeating myself.

She sipped her drink and placed it on the small table next to her. "If I remember correctly, I believe someone gave me his name."

"Do you remember who?" I said.

"No, I don't. I was just trying to get my business off the ground back then, and—"

"You were a writers' agent?" I said.

She shrugged with a crooked smile, nodded her head. "I guess so. I was a writer myself back then, although not a very good one. I started off with a pen name—that's where May Leigh came from. It was my pen name."

"So you decided to become an agent? And use the same name? Why not just go with Margaret, or…"

"I didn't think I should use my real name. There was some controversy with my job at the time, which had been well-pub-licized. I'd actually hired an agent myself, when I first wrote my book and was looking to get it published. She was the one who suggested I use May Leigh. I guess it was close enough to Margaret Langford. She said it would be easier to brand myself, but none of it really worked out that way." She picked up her drink and took another sip.

"Okay, so what did book publishing, or whatever you were doing, have to do with Stuart Graves? He'd written a movie script. Isn't that right?"

She nodded. "Oh, well, I was going to… I mean, I represent-ed all kinds of writers. Or that was my plan. See, I used to be in the radio business, and had some old contacts. In fact, I had a friend out in LA, someone I used to work with, who knew some people in the movie business."

"Are you the one who sent him out there?" I said.

"To LA?" She shrugged. "I gave him a couple of names, but I don't think it turned into anything. We'd only met a couple of times at this bar, where I remember he said he used to go to write. He was a little strange, to be honest. At first, he wasn't even going to let me look it over."

"The script?"

She nodded.

"Did you read it?" I said.

She nodded. "Not exactly. He gave me a disk, like one of those old floppy disks. I didn't even have a computer back then. The book I wrote, I used a typewriter." She smiled. "He told me not to show anybody or talk to anybody about it until I read the whole thing."

"But you didn't read it?"

"Like I said, I didn't have a computer back then. And by the time I had one, Stuart was already gone. A couple of years went by, and he called me, looking for the disk. He left me a message on my machine, but I never heard from him again. A week or so later, he was dead."

"Did you tell the sheriff's office he'd called you, looking for it?"

She stared at me, eyes wide, shaking her head. "Should I have? It didn't even cross my mind. Why? Do you think—"

"Is there any chance you still have it?" I said.

"The disk?" She got up from the chair and started down the hall. "My husband gets so mad I never throw anything away. I bet it's back here somewhere." She disappeared into another room.

Alex and I both glanced at each other, and I wondered if Mrs. Jordan was going to come out of that room with the old disk in her hand.

I said to Alex, "Do you have any way of reading a floppy disk?"

She nodded. "Billy used to keep all of his financials on floppy disks. He kept them in a safe. I know he still has them, but can't say for sure he has a reader. But we can find one."

I kept my voice low. "I suspected at first someone put her up to going to talk to Stuart. But now I'm not so sure."

"She could be lying?" Alex whispered.

We waited another few minutes, and Margaret finally walked out, holding a yellow envelope. She undid the clasp and removed a floppy disk, holding it in her hand, looking it over. "I think this is it."

I said, "Do you mind if I take it? I'll get it back as soon as I can."

She dropped it back in the envelope and handed it to me. "I don't think I need it back."

Chapter 36

We stepped out of the Jeep behind Billy's Place and headed for the entrance. We turned the corner toward the front lot, and I looked over near the street, where the body of the man Alex had shot had been, just a couple of days before. I glanced at Alex, and she was looking in the same direction.

"You all right?" I said.

She nodded but didn't say much else.

We went inside the restaurant and up to the bar, Chloe behind it. She waved as soon as she noticed us. "Billy's in his office," she said.

We continued all the way around the other side and down the short hall to the open door. Billy was at his desk and stood when we walked in. In front of him was an open box with plastic packing bubbles hanging out of it.

Alex looked around the office. "Didn't this used to be a storage room?"

Billy nodded. "It was. You like it?"

"It's nice," she said, nodding. "Classy." She looked in the direction of the window where you could see past his outdoor patio to the St. Johns.

I started to wonder if he remembered I'd told him not to say anything about my proposal to Alex, although I had a feeling she'd know I told him. It would be odd for me not to.

I pointed at the box on his desk. "Is that it?"

He reached in and pulled out a floppy disk drive. "All yours," he said.

I picked it up and looked it over. "So, why do you still have this?"

"Somebody told me disks were the safest place to store sensitive information. At the time, I didn't have much faith in the cloud. I'm still not sure I do, but..." He took it back from me and looked it over. "So what exactly do you need this for?"

"We have Stuart Graves' movie script," I said.

"You got it?" he said. "But it's on a floppy disk?"

I told him about tracking down Margaret Jordan, and how, for some reason, she seemed to be the only person Stuart allowed to read his script, even though he hardly knew her.

Billy said, "And you think whatever's on the disk has some kind of clue related to his murder?"

"Maybe," I said.

"Is there something specific about it, that—"

"I'll have to let you know once we have a chance to look it over," I said.

Alex had the envelope with the disk, in her hand.

"You should be able to plug it into my computer, right?" Billy said. "This isn't the same machine I had it hooked up to back when I was using the disks. So I'm not sure if it connects." He reached into the box and looked over the wires.

Alex took them from him and looked them over, shaking her head. "We're going to need a converter, so I can plug it in with a USB. We'll have to pick it up, and I'll just use my laptop."

"You don't have it with you?" Billy said.

"The laptop?" She shook her head. "It's at the hotel."

Alex's phone rang, and she glanced at the screen. "It's Mike," she said, answering right away. She put the call on the speaker.

"Hey, Mike," she said.

"Oh, I'm glad to hear you're all right," he said.

"Why wouldn't I be?" She waited, then said, "By the way, you're on speaker with Henry and Billy."

"Where are you?"

"At Billy's restaurant."

"I'm on speaker? In the middle of a restaurant?"

Alex said, "No, not in the middle of the restaurant. We're in Billy's office."

There was a pause. "Okay, listen. What I told you before, about Omar Flores's brother, Alejandro? It turns out there's more chatter coming through. We haven't been able to verify it, but there's enough evidence to suggest he's planning a retaliation."

"Retaliation?" Alex said. "Against me?"

Billy and I looked at each other.

Mike took a moment before he responded. "Intelligence believes he's out there right now, waiting to make his move. So you need to be careful. I don't think it's safe for you—or Henry—to be anywhere right now without some kind of protection."

"You took my Glock," she said, but reached around and removed the .45 from her waistband. "But I should be okay."

"Alex, you're not listening to me. I want you to stay where you are. I'll send over a couple of officers, then head over there myself. Can you wait for me?"

Billy walked to the window at the back of his office and closed the blinds.

Alex said, "I need to get back to the hotel."

"No," Mike said. "You need to stay where you are."

The phone went quiet.

Alex said, "What makes you think he knows we're here?"

"He may not. Not yet. But he obviously knows where his brother was killed. And he knows Henry's office is upstairs."

"Then I should go back to the hotel," she said.

Alex glanced at both me and Billy, although she didn't appear to be as worried as I felt she should've been.

"I think we should listen to Mike," I said.

Alex laughed. "*You* think we should listen to *Mike*? That's a first, isn't it?"

"What's the big deal, waiting here?" I said. I wasn't sure why she was being somewhat stubborn about the situation. I guess I wasn't one to talk, but I wasn't willing to take a chance, not when Alex's life could be in danger.

Alex said, "Mike, why don't you tell the officers to go to my hotel. We'll head over now. Billy doesn't need any more trouble at his restaurant."

Billy opened his mouth, about to say something, but stopped.

Mike said, "I can have them in Billy's parking lot in five minutes."

Alex sighed. "Just send them to the hotel. We're going there now." She ended the call and slipped the phone into her pocket.

Billy looked concerned. "Who is this guy he's talking about?"

I said, "The brother of the man who was shot in the parking lot."

"No, I mean, who is he? What's his deal? Is he some kind of—"

"He's a hired gun," I said. "It's what he does."

"Kill people?" Billy said.

Alex and I both nodded.

"So Mike thinks he's going to show up here? At the restaurant?" He opened his office door and looked down the hall, toward the dining room. "With all these people out there?" Billy stepped around his desk, took a key from his pocket, and leaned over a drawer he'd opened. He pulled out a gun that looked a lot like the .45 I'd given Alex.

He placed it on top of the desk and reached into the drawer again, this time coming up with what resembled a .38 revolver. He nodded toward both guns. "Take your pick."

I hesitated, then grabbed the .38.

Billy picked up the .45 and walked out of the office. "Follow me." Alex and I were right behind him, cutting through the kitchen and out the back door.

I stepped ahead of Billy and pulled open the door to look outside. It had gotten dark since we first got there. I looked out at my Jeep, just a few feet away, and said to Alex, "You really don't think we should wait?"

She shook her head. "I don't like the idea of being a sitting duck, along with all these people. Besides, if we can trap him somehow..."

"Trap him?" I said. "Are you serious?"

She held up the .45. "Would you rather put everyone's life in danger?"

She grabbed my arm and pulled me toward the Jeep. Billy stood, the gun in his hand and by his side, looking around the parking lot, ready to lend a hand if we needed it.

"I'll call you," I said, opening the passenger door for Alex.

She climbed in, and I hurried around to the driver's side.

I started the engine and looked over at Billy. He still hadn't moved. I put down the window and yelled to him. "Why don't you get back inside!"

Billy stood just outside the doorway, watching us.

I backed out of the parking space and drove across the lot. I looked in the rearview when a set of lights turned on somewhere behind us.

"What is it?" Alex said, turning to look out the rear window.

"Probably nothing," I said, placing the .38 in the center console.

Alex had the .45 rested on her lap.

I turned right, out of the parking lot, and looked in the rearview again. The vehicle headed in our direction, and I glanced at Alex, still looking . "It's nothing," I said. "Just a car leaving the restaurant."

The car had stayed back a ways, and when I took North Main Street, it did the same.

Can you tell what kind of car it is?" she said.

I shook my head, and she slouched down in the seat, trying to get a look out the side-view mirror. She adjusted it, moving her head around to try and get a look. "It's an American make, actually looks like a Crown Vic, from here."

"Is it Mike?" I said.

She straightened up in the seat. "He wouldn't follow without letting us know." She started to dial her phone.

"You calling him?"

She nodded. "Mike? Hey, are you following us?"

I pulled over into the Sunoco gas station, which at first I thought might've been a foolish move if it wasn't Mike behind us.

Alex said, "It's not?" She paused. "I don't know. Someone in a sedan is following us. I thought maybe it was your Crown Vic."

After pulling up to a gas pump, the car drove past the Sunoco, then turned onto Tallulah Avenue. I said, "It was green, and looked to be a Ford LTD," I said. It wasn't a Crown Vic, although they looked somewhat similar.

She pulled the phone from her ear. "That's what he said. It's not him. But he's heading this way now."

Alex put down the phone, looking out at the street. "Where'd it go?"

I pointed down a block across Main Street. "They went down Tallulah."

I shifted into drive and pulled back onto the road, heading toward 95, still fifteen minutes from Alex's hotel. But as we drove past the turn where the car had gone, I saw it parked, facing us, with its lights on. "There it is," I said, and slammed my foot down on the pedal.

I was doing sixty, with at least a mile to go before we hit the highway.

Alex looked out the rear window. "You sure that's the same car?"

I nodded as the headlights moved closer.

The Jeep wasn't brand new, and had over a hundred thousand miles on it already. It certainly wasn't in any condition to be in a car chase. "Call Mike back; tell him we're going to lead them to the hotel."

"If we make it that far," she said, flipping down the visor to watch our tail without turning around.

I pushed the Jeep to seventy-five as soon as I hit the Main Street Bridge, the Ford behind us, keeping up. I was almost on two wheels at the Route 10 curve, but eased up to maintain control, continuing onto 95.

But the LTD had more power than the Jeep, and in a matter of seconds, pulled up along the passenger side, driving in the breakdown lane. The windows were tinted, almost black, so it was too dark to see who was inside.

A man climbed out from the passenger side and rested his arms on the roof with some kind of rifle, taking aim at us.

"Get down!" I yelled, and slammed my foot on the gas to get ahead of them.

Alex slouched down and had the .45 up, ready to take aim.

I'd expected shots to be fired, but then another car came out of nowhere, going full speed, and smashed into the rear end of the Ford LTD driving alongside us. The car went spinning out of control, and the man who was hanging out the passenger side flew out of the car, disappearing like he was sucked up by a Hoover vacuum. I looked back and saw him land somewhere on the highway behind us.

Horns blasted all around, tires screeching, as the Ford spun into the barrier, flipped over it, and veered off the highway. The vehicle landed somewhere below, on Atlantic Boulevard.

I'd slammed on the brakes, along with every other car on the road. Blue lights were already coming up fast, behind us.

I still wasn't sure exactly what had happened.

Alex and I both jumped out of the Jeep and looked at the maroon Crown Vic, front end smashed, hood open with steam and smoke pouring from the engine.

Alex yelled, "It's Mike!" and ran toward the vehicle.

I ran to the edge of the highway and looked over the railing, down at Atlantic Boulevard. The Ford was on its roof, flipped over. A man was on the ground, bloodied, and barely moving.

Within thirty seconds, we were surrounded by sheriff's vehicles, the highway traffic backed up along the Route 10 ramp and both north and south sides of 95.

I yelled for one of the officers and told him about the vehicle that went off the highway, then ran over to Alex, helping Mike get out of his car. His face was badly bruised and bloodied, the airbags already decompressed. He walked by himself from the car, although appearing a bit dazed.

Chapter 37

It was close to midnight by the time Alex and I made it back to her hotel. We'd stopped by the hospital to check on Mike, who had suffered a broken arm and a concussion, with twelve stitches over his eye, apparently from the airbag. The doctor wanted to keep him overnight for observation.

Against his wishes, of course.

As it turned out, the man behind the wheel of the Ford LTD was—as we'd suspected—Alejandro Flores, the brother of the recently deceased Omar Flores. Alejandro was injured in the car when it landed twenty feet below onto the eastbound lane of Atlantic Boulevard. In the ICU with half his bones broken, and in a coma, he was not able to speak. That meant asking who hired him and his brother would have to wait.

Whether or not he'd even make it through the night was the question. But for the time being, he was alive.

The same couldn't be said for his friend who fell out of the vehicle's window.

I pulled up in front of the hotel and reached into the back seat for Billy's disk drive, handing it to Alex.

"Aren't you coming up?" she said.

"Can't I drop you off at the entrance?" I smiled. "I'll go park, meet you up there."

She took the disk drive and had the yellow envelope with the floppy disk in her other hand. "You're a gentleman," she said.

I wasn't sure if she was being facetious.

"Can those things go bad?" I said.

"You mean the disk? Or the drive?" She held up both.

"Either one."

"I'm not sure. I guess it's possible we could have a disk issue, considering the fact it's been sitting in that woman's house for, what, fifteen years?"

"About that," I said.

"I guess we'll find out." She closed the door with her shoulder and started for the entrance. "I'll wait in the lobby."

I said through the open window, "No, that's all right. Just go up."

She gave a quick nod and stopped one more time as the entrance doors slid open. "Oh, it's room three-oh-one-seven."

I drove away and parked the car at the back of the lot, the only available space I could find. I waited a few minutes, sitting in the driver's seat, trying to gather my thoughts. I played through different scenarios in my mind of what could possibly be in that movie script, if anything at all. I started to wonder if Jane Ryan was wrong, or for some reason had lied. Part of me wondered if it was all just a waste of time, tracking down that script. There was a chance Alejandro would come out of his coma and start talking, although Mike said he wouldn't count on it.

I walked into the hotel and across the lobby, stopping in front of the elevator. That's when I realized I'd forgotten Alex's room number.

For the most part, I was usually good with details. But my mind had been somewhere else since we'd left the hospital. I was having trouble putting everything together, not to mention when I pulled up to the hotel, I was thinking of Trish. It was a different hotel, of course. But I thought about seeing her there, and about her checking out earlier than planned. How her father was in St. Augustine, expecting to meet her, when she was killed.

I felt a deep sense of guilt for how things went down.

I sent Alex a text:

What's the room number?

The elevator door opened, but I waited for Alex to respond to my text. When the door started to close, I stuck my foot out to keep it open. I glanced back at the front desk where the woman behind it watched me with a look of suspicion. I gave her a grin and looked back at my phone.

The door slid closed, and this time I let it go. At least a minute passed without a reply from Alex. I had to assume she'd put her phone down for one reason or another, or was perhaps on a call. But I couldn't help it; I started to worry.

Even if the two brothers weren't a threat, the person who hired them was still out there.

I dialed the phone, and Alex answered right away:

"Where are you?"

"In the lobby. I sent you a text."

"Oh, sorry. I took a quick shower." She paused for a few seconds. "I thought I told you? It's three-oh-one-seven."

"On my way," I said, pressed the elevator button again and waited another minute for the bell to ring when the door slid open.

A quick trip up to the third floor, and I walked down the hall to her room. The door was ajar and I checked the .38 Billy had given me, tucked in the front of my pants.

I eased the door open. "Alex?"

She poked her head out of the bathroom, hair wet, a towel wrapped around her. "Give me a minute."

"I don't think it's a good idea you have the door unlocked like that."

"You said you were on your way up," she said from inside the bathroom.

Her laptop was on the small desk on the other side of the room, tucked in the corner by the window. The disk drive appeared to be connected, a document up on the screen:

Title: One Fatal Night

By: Stuart F. Graves

Alex walked out in shorts and a T-shirt, wearing flip-flops, and rubbing her hair with the towel. It looked longer, being wet. "That feels better," she said. "You want to shower?"

"Is that a hint?" I sniffed myself, and thought maybe it was a good idea, although I, of course, didn't have any clothes other than what I was wearing. I pointed at the laptop's screen. "Did you look at any of this?"

"No, I just plugged it in and opened it. It has to be copied onto my hard drive."

I pulled the chair back from the desk and sat down, scrolling through the document. "I wish we could print it out," I said.

She picked up a duffel bag and reached inside, pulling out a tablet. "I can read it on this, if you don't mind reading on the laptop?"

I nodded and stood again. "I just hope we're not wasting our time," I said, and headed to the bathroom. "If you're sure you don't mind, I'm going to rinse off."

I went into the bathroom and could smell whatever lotion or shampoo Alex had used, the sweet scent mixed with the dampness hanging in the air.

I closed the door and got into the hot shower, closing my eyes with the water's pressure giving me a sense of relaxation I didn't experience often. The shower on my boat was more like a hose with water that barely dripped from it. And it was usually cold.

Alex knocked on the door. "Henry, get out here. You have to read this."

"Be right out," I yelled. I'd have to try a real shower again some other time. I turned off the water and reached for a towel with my dripping hands, then wrapped it around my waist. I walked out into the room, my feet still wet, and stood by the bed where Alex sat with her tablet.

She said, "That woman, the one who went off the road into the Nassau River..."

"Elizabeth Sutton?" I said. "Does it have something to do with her?"

"I'm not sure yet." Alex took her eyes off the screen and looked me over, in nothing but the towel.

"Sorry," I said, and walked back into the bathroom and yelled out, "Go ahead, what did you find?"

She raised her voice so I could hear her. "You said she was pregnant, right?"

"Yes." I pulled on my shorts and the T-shirt I'd been wearing all day and stepped back into the room. "What did you find?"

"This sounds quite a bit like everything you've told me so far about Stuart Graves and his friends, all hanging around some local bar. The main character's lover is pregnant and drowns when her car goes into a river."

I sat down at the desk and started scrolling through the document. "How much of it did you read?"

"Not enough. But…"

Almost under my breath, I said, "Could this be about what happened to Elizabeth Sutton?" I looked at Alex, staring back at me.

"None of the same names," she said. "At least from what I've read so far. But it's…" She shook her head. "This is strange."

I said, "But this is what Jane Ryan said. This script had the answer. She was telling the truth."

"You thought she was lying?"

I shrugged. "She was being so vague. I didn't know what to think, but I wasn't about to ignore it either."

"We need to read the whole thing," I said. "But why would someone do this? Why wouldn't he just go to the police if he knew something?"

"This is hardly going to be evidence," Alex said.

"Yeah, maybe not something that could hold up in court, or for Mike or the sheriff's office to make any kind of definitive move. But if it gets us a step closer to figuring this thing out…"

Alex said, "Okay, then what if we split this up. I'll read the first half, you read the second."

"How long is it?" I said.

"A little over a hundred and twenty pages. Double spaced. It's not like reading a novel. But if we split it up, I bet we could get through this in an hour."

I pulled my watch from my pocket, strapped it on my wrist and scrolled to about halfway through the document. "I'll start on page sixty, read through to the end."

Alex nodded, fixed the pillows she was leaning against and picked up the yellow legal pad she had next to her. It looked like she'd already taken some notes.

We were both quiet, reading the document for at least a good twenty minutes, when I saw the words that stopped me cold. I looked over at Alex on the bed. "If this story has anything to do with reality—and right now it appears it may—then Elizabeth Sutton's death wasn't just an accident. She was murdered."

Chapter 38

ALEX AND I WERE at the hospital at 7:00 a.m., Alex using her badge to get us in to see Mike before visiting hours had started. He was already dressed when we walked into his room, his back to the door, looking out the window before he turned. His face was a bit more banged up than it appeared the night before. Even his eyes were swollen, with a bandage on his forehead where they'd stitched him up. He had a cast on one arm.

"Oh good," he said. "I'm supposed to get discharged this morning, but for whatever reason these people can't seem to get their act together." Mike was clearly agitated, shaking his head. "Only reason they kept me here is to be able to whack the sheriff's office with a few extra grand in fees. I know how this hospital business works."

Alex had a backpack she placed on the bed, walked over to Mike and brushed a strand of hair from his face, looking him over. "You have a severe concussion," she said. "If you're cleared to go, we'll take you home."

"Home?" he said. "I gotta get to work." He looked at his watch. "I'm already late, and probably walking out of here, if someone doesn't show up in the next few minutes with my discharge paperwork."

"Mike, listen," I said. "I appreciate what you did for us," I said. "You could've been killed."

Mike acted like he didn't even hear me, turning to Alex. "I don't know why you didn't just stay at the restaurant, like I told you to." He paused, like he was hesitating. "I still haven't heard if Flores made it through the night."

Alex said, "Mike, listen. We found something last night."

"Found something? What about?" He tried to fold his arms but stopped, with his cast making it impossible.

"Stuart Graves," I said. "And potentially a clue about what happened to both Trish Williams and Sherry Carter."

Alex said, "We read the movie script. The one Stuart Graves wrote."

"Movie script?" Mike laughed. "I told you already; it has nothing to do with—"

"That movie he wrote. It was about Elizabeth Sutton," I said. "It matches her story, and everything that occurred, leading up to it."

Mike had a twisted look to his face, like he was ready to say something about how foolish it sounded. And he didn't disappoint. "You really expect me to take some guy's pipe dream about making a movie, and consider it some kind of evidence?"

Alex said, "Mike, he gives all the details and recreates the scene of the bar he used to hang out with his friends, and how Elizabeth Sutton started hanging around. Of course, he didn't use any names, but the whole thing comes so close to the actual story. I mean, it's almost like he wrote a *True Crime* story, but he doesn't exactly reveal who did it. The ending was never wrapped up."

"So, what you're saying is you have nothing?"

I shook my head. "There's something there, but he didn't spell it out. Maybe we're wrong, but I think I know who might be able to fill in some blanks."

Mike said, "Okay, so are you going to tell me what you have so far? Or am I supposed to guess, like this is some kind of game." He sat in the chair next to the window and looked up at me, waiting.

"She was already dead," I said. "Somebody—and it may've been more than one person—put her in that car and pushed it into the water."

"This is what you read in the script? Can I see a copy of it?"

Alex pulled out the tablet and tapped the screen, then handed it to Mike. "You can read it if you want, or we can tell you what we found. But if you look at the stories behind Elizabeth Sutton's death, you'll see how similar everything is."

Mike held his gaze on Alex, reaching for the tablet. "But you said it wasn't finished?"

"It was finished," I said. "But he leaves it hanging. I don't know for sure if he ever really knew how it ended."

Mike took a deep breath and exhaled, looking down at the tablet.

"Okay, so can you explain to me what I'm supposed to do with this thing? You're telling me no real names were used, and there's no real ending? And how does this give us anything close to what I'd need?"

I took a step closer to him. "One of the characters is a photographer. As you know, Jack Carter's a photographer. There's a character who's a businessman, who seems to be Rick Lilly. The photographer is married to a woman who wants to open her own pottery studio. Clearly, Sherry Carter. And the main character... It's hard to tell who he is. But it appears to be Graves. He believes he knows who killed the woman."

Mike put up his hand, the one with the cast on it. "Wait a minute. Let me get this straight; the main character is Graves. And the others are all his buddies? And his girlfriend?"

"The woman who was killed was his girlfriend at the time. The photographer's wife, her character's based on Sherry Carter, from what I can tell. But this all takes place before Sherry and Stuart Graves were together, as a couple."

"Then who's the killer?" Mike said.

I said, "That's the problem. There's no ending. It's like, either he didn't finish it, or he just left it hanging."

Alex said, "Or maybe he left it out on purpose. Remember, this is the file he gave to Margaret Jordan. Or, better known to him at the time as May Leigh."

Mike looked at me like I was a fool. "So, you're coming to me with this crazy idea the answer to these murders is in this script. But it's actually *not* in the script?" He laughed. "You've really outdone yourself this time, Walsh."

"But there's another character we can't seem to match up with anybody I read about in any of the reports, or anyone I've spoken to about Graves' death."

Mike watched me, a condescending grin on his face.

"There's this character; his name's Hank in the script, and the main character, let's just call him Stuart, to avoid any confusion: the main character, Stuart, doesn't like this guy because he shows up to meet with the photographer—he's apparently a client—and starts hanging around this bar. The main character knows him, but he doesn't say how. Next thing you know, this guy, Hank, is leaving the bar with the woman."

Mike's expression made it appear like he was having a hard time following. "*Which* woman?"

I said, "The one who's killed, or drives her car off the road, into the river."

Mike held his gaze on me for a moment, then faced Alex. "And you really believe this? You think these people represent some kind of answers I'm supposed to be able to do something with?"

He held his gaze on her, waiting for an answer. But she just stared back at him, until she shrugged, without saying a word.

Mike said, "See? You're not even sure yourself. You know what I think? As soon as you start hanging around Walsh, his crazy ideas start to rub off on you, like they always have. It makes you look as crazy as him." He shook his head, like a disappointed parent. "You know what I think? I think the best thing you can do is get back up there to North Carolina, and get your career squared away. You don't need to be fooling around with this clown any longer."

Alex stared back at him. "I just think we should have an open mind," she said. "Some of it makes sense."

He laughed. "Some of it? Yeah, you can make sense of anything, if you want to. But I choose to be a little more objective when it comes to solving crimes. That's why I wear the badge." He nodded my way. "And he never will."

The first thought in my mind was to defend myself. Especially in front of Alex. But I'd learned over the years how to deal with Mike, and I wasn't going to let his grumpy, foolish, black-and-white way of thinking get under my skin.

I said, "So then, how do you explain the similarities to these characters?" I said. "Everything about it is spot on."

Mike said, "Yeah, it's called writing a story. You think someone just makes up some characters off the top of their head, without basing it on someone real?"

"Oh, I forgot you were an expert on writing," I said, shaking my head. I was tempted to walk right out the door, but Alex grabbed me by the arm.

Mike handed the tablet back to Alex. "I'm sorry, but there's nothing here I can work with, unless I want to be laughed right out of the department." He looked me in the eye. "Don't you think if this guy really knew something about a crime, he'd just come to the sheriff's office? Isn't that what any normal human being would do?"

It was the same question I'd asked Jane.

"I don't know," I said.

Mike looked at his watch, got up from the chair, and walked out into the hall.

"Where's he going?" I said.

But before Alex answered, Mike yelled out, "Hey, I need a nurse in here. I don't have all day to sit around this place."

He walked back into the room, shaking his head. "I can't think straight in this place." He rubbed his temples.

A young female nurse came into the room, pushing a wheelchair. "I'm sorry for the delay, Detective."

Mike cleared his throat, nodding. "I hope you understand my frustration, but..."

The nurse handed him a clipboard. "Sign these papers, and we'll get you out of here." She said to me and Alex, "Are you his ride?"

"If we have to be," I said.

She looked at me like she wasn't sure I was serious and moved the wheelchair closer to Mike, "Have a seat, Detective."

Mike didn't have anything else with him besides the clothes he was wearing. He sat in the wheelchair and flipped through the papers, signing each one without reading any of it.

"Are you sure you know what you're signing?" Alex said.

He handed the clipboard to the nurse without responding to Alex. "All right, let's go. Get me out of here."

The nurse pushed him out of the room with Alex and I following the two. We continued down the hall and onto the elevator.

Mike looked up at me. "Oh, by the way, those files you didn't tell me were stolen from your office were in the trunk of Flores's car. Drop me off at the sheriff's office. I'll get you your laptop."

Chapter 39

Billy walked into the office as soon as Alex and I arrived, soon after dropping Mike off at the sheriff's office. I was on the couch and had just opened my laptop, checking out the cracked screen and broken lid. But after plugging it in, I was surprised it still worked.

"So how's Mike?" Billy said, closing the door behind him.

Alex was across the room, sitting at my desk.

"He's back to being himself," I said. "Maybe worse."

Billy chuckled, but his expression changed as soon as he realized I was serious.

I had already spoken with Billy on the phone and got him up to speed, but went ahead and filled him in on the rest of the details about the movie script. And he wasn't surprised Mike didn't believe there was much to run with.

"I hate to agree with him," he said. "But it does seem strange to think Graves wouldn't just go to the cops, instead of going through all the trouble."

I said, "I'm with you on that, but I can't help but think there's something to it. Maybe he didn't want to bring anybody down as much as make it known."

Billy said, "You mean, like that story where it was rumored Phil Collins allegedly wrote 'In the Air Tonight' about a man who didn't help a boy who was drowning, and invited the guy to his concert to hear it?"

"Yeah, but that story's not even true," I said.

"I know," Billy said. "But I'm just saying..."

Alex looked over from the desk. "The fact is, there's a reason Stuart Graves was murdered. And nobody's been able to come up with anything. It obviously wasn't some random homicide, so now, if we look at this woman's death..."

Billy said, "But then, what was his plan, considering the movie never saw the light of day?"

"We may never know," I said. "We can still assume Graves was trying to tell someone *something*, except the fact he might've wanted to do it in his own way. I'm at a point now I'm not even sure we need to discuss the script, and just taking what we believe may lead us to something, regardless of the fact the man did things his own way."

"Reminds me of someone I know," Billy said, giving me a nod, a slight smirk on his face. "I mean, the part about doing things his own way."

Alex looked up from the computer and waved me over. "Henry, look at this."

I walked over and stood behind her, looking at her laptop's screen.

She said, "Didn't you say Steve Ryan owned some kind of commercial leasing business?"

Billy said, "Who's Steve Ryan?"

"Stuart's sister's husband," I said.

Billy walked over and stood next to me.

Alex had the Carter Photography website up on the screen. "This page has all Jack Carter's past clients." She pointed at one of the names. "Is his company Ryan Commercial Leasing?"

"Was," I said. "He sold it."

"It looks like he was one of Carter's clients, at least at one time." Alex's eyes met mine. "Nobody's ever mentioned that to you?"

I shook my head.

Billy said, "Am I missing something?"

I looked at Billy but didn't give him an answer. I wasn't sure he was the only one not completely clear where Alex was going. "What's the significance?"

Alex opened another browser window and typed in Ryan Commercial Leasing. The first result was a Georgia-based company with a modern-looking website. She clicked through some of the pages, then opened up another window. "Let's go to the Wayback Machine."

Billy said, "The *what*?"

"The Wayback Machine," I said. "It's a website where you can look up the historical pages of any website that's out there," I said.

"Okay," Billy said. "But I still don't see what this has to do with—"

"The script had a character who hung out at the bar and happened to be the photographer's client at the time."

Billy nodded toward the screen. "Looks like he had quite a few clients. Is there something about this Steve Ryan guy?"

Alex glanced at Billy and shrugged. "Just a shot in the dark."

The expression on Billy's face said he wasn't buying it. "I'm sorry," he said. "I know you two are the detectives here, but..."

"You never know," I said, my gaze on the screen.

Alex stopped on one of the images and pointed at one. "This one's from sixteen years ago," she said. "Ancient, in internet years." She clicked through until an image caught my eye.

"Wait!" I pointed at the screen. "That photo's hanging on the wall in Carter's studio."

· · · • · • · · ·

I walked into the reception area at Carter's Photography, and the same woman I'd met there the first time was seated behind the desk. She smiled, as if she remembered me. But I wasn't sure she did.

"May I help you?" she said, watching me as I approached her desk.

"Is Jack Carter available this morning?" I said.

She shook her head. "I'm sorry. He's out on a photo shoot."

"May I ask where?" I glanced to my right, toward the wall with most of the framed photos. I looked directly at the one from Steve Ryan's old website.

"Over at Ortega River Marina." She tapped the keyboard in front of her, gazing at the computer screen. "He should be back in about two hours. I can send him a message, let him know you were looking for him?"

I walked from the desk, over to the framed photo. "Was this photo taken for Ryan Commercial Leasing?"

The woman nodded. "They were one of Jack's first clients. He doesn't love it, but it signifies the beginning of his career, so he keeps it up there."

I studied the photo. I still couldn't tell exactly what it was, other than some kind of machine with gears. Some of it was blurred, like there was movement in the photo. No doubt, Jack Carter had a talent for making something boring look interesting.

"Do you happen to know the owner? Steve Ryan?"

She shook her head. "I was only working for Jack part-time back then. That's when he was working out of his apartment."

I looked at my watch. "You said he'd be at the marina for another two hours?"

She nodded. "Would you like me to send him a message?"

I shook my head and headed for the door. "You don't have to. I'll catch up with him soon."

· · · ● · ● · · · ·

Jack Carter was up on a yacht big enough to put four boats the size of mine inside it. He was on the upper deck, camera in hand, holding it in front of his eye, moving around the deck, standing, crouching down, turning the camera...

"Jack," I said, standing on the dock below, looking up.

He pulled the camera from his face and looked around, like he didn't know where the voice came from. He had a look as though he'd just been woken from a nap.

"Down here," I said.

He finally glanced my way, and by his expression, was clearly surprised to see me. "What are you doing here?"

He really *did* look like a sea captain with his white beard and the black cap he had on his head. If it wasn't so hot out, I could see him wearing a turtleneck, maybe smoking a pipe.

"I know you're in the middle of a shoot," I said. "And I'm sorry to bother you. But we need to talk."

He looked at his watch. "I really don't have time right now." He glanced up at the sky, squinting his eyes. "I'm already behind schedule, the way the sun's positioned."

I walked across the ramp and climbed aboard the yacht. "It'll only take a few minutes," I said, continuing up the steps to the upper deck, where Jack stood watching me.

"Is this about Stu again? Because—"

"Actually, it's about Elizabeth Sutton."

He backed from the top step and watched me walk past him.

I looked out at the Ortega River. "You told me you didn't know much about Elizabeth Sutton or what had happened to her," I said.

"I don't."

"Why do I get the feeling you're all hiding something. I don't know exactly what it is, but—"

"I'm sorry you feel that way."

"Which one of you was sleeping with her, behind Stuart's back?"

He laughed. "I have no idea. But I'm not sure what you mean when you say, 'behind his back.' I already told you Stu and Elizabeth never had much of a relationship. At least not what he thought it was."

"You say that like it amuses you that he thought there might've been something more between them."

He shook his head. "I couldn't care less. That was all a long time ago. We were young."

"But the fact is, there *was* something between them. And if she was carrying his baby..."

Jack stood, quiet, like he had something to say but stopped himself from saying it.

I continued, "You ever have any clients hang around The Crow, back when you were all regulars? Back when Elizabeth was still alive?"

He pulled at his beard. "I'm sure I might've at some point. How do you expect me to remember? That was such a long time ago, I..." Jack cleared his throat, looking down at the camera he held, before raising his gaze. "You want to tell me what you're trying to get at?"

"Sure. What I'm wondering is if you had a client who might've fooled around with Elizabeth Sutton."

"A client?" he said. "Who slept with Elizabeth Sutton?" He did another nervous throat clearing, shaking his head. "I'm sorry, but like I said, that was a long time ago, and—"

"Too long to remember if perhaps one of your clients might've had something to do with what happened the night Elizabeth Sutton allegedly drove into the Nassau River?"

"Are you trying to say I know something about what happened to her?"

I hesitated. The truth was I didn't know where I was going or what I was trying to accuse him of. I didn't have much and was basically prodding Jack Carter, hoping something might come out. I wasn't about to tell him the only clue I had was his dead friend's unfinished movie script.

"I believe she was with someone else that night. And it wasn't Stuart."

"And you think it was a client of mine?" He shook his head, eyeing me like I was crazy. He looked at his watch. "Listen, I can't blow this photo shoot. I barely remember two weeks ago; you're expecting me to answer questions about fifteen, twenty years ago?"

"How many clients did you have back then? Couldn't have been too many, right?"

He didn't answer.

"I'm not sure what any of this matters," he said. "Elizabeth Sutton drove her car off the road," he said. "She was drunk, as she usually was. I don't know what else you're looking for."

"Is that really what you believe?" I looked him straight in the eye, and he didn't flinch.

Jack shook his head. "I'm sorry. But I can't help you."

I started for the steps. "I know the truth, Jack. I'm just not sure why you're hiding it."

Chapter 40

MAC WAS BEHIND THE bar at The Crow. "Hey, Henry!" he said, reaching for a glass he filled from the soda gun and placed on a coaster in front of one of the empty stools. "Ginger ale?"

I liked the guy. If I was still drinking, I could see myself at his bar a little too often.

I sat and picked up the glass, raised it for a quick toast and took a sip. "Thanks." I reached for my phone in my pocket and tapped the screen to unlock it. I said to Mac, "You recognize this guy?"

I showed him a photo of Steve Ryan.

He pulled a pair of glasses from his shirt pocket. "Never thought I'd be the age I am to slip these on just to be able to see a picture."

I placed the phone on the bar and Mac picked it up, looked closely at the phone, and slowly nodded. "He looks familiar. This a recent photo?"

"Not really. I'd say that's from about ten years ago."

"Oh," Mac said. "He used to come in here?"

"That's what I'm hoping you can tell me," I said. "Remember I asked you about Elizabeth Sutton?"

He nodded. "Yeah, of course."

"I'm trying to figure out who else she might've been, uh, in some kind of a relationship with. Besides Stuart Graves."

"Oh, well..." He grinned. "I think I told you, she wasn't the type who was looking to settle down with one guy, if you know what I mean?"

I nodded. "Yeah, I get that. But I have someone in mind who she could've potentially gotten involved with, around the time of her death."

He cocked his head back. "You think this guy had something to do with what happened to her?" He looked at the image on my phone again. "You know, he does look familiar, but..."

"He's married to Stuart Graves' sister."

"Ohhh." Mac nodded, pulling at his chin. "That's why I recognize him. I remember now." He pushed the phone toward me. "I don't recall whether or not he was involved with Elizabeth Sutton at any time though. I'm not even sure I remember him being here with Stuart."

"He might've been here with Jack Carter. He was his client."

"Jack was his client?"

"No. Steve Ryan was Jack's client. One of his first, from what I understand."

"Oh, okay." He put up a finger. "Give me a sec." He walked away, filling up some of the glasses and replacing beers down the other end of the bar.

He walked back over and pointed his thumb over his shoulder toward the phone hanging on the wall. "You want me to call my dad, see if he knows anything about him?"

I picked up the soda. "It'd crossed my mind to stop by and see him myself. But if you could save me a trip?"

Mac stepped away and reached for the phone on the wall. He dialed it and held it between his shoulder and ear, wiping his hands with a towel.

"Dad?" he said, leaning with one hand on the bar. "Hey, listen, you remember a guy used to come in here, name's Steve Ryan?" Mac listened, nodding. "Yeah, that's him, the brother-in-law." He was quiet, looking like he was focused on every word his father was saying. "What about Elizabeth Sutton? Did he have anything to do with her, that you remember?" Mac laughed at whatever his father said on the other end, then nodded once again. "Yeah, that's what I said." He listened, nodding. "All right, yeah. Thanks. Uh-huh. Yes, Henry Walsh. I will."

Mac hung up the phone. "Dad says hello." He glanced at the small crowd at the other end and leaned closer to me. His voice hushed, he said, "Dad said in the old days you'd have to put a gun in his mouth to get him to talk about someone messing around with another woman at his bar, but he knows why you're doing this." He cleared his throat, lowering his voice even more. "He said he remembers this guy Steve, because he started coming in, hung around for a couple of months. He said he asked about Elizabeth Sutton a couple of times, and is pretty sure he remembers them having drinks together."

"Did he sound sure they were involved in something together?"

Mac laughed, nodding. "You can't hide much from him," he said. "If he felt someone was sneaking around like that, he knew."

I called Alex on the ride up to Georgia and filled her in on what Mac had told me. We still didn't have much, outside of the possibility that the character in that movie script, who was the photographer's client, fooled around with the woman who drove into the river.

"I've been digging into Steve Ryan's background," she said. "And I found a few things of interest."

I had the windows down, with the warm air being somewhat bearable compared to how hot it had been, but put them up so I didn't miss a word.

She said, "Did you know he's from Miami?"

"Steve Ryan?"

"Yes."

"What's the significance?"

Alex paused on the other end. "He was friends with Parker Collins, played on the high school football team with him."

I had to think for a moment. "Who's Parker Collins?"

"The man doing life in Raiford for hiring the Flores brothers to kill his wife."

"Are you saying…"

"I'm saying there's a connection. That's all. But you have to wonder…"

"Steve Ryan knows them. The brothers."

"Of course," she said, "they're also from Miami."

"Can we tighten this up?" I said. "We'd need a little more than the fact he knew Parker."

Alex said, "It wouldn't be enough for Mike, if that's what you're asking."

I stared straight ahead at the road. "Not even close."

Alex was quiet for a moment on the other end. "I don't know what kind of friendship Ryan and Parker had after high school. But I was thinking I'd make some calls, see if I can get visitation records for Parker."

"You mean, see if Ryan visited? What would it prove if he had?"

"It's just another link," Alex said.

I thought it through for a moment, taking the .38 Billy had given me from the center console. I already had my plan. "I'm on my way to Ryan's house right now."

"What good is that going to do?" she said. "Can't you wait, let me at least see what else I can dig up?"

I looked at the clock. "I'm just not sure what good it's going to do, but I guess I can wait." I pulled off Route 17 into the parking lot of a place called Carl's Lounge and Liquor. It looked a bit seedy, and not a place I'd want to hang around for long.

Alex said, "I'll call you back," and hung up without another word.

I sat in the Jeep, windows down, with the odor of grilled meat coming from the smokestack on top of the brick building's flat roof. At first glance, it didn't appear that Carl's Lounge and Liquor was a place to get a good meal. But sometimes the seediest dives had the best food.

I was getting restless, waiting for Alex to call back. Fifteen minutes had passed, and I was tempted to go into Carl's and get something to eat. But then my phone buzzed.

I answered, and Alex said, "Steve Ryan visited Parker Collins in prison twice in the past three years. One time was six months ago."

I turned the key in the ignition and skidded across the parking lot, kicking up the dust and stones behind me. I took North 17.

"Maybe you should come back here," she said. "I'll call Mike, let him handle it from here."

"I don't think so," I said.

Alex had started to say something else, but I hung up and gripped the wheel with both hands. Even if we could tie Ryan to the Flores brothers, it still wasn't enough. I had the unloaded .38 on my lap, the windows down with wind blowing through the Jeep, as I slammed my foot down on the gas and crossed over the Georgia line.

Chapter 41

I stood at the front door of Steve and Jane Ryan's home. There were no cars in the driveway, and the windowless garage door was closed. I'd already knocked twice and rang the doorbell, but nobody answered. I heard a vehicle out on the street and spotted a blue BMW. Steve Ryan, Stuart Graves' brother-in-law, was behind the wheel.

He pulled into the driveway, and the garage door made a quiet hum, lifting as the BMW slowly disappeared inside.

I watched, waiting to see if the garage door would close behind him. But it didn't, and Steve Ryan stepped onto the driveway wearing sunglasses and what looked like tennis clothes.

He walked toward me, standing on the walkway.

"Remember me?" I said.

He walked closer, nodding, his face red and sweaty. "Is there something I can do for you?"

I took off my sunglasses. "Can we talk?"

Steve hesitated, chin lowered. "Does this have something to do with Jane's brother? Because, as I told you last time you were here, I'm not going to—"

"I'm here about Elizabeth Sutton," I said. "And your relationship with her."

He stared at me through his sunglasses but didn't respond.

"Your silence speaks volumes," I said.

"I don't know what you're talking about. I never had any kind of relationship with that woman. I hardly knew her."

"Hardly?" I said. "That's not what I've heard."

"Whoever told you otherwise is lying."

I grinned. "Is that so?"

He looked me over, taking his time before reacting. After a couple of moments, he started back to the garage. "Maybe we should talk inside."

I felt around the back of my pants for the .38. It was unloaded, but would do the trick if things went off the rails, as I somewhat was expecting. I followed Mr. Ryan into his garage.

I didn't trust his calm demeanor.

We continued through a door and into his kitchen. Steve went to the refrigerator and took out a small plastic bottle of water, drinking half of it before saying a word. He pulled the bottle from his lips. "So, what is it you've heard?"

I stepped around the other side of the island and stood across from him. "I have my sources," I said. "That's why I believe you were having an affair with Elizabeth Sutton around the time she allegedly drove her car into that river."

"Allegedly?" he said. "You don't believe it's true?"

"Let's not play games," I said.

He stared back at me across the island. "I'm sorry to disappoint you, Mr. Walsh. But you've been given some bad information."

"Have I? So you're going to tell me you never hung around with Elizabeth Sutton at The Crow?"

He shrugged, trying to hide his swallow. "Just because we were there at the same time, doesn't mean there was something between us."

"So, you never left with her?" I said. "Or did your timely departures just happen to be a coincidence?"

"It was all a long time ago," Steve said. "Do you really expect me to remember who I might've walked out of a bar with?"

"I think most men would remember every detail of an affair. But you know what? I'm not here to argue about it. I don't care if you're a cheater. I don't even care that you were caught up in some kind of love triangle with your own brother-in-law. That's not what this is about."

It was time to put on a show. I pulled the .38 from my pants and pointed it at him. "You're going to tell me the truth. All of it."

Ryan put his water bottle on the counter, his eyes widened, looking at the gun. "What the hell are you doing?" He hurried around the island toward a landline phone, lifting the handset. "I'm calling the police!"

I stepped toward him and ripped the phone from his hand, slamming it down on the base. I had the .38 pointed at him. "You know what I think? I think you killed your own brother-in-law because he found out you were screwing around with his girlfriend. The one thing I haven't figured out is why you killed her. My best guess is you did it because she was carrying your baby."

He turned, raising his hands. "This is preposterous!"

"The only thing that's preposterous," I said, "is the fact you somehow got away with murder."

Steve shook his head. "You have no proof of anything. You're making assumptions, because that's all you can do. You have nothing that..."

I pulled back the hammer on the .38 and had the muzzle inches from his temple.

The man looked like he was going to cry. "Please! I swear. I didn't kill anyone." He cleared his throat, looking around the kitchen, beads of sweat dripping down his colorless face.

He didn't look very good.

"I need to sit," he said.

I pulled a chair from under a table in the corner of the kitchen and slid it across the hardwood floor toward him. "Go ahead. Sit."

But instead of sitting down, he grabbed the chair with both hands and swung it at me. I raised my arms to cover my face, and felt a crack when it hit my elbow. The chair fell to the floor and Steve started to run out of the kitchen.

He stopped short when his wife came around the corner holding a gun.

She pointed it at him. "Go sit down, Steve. Don't make me do this."

"Jane? What are you..." He looked at me, then back at Jane. "What are you doing?" He pointed at me. "Shoot *him*. He's going to kill me."

"Not if I do it first," she said, stepping into the kitchen's light just inside the doorway, her gun—a small revolver—still aimed at her husband. She shifted the gun toward me. "Put your gun down, Mr. Walsh."

She'd caught me off guard, starting with the fact she showed up out of nowhere with the gun pointed at Steve.

I said, "You knew it was him?"

"Did I know *what* was him?" she said. "I knew he was sleeping with that whore. But..." Jane shook her head, with a look like she was thinking things through. "I'm sorry, but I don't believe you have the story straight."

"I know what he did," I said.

She shook her head. "No, you don't."

Steve said, "Jane, don't tell him anything."

"Sit down, Steve." She turned the gun toward him. "Don't make me tell you again."

He dragged another chair out from under the table and eased himself into it.

I gave him a quick glance. "I take it she wasn't happy you slept with her brother's girlfriend?"

Jane said, "He always thought I was a fool."

"That's not true," he said, pleading. I could see in his face he was scared of what she might do.

I said to her, "Did he kill Elizabeth?"

Jane paused before she shook her head. "No."

It wasn't the answer I was expecting. "Did your brother do it?"

"Please," Steve begged. "You don't have to tell him anything! What good is it going to do?"

I looked back and forth between the two. I wasn't clear about what was going on, or what kind of game they were trying to play.

"*I* killed her," Jane said. "*I* killed Elizabeth Sutton. That's the truth."

"No!" Steve said, shaking his head. "Don't listen to her."

She held the gun on him. "Shut your mouth, Steve. I'm done lying. I'm done living my life covering up our lies."

I held my gaze on Jane. "*You* killed her?"

"It was an accident," she said. "I mean, it wasn't that I didn't *want* to kill her. But when Stuart came to me after he found out his own brother-in-law was sleeping with his girlfriend..."

"He knew?"

Jane paused, then nodded.

Steve rose from the chair. "Jane! That's enough. Stop this right now, before I—"

She pulled the trigger and fired two shots into her husband's chest. He fell back into the chair, sliding off it and onto the floor.

I didn't know what to do. I didn't even have the .38 in my hands, not that it would have been much help. I glanced at Steve Ryan's lifeless, bloodied body.

"It's over," she said. "I was never able to forgive him for what he did. I should've just left him when I had the chance. But we got so wrapped up in trying to hide what happened."

"Did you really kill her?" I said, taking my eyes from the bloodied body a few feet from where I stood. I had trouble believing it.

Jane nodded.

"What about your brother? Did you kill *him*?"

"No, of course not. Steve found out Stu was going to tell the story, in his own way. He didn't want to take the chance. We all would've paid the price."

"I don't understand," I said.

Jane had the gun lowered by her side. "How did you figure it out?"

"I found Stuart's script," I said, glancing at Steve on the floor. "I was sure it was him."

Jane said, "When I first found out he was screwing around with her, I was so upset. I couldn't control my anger. So I went looking for her. All I wanted was her to admit the truth about what I'd heard. I went to her apartment. You know what she said? She told me she was in love with him. With *my* husband. She wouldn't apologize for anything. And when she told me she was pregnant... that Steve was the father... She said he was going to leave me. I—"

"You killed her?" I said, still having a hard time believing it.

"We fought like a couple of teenagers rolling around in a high school parking lot. I pushed her, and she tripped over her own feet. Even though she was pregnant, she'd appeared to be drinking. When she fell, she hit her head on the corner of the coffee table. I think I knew right away she was dead, although her eyes stayed open." Jane took a deep breath, closing her own eyes. "I called Stu first, and told him where I was. I didn't say what had happened, just that he needed to get right over. I waited, but he didn't show up. But you know who did?" She laughed, nodding with her chin at her dead husband. "This one. He walks in the door with flowers in his hand."

By that point, it was clear what they had done.

"I was so scared and upset," Jane said, "I just wanted to leave her there. But Steve wouldn't do it. He knew I'd be in trouble. I remember him telling me how sorry he was. Even as we carried her out to the car, he begged for my forgiveness, promised me he'd change."

I said, "I still find it hard to believe you stayed together all these years."

"Sometimes secrets keep people together," she said, looking at her husband's body.

"So, you drove her to the river?"

"Steve did," she said. "I know how hard it was for him, but..."

"Your brother never showed up?"

"Not when we were there. But he must've gone to her apartment at some point. He never spoke to me or Steve again."

"But he never knew the full story?" I said.

She shrugged. "How could he have?"

"You never told him?"

Jane didn't respond.

"That's why, the script he wrote, it wasn't clear," I said. "He never finished it."

"Where did you find it?" she said.

I told her about Margaret Jordan aka May Leigh.

Jane said, "Sherry knew what was in that script."

"But she told me she couldn't find it," I said.

Jane shrugged. "She lied to you. She lied to everyone. Even the cops."

"Why?" I didn't understand.

Jane just stared back at me, like she didn't have the answer. "I told Trish Williams to ask her about it. I couldn't live with it anymore."

"Why didn't you just tell her what happened?"

Jane, again, didn't answer.

"Did you kill them both?" I said.

She shook her head, glancing at Steve's lifeless body. "He overheard my conversation with Trish. He lost his mind. I thought he was going to kill me, but then he gets on the phone, tells me I've left him with no choice; we'd both end up in jail. But I didn't care anymore."

"We have to call the cops," I said.

"Call the cops?" She raised the gun and had it pointed at me. "Why would I do that?"

"Don't you want to confess?"

"I just did," she said, smiling. "I already feel better."

"You don't have to kill me," I said.

Jane was about to take aim, her finger tickling the trigger. But she stopped and turned when a woman's voice yelled out from the darkness, coming out of the room behind her.

"Police! Drop your weapon!"

Three Kingsland police officers—two males, with the one female leading—stepped behind Jane, guns drawn.

"Ma'am," the officer yelled. "Put down your weapon."

Jane kept it on me for another moment, then slowly shifted her grip. But she didn't lower the gun. She turned it around, pointed it at herself, and stuck the barrel in her mouth.

"No!" I yelled, rushing toward her.

Before I could get to her, she pulled the trigger.

Chapter 42

I WAITED OUTSIDE THE security gate at Jacksonville International, feeling my heart race—in a good way, this time—when Alex turned the corner after exiting her flight. The smile on her face made the hair on the back of my neck stand on end, watching her hurried pace as she came toward me. The diamond on her finger sparkled with the way she gripped the strap of her backpack to keep it from falling from her shoulder.

She jumped into my arms, and we stayed there, holding each other, as everyone walked around us. One or two people bumped into us, maybe even on purpose. But neither of us cared.

It was September, and I hadn't seen Alex in two weeks. It seemed like forever.

"I wasn't sure you'd show up," I said, looking into her big brown eyes.

She laughed, took my hand, and pulled me toward the airport's exit. "Let's get out of here. I need to see Raz."

Last time I saw her, two weeks prior, I'd driven up to Selma to get some of Alex's things, including her dog, Raz. *Our* dog, Raz.

Alex had already resigned from the Selma Police Department. But she didn't want to leave them hanging, so she stayed on through the summer until they were able to find and train her replacement. Even after I told her I'd move to North Carolina if she wanted to keep the job, it turned out she had more than one reason to come back to Florida.

Our wedding was a little more than a month away, set for late October when we could have it outside in the backyard of the house we bought together in Fernandina Beach.

No way I got rid of the boat.

But Alex and I ended up buying the house I grew up in. The day I heard it'd been put up for sale, I knew it was something I had to do. I never thought I'd ever own a house. After all, it was a money pit, as my dad used to call it. But sometimes it has less to do with what something costs and more to do with knowing when something feels right.

We pulled up in the driveway, and Raz was in the window, his big paws scratching at the glass. Alex jumped out of the Jeep and ran to the door. She turned to me with her hands out, and I tossed her the keys. I'll admit I got a little choked up when she opened the door and crouched down when Raz charged her, stood up on his hind legs and hung his paws over her shoulders, licking her face.

She laughed. "Oh, Raz. I missed you too."

Billy pulled into the driveway in the old convertible Mercedes he'd picked up from the auction that morning.

"I thought you were done buying cars," I said.

Billy stepped out and shrugged. "This is the last one." He gave me a nod. "Maybe it'll be your wedding present."

Alex came down from the front porch with Raz and gave Billy a hug.

"Welcome home," he said.